The Secrets of Lilypond Lane

Contents

Welcome to Lilypond Lane

Lilypond Lane is a fictional street, though in some form, it exists in many towns. Wealthy suburbia. The kind of manicured street whose houses all have closed doors and twitching curtains, filled with desperate housewives and pretty little liars. A street where rumours both stop and begin. Where questions are asked too often, or not at all.

Once you've read these stories, you might never look at your own neighbours in quite the same way again.

The authors of this anthology are from across the globe. American or British English is used according to the author's native language.

Turn the page, delve in, and knock on your first door of Lilypond Lane.

See Her

BY EMMA ELLIS

When Katarina used the lilypond to hide evidence of her crime, she had no idea what other secrets lurked beneath the water.

"DNA can't survive in water," Christopher Morely says with such an air of authority, I know he's done this before. It's the same confidence he has when he kisses me or shoves his hand up my skirt, like doubt has no place and cowers away. "I mean, it survives, but it washes away. They can hardly DNA test every molecule in the whole pond."

He throws the rock in, and then the next, and we watch as they sink below the inky water. I hold my breath as each one disappears, imagining tendrils of DNA—both ours and the man in the orange Range Rover—floating up and dancing like feathers in the wind. The pond is black under the night sky; the blood doesn't even leave a trail in the bubbles.

"Anyone can bang their head on a rock," he says. "It's the best way to kill someone."

There are other rocks across the bank of the pond, and I wonder how many there are on the bottom. How many people's blood mingles in the water.

I look up at him, his tight lips, unblinking stare. He's a Christopher, not a Chris. Chris is too common, he claims. Three syllables is the minimum he deserves. His clothes are still neat and pressed. He probably has a maid to do that, as well as an expensive lawyer to cover for him if he ever gets in trouble. He didn't want to toss the rocks into the river by his neighbourhood. People always want to find the richest guilty of something, he said on our way over here. Far better to leave the evidence by a poorer neighbourhood.

Lilypond Lane is poorer than his, but hardly poor. Each house is easily four times the size of mine. The houses down his street though are fenced with electric gates, swimming pools out the back and security dogs out the front.

Everyone knows who Christopher Morely is. His famous mother and billionaire father make him cannon fodder for the press and local gossip. If he gets caught doing this, I know it'll be me who goes down instead. People like Christopher Morely are untouchable.

The third and final rock splashes, the water rippling out in concentric circles until they hit the grass next to where we are standing. Little tsunamis, carrying our guilt.

He pulls me in close, his arms locked around me, my body pressed into his. He may only be seventeen but after a decade of playing rugby, he's as built and strong as any man, though his hold is still not enough to stop me shaking.

"You know what this means now, right, Katarina?" he says, his nose less than an inch from mine. His hands are clasped behind me and his biceps dig into my ribcage. "We're bonded. Knowing what we know about each other. This means you're mine forever."

I swallow and nod, and he kisses me. Still so confident. So unyielding.

We run now, hand in hand across the grassy bank of the pond, then down the street. The last house is my aunt's and for a moment, I consider knocking on her door and curling up on the sofa with a hot chocolate, a shot of rum in it while she tells me not to tell my mum she's giving me booze. As if she'd care, but we like to have our secrets.

I drop his hand, though with his grip so tight he doesn't let go. I yank mine away more firmly this time, and stop running.

"What?" he says between panting breaths.

It's winter but despite the cold temperature and my overly revealing clothes, I'm sweating. "I think I'm going to go see my family now."

"No, Katarina. You're coming with me."

I step back. "I'll catch up with you later. I just really want to see my aunt. She's ill. I just want to check she's okay."

He grabs my wrist, with such force it'll leave bruises, and pulls me close to him again. His breath heats my face. "I mean it, Katarina. We're bonded. You know how powerful my family are." With his other hand, he squeezes my breast. "I'll see you tomorrow. You'd better be there."

His eyes glint in the moonlight, like shards of glass, and I nod again before he releases me. His physical hold may be gone, but the mental one, I don't know if I'll ever be free of that.

I run back to my aunt's house and knock on the door.

"Katarina, darling. Come in." She greets me with her forever smile and warm hug. Despite my body being clammy, the hug soothes me.

"You're shivering dear, dressed like that I'm not surprised. Let me make you a hot chocolate. Little shot of rum?" she asks with a wink.

I nod and take my shoes off before walking through to the living room, the smell of turmeric as overpowering as ever. It helps with inflammation, Aunt Camilla says. As if that's all her cancer is. Looking at her now, with her thick dark hair like everyone in our family has, her grey roots only just showing, it would be easy to believe she isn't sick.

My toes poke out the holes in my tights revealing chipped red nail polish on my toenails. The carpet doesn't look like anyone has ever bothered taking their shoes off before walking on it, it's so trodden and stained. Aunt Camilla's house may be meticulously presented on the outside with its manicured lawn and pruned hedges, but she has never been house proud on the inside. She's on borrowed time now, the cancer will get her soon and so bit by bit, the house is falling into more disarray.

"What's the point?" she always says. "I only invite inside people I like, and if they turn their nose up at my home, then I won't like them anymore nor invite them again."

The state of the place is, like so many things with Aunt Camilla, a test.

"I'll come help you," I say as I walk through the house.

"Not a chance, young lady. I'm still capable."

I know better than to have this argument with her. She'll refuse all help until the end.

I sit on her sofa, sinking into its softness, and my shaking abates a little. It's so warm in the house, and the switch in temperature makes me sweat all the more. She comes through with two over-filled mugs of hot chocolate, slopping over the rims and onto the tray, and she puts one on the wooden coffee table next to me.

"Give it a moment," she says. "It's hot."

She sits on the next chair, her feet dangling. What little height she had, time is rapidly reclaiming. A slipper slips off her foot and I smile at her nail polish. The same colour as mine, and just as chipped.

With my first sip of hot chocolate, my heart rate calms, and I relax back into the cushions. Aunt Camila talks, filling every second with neighbourhood gossip. There always seems to be gossip on Lilypond Lane. Always some antics or adultery. I say nothing but sit and listen.

"And that Jermey whatshisface," she says. "The twat across the road thinks, just because he's minted, he can say what he likes."

I frown. "I don't know this guy?"

"Oh, you know him. You've definitely seen him. Jeremy...oh, what's his damned name again? Jeremy Dos Santos. That's it. Your mum thinks he's the bee's knees because his surname sounds

Spanish. I think they've been dating, I'm sorry to say. I don't think he's even Spanish. Maybe his great-grandfather was or something. We had that potluck dinner here with all the neighbours and she was fawning over him like some teenager. No offence."

I laugh and wave away her comment.

"Anyway, how are things at home?"

"Shit, obviously, if mum is prowling after your neighbour."

"He just thinks he's the mutt's nuts because he wears his fancy suits and drives that orange Range Rover like he's some middle-aged gangster."

I don't swallow my next sip. It lingers on my tongue a while as my muscles tense. The sight of the orange Range Rover flashes before my eyes again. The man stumbling out of it. The coolness of the rock in my hand.

"Awful car," she continues, though she sounds a million miles away as my mind drifts, as if I'm one of those rocks underwater. "So pretentious. Definitely not good enough for your mum."

Aunt Camilla is twelve years older than my mum, and no man has ever been good enough for her baby sister. She struggled to contain her glee when my dad did a runner several years ago. I never heard from him again but she stepped into his shoes, being more of a parent than he ever was. And my mum, if I'm being honest.

"Anyway," she continues, and my attention is snapped back to the here and now. "I shouldn't gossip, but he's not good enough for your mum. Or any woman. I can tell. Not an ounce of kindness in him. Just another pervert."

I've never heard the full story of what happened to my aunt and mum in their childhood, all I know is that my grandfather is still serving prison time for it, and my grandmother killed herself because of it. I don't need the details. Those sentences and my aunt's overprotectiveness tell me enough.

"Your mum has never needed a man. She always thinks she does, she's got no confidence on her own and the predatory men prey on that. I'm so glad you don't take after her."

"Thanks," I say. Christopher's hand on my breast now feeling like a bite from a hyena.

"So what's wrong?" she asks, peering at me from the top of her glasses. "I know something's wrong so don't try to say nothing."

I sip my hot chocolate, and sift through the list of things that are wrong, choosing what to tell her. She'd got a sixth sense for scandal. So, I add to our secrets and tell her about Christopher Morely. His forceful nature, though I don't mention the rock, the lake, the crack.

She tuts, and slurps the last of her hot chocolate. "These young men these days. No respect. Are others like this?"

My cheeks heat. I so want to be as strong as her. "Some."

She puts her mug down and leans towards me. "You're a tough girl. I see a lot of me in you, though you could do with some more self-respect. Don't let him think he can get away with it."

A little bit of determination bubbles inside and I sit straighter, like my dying aunt's words have sprouted me a backbone. "I won't. I'll kick him in the balls next time."

She laughs. "That's my girl."

I finish my hot chocolate and walk home, picking up my pace as I skirt the edge of the grassy bank by the pond, then breaking out into a jog as I divert at Bell's Lane to avoid the top of the road, where the orange Range Rover is still parked. Where that Dos Santos guy probably still lies.

I search the sky for flashing blue lights, listen for sirens, but there's nothing besides a screech of a tawny owl. Bell's Lane is a quiet street. I doubt anyone will go down there until the dog walkers and joggers wake early.

I never got a good look at the guy. He only cut Christopher up at the traffic lights. A dickhead overtaking move, but not so bad that he deserved what he got. We were meant to tease him a bit. That's all. It was Christopher who put the bag on his head. It was Christopher who handed me the rock. I was drunk, adrenaline-pumped, goaded on.

"Do it," he said. "Just a whack."

That's all it was. The kind of tap that wouldn't even cut. Then Christopher did it again, harder. And again until the man shut up and went limp. There's a rockery at the end of the street. We lay him there and took the rocks we had touched with us.

He's probably not dead. Concussed and in need of stitches. Not dead.

I sit on the swing in the park for a while on my way home. My breath steams in the winter night and glows orange under the streetlight. Adrenaline has left me and the coldness of the night creeps over my bones. Frost is settling on the grass already. What was that guy wearing? I can't remember if he had a coat on. The blood pooling beneath him would be turning to ice.

I walk home, my arms folded across my chest and my shoulders raised and stuff. Every noise makes me jump. A baby cries from one of the houses, a dog barks, a gate swings on its hinges. All such sounds taunt me, whisper at me, divulge my guilt as I jump and jolt.

It'll be fine, I repeat to myself over and over. He's probably not dead.

But he is. The next day, the news says so. Local man found fallen, died of head injury and exposure. A resident of Lilypond Lane.

Crack. I can still hear it.

It's all I can think about at school as I stare out of the window at the grey sky and drizzle. Did he feel the cold or did he stay unconscious? Did he have a family? Aunt Camilla seemed to think he wasn't a good guy, but she thinks all men are bad.

A teacher shouts at me for daydreaming, my friends ask if something is wrong, not that they care. Gossip is their main focus.

The night before plays over and over again. The orange Range Rover. The weight of the rock. The way his struggling limbs went limp.

I hear the noise everywhere. A locker slams shut: *crack.* A car door closes: *crack*. Some books are dropped: *crack.*

I spend my lunch break throwing up in the toilets. The other girls will gossip: she's making herself sick again. She drank too much last night. She's pregnant. Such rumours I would normally put a stop to, give anyone saying it a shove, use my popularity to bolster me up. Today though, the rumours don't seem too bad. Better than the truth anyway. Pregnant is better than murderer.

Christopher Morely goes to the expensive college down the road, so at least I don't see him during the school day. I walk home with my friends as usual, though I walk quietly as they all laugh and giggle at god knows what. No one notices I'm not my usual lively self. The tidbits of conversation I do hone in to, I wonder why I am friends with these people. They're all so shallow, so vacuous. They don't even care when one of the older boys gropes them; they act like it's a badge of honour.

I've been friends with these girls forever, but I can't tell who's talking unless I look at them. How had I never noticed before? They all sound the same. The same screechy laugh, the same overexcited voice. Do I normally sound like that? Even when I turn to look at them, they're indistinct. Just a homogenous blur of fakery.

We stop off at the corner shop to buy booze, or rather, get someone to buy booze for us. It's dark already and the usual hang out outside the corner shop is lit by a single streetlight. Its glow feels like an interrogation lamp, highlighting my shame. I sit on the bench with the others, shuffling to the end that is in the most shadow.

Christopher Morely and his best friend arrive, to the cheers of the girls I am sitting with. My chin is dipped, but I glance up and meet his steely gaze, and the evening suddenly is even colder.

Callum Peters offers to buy us alcohol. He's Christopher Morely's friend, a few months older. The two of them are a pair of wealthy thugs who think they own the city and also think it's okay to feel up who they like. Christopher stands just a few metres away. He sees it all. He sees it when Callum pins me against the wall and helps himself to a grope in my underwear. It's not the first time Callum has done this, not the first time Christopher has watched him do this. His eyes lock on mine and his lips press together into a grim line, like he's daring me to say no, daring me to speak at all.

I struggle free and elbow him away. Christopher and Callum high-five afterwards, before Callum does the same thing to another girl who resists less.

I want to throw up again. I want to rip off every bit of skin he has touched. Aunt Camilla would tell me to hit him, to scream at him and tell him to fuck off. But it's hard to be so confrontational when under the dazzling glare of popularity. Can I ostracise myself that much?

There's this girl at school, always alone, studious, spends break times among the trees and birds. Is that what awaits me if I stand up to these people? An outcast with just bugs for company. A glance around at my current friends and bugs don't seem so bad. Maybe I should befriend her, just in case.

Christopher walks over to me, puts his hands around the back of my head and kisses me, so firmly it's like he's marking his territory in front of his arsehole friend. He'd never tell Callum to back off. It would be my fault if Callum oversteps the line.

I push Christopher away and wipe my mouth.

"You shouldn't let him touch you like that," Christopher hisses in my ear, quietly enough that Callum doesn't hear.

"I shouldn't let you either."

His hands press down on my shoulders and rests his forehead on mine. "Remember, Katarina. You're mine."

I shove him and step away.

"What's with you, Kat?" Amelia, who is meant to be my friend, talks to me in such a snooty way I want to shove her next.

"Nothing," I say, aware of Christopher's glare. "Just not in the mood."

She steps closer and puckers her lips. "How'd your date go with Christopher last night?"

I shrug, but before I answer, a car beeps. It's Aunt Camilla in her car. It's parked, the engine isn't running.

"Kat, darling, I need to take you home. Your mother needs you," she shouts.

I wave at my friends and run to the car, flicking Callum and Christopher a V sign, leaving the sound of their laughter behind me.

"How long have you been parked here?" I ask as I get in.

"Long enough. That those boys?" she asks.

I nod, and she pulls away.

"Sorry if I embarrassed you," she says.

There's a box of chocolates on the dashboard, and I help myself to one. Sweets are about all she can stomach these days. Any time my mum suggests she eats more healthily, she's met with conflict. Camilla says she's dying, and so she'll eat what she damn well pleases. The way her skin hangs off her, I figure any food will do.

"You didn't embarrass me," I say. "What's up with mum?"

She releases a slow exhale. "That man she was dating, he was found dead."

"Oh." I say. "He's that guy."

"Yeah. The one on the news—"

Crack.

"—It seems after their two dates she thought he was to be the love of her life. You know how she gets."

I nod, knowing all too well.

When I get home, mum is beside herself. Her face is red and puffy from crying, her hair a knotted mess over her face.

"Every man I date, this happens. They die or disappear or end up in prison." She sobs into her vodka coke. By the sound of her slurring, it's not her first drink.

Aunt Camilla puts her arm around her as I stare blankly at the wall, trying to keep my mind elsewhere and not on my guilt.

"You don't need a man," Camilla says. "He was no good anyway. Drink driving, did you hear? That's what they're saying. So drunk he fell over and smashed his head getting out the car. He was just no good."

She shrugs free of Camilla's embrace. "They're never any good though, are they?"

Mum runs upstairs, stamping her feet and slamming doors like she's the teenager of the house, and Camilla sits at the table. For someone on death's door, she has so much energy still. Stubbornness, most likely.

She reaches for my hand. "When I'm gone—"

"Don't say that." I snatch my hand back.

"It needs to be said. I'm not going to be around forever." I know this. I just don't like talking about it. The thought of no Aunt Camilla makes my chest cave in. "It's not up to you to look after your mum," she continues. "I just want to know you're not going to end up like her. Those boys today, I saw enough. Don't ever let them take advantage of you. You don't need them. You're too good for that."

Mum comes downstairs with a bag packed. "I'm going away for a while. I need a few days. Can you drop me at the station? Katarina can stay with you."

"Mum —"

"No arguments. I just need to be alone. I'm going on a yoga retreat."

Impulsive would be being kind to my mother. Her thoughts jump from one to another so quickly, it's like she doesn't really think at all.

Aunt Camilla nods, tells her of course, and I plod upstairs to pack a bag. It's still half packed from the last time my mum had her heart broken. What was his story? Just did a runner, I think. Disappeared, no note, never to be heard from again. Much like my dad. Same story again and again. Like my mum is some inverted magnet and pushes them all away. She gets so obsessed so early on, it's hardly surprising. Every man who pays her a compliment is to be her knight in shining armour, to rescue her from her loneliness. It's clear why Aunt Camilla worries about me, but no way am I going to end up like that.

My bedroom at aunt Camilla's overlooks the pond. I sit at the windowsill, boozy hot chocolate in hand and stare at the water, imagining what secrets it holds. How many DNA-tainted rocks. There are a few ducks on the water. If they could talk, what would they say?

My phone buzzes frequently from my friends.

Where are you?

We're going for a drive, join us?

We're going to the southdowns for a smoke, come. It'll be fun.

I ignore them all, silence my phone, and throw it across the room. I'm sick of my friends. I'm sick of everything about being Miss Popular. Everyone expects me to act a certain way, dress a certain way, like certain things. And put up with certain things. I'm an object, an accessory to the boys and girls alike. There's no room for individuality in a group like that. It's not okay to hate those boys, to say no. And no is all I want to say, as well as some curse words.

My thoughts wander to that girl at school again, who seems to have no one. She's quiet and dresses badly, but she's always interested in nature and doesn't give a toss about all the other crap. How satisfying it must be to find contentment in nature. If I want some new friends, maybe I should start there. I'll speak to her tomorrow. The others may mock and tease her, but right now, that seems preferable to having to put up this constant façade.

There's no time to befriend anyone else. I miss one evening of socialising with my so-called friends and they spend every second giving me a blow-by-blow account of what they got up to. I don't want to hear it. I want to cover my ears and scream and tell them all how conceited and shallow they all are. I want to cover every inch of flesh I have on display under a thick fleece blanket and hide, somewhere quiet and warm, and just try to figure out who I am.

Callum helps himself to a handful of my flesh again on the way home. Christopher Morely sits on the wall, laughing, as if I am a piece in a game instead of a human being.

No more. I can't take it anymore.

I push him away, scream at him, tell him I'll kill him if he does that again. In my bones, I mean it. I am so sick of it.

I see that quiet girl run past. She escapes all the insults this time. Instead, she slips by unnoticed. How great it would be to draw less attention. She can hide. No one bothers her, not really. No one expects anything.

I can't watch her for long. It's Christopher Morely's turn now. He's behind me, Callum in front. I'm squashed between the two of them as they laugh, tell me not to be so frigid, and call me a slut.

I land a punch squarely on Callum's nose and a kick in Christopher's crotch.

I escape their grasp and stare at them both a moment, wide, unblinking eyes as they both double over and groan. I am so dead. I know this now. Two wealthy thugs from families of thugs.

The girls laugh, repeat the claims of frigid, and other words I don't hear as I run as fast as I can away.

I arrive back at Aunt Camilla, in tears, and I tell her everything. Almost everything. Still nothing about the orange Range Rover.

"It's okay, dear," she says, in such a way I believe it. "It's going to be all right."

All night I still hear cracking skull, feel the coolness of the pond water on my hands. All night I feel his hand on me.

A broken skull is how Christopher Morely deals with people who piss him off. I should learn a lesson from him.

The next day, I make plans with that quiet girl. She holds a bird in her hand, dazed from flying into a window. She holds it until it is recovered and ready to fly again. The sound of my usual friend's laughter and banter makes my skin crawl. I just want to be around people who are caring, real, none of the fakery and façade.

It's just past lunchtime when I get a call. The school receptionist comes to find me and passes on the message.

"You need to go to your aunt's immediately, Katarina."

My stomach drops. It takes a few seconds for it to sink in as those words turn my blood to ice. I know what she means. Aunt Camilla hasn't got long.

The doctor leaves as I arrive. A fall, the doctor says. She was so weak anyway, it's too much for her system to cope with.

"It won't be long," the doctor says as he walks to his car.

Aunt Camilla is in her bed, ragged breaths and pale. Purplish bruises on her forehead and shoulder. I hold her hand; it's freezing and so weak I fear I may break it. She doesn't look my way, instead her half-closed eyes stare up at the ceiling.

Blue lights flash outside, but it's not an ambulance. She's refused doctors for months. "When it's my time, it's my time," she said.

I forgot I was going to meet that girl after school. It's too late now, I'll explain tomorrow.

The blue lights stop at the lake but keep flashing. There's the sound of people walking, several people, the clang of metal equipment.

As Camilla dozes, I watch out the window. A gathering of other school kids and parents, the residents of Lilypond Lane, all stand around as forensics teams in hazmat suits put up a tent and cordon off the grassy bank. I open the window to lean out further. Among the onlookers is Christopher Morely.

He looks my way, clocking my gaze. He's paler than my aunt.

The police cars still have their lights flashing, and I shiver.

Aunt Camilla stirs, and I take her hand again and tell her I'm right here.

She says in a breathy voice, "They won't hurt you anymore. Go and see."

I lean away from her and glance towards the window again. There's a splash from the lake, people entering the water, some shouts from the crowd. A pit lodges itself in my stomach, my mouth running dry. They can't be looking for our rocks, surely not.

Camilla is asleep again, so I leave the house for a few moments, and stand next to Christopher Morely.

Looking his way, I note his wide eyes, a tremble to his chin.

There's gossip in the crowd. Little pieces of information passed around in hushed whispers.

"Murder, they're saying."

"Someone missing."

"They found blood leading to here."

"A shoe, a bag, or something. They think he's in the lake."

The crowd is silent then as we all watch the divers haul out the body. Swollen and blue, torn flesh down his head. My hands go to my mouth as my stomach lurches. As they drag the corpse to the grassy bank, it's clear who the body is. Was.

Callum Peters.

There's a gasp from the crowd, a few cries, as I turn my head to watch Christopher Morely blink his tears away. "DNA can't survive in water," I say, the same way he said it.

Then I turn to go back in. To say my final goodbyes to Aunt Camilla.

She stirs a little, and her glassy eyes focus on me. "You're going to be just fine," she says. "I never let any of them hurt you. Have a look in there," she points to her drawers. I open the bottom one and take out a box. Trinkets of car keys, mobile phones, credit cards, human teeth. "Might want to hide those," she says. "Don't want your mum finding them."

All things I recognise. Each item is from one of my mum's toxic exes. My dad's car keys. Plus Callum Peter's wallet.

"Kill or be killed," she said. Then she croaks her final breath. Her eyes now unfocussed anywhere, her mouth frozen in a half smile.

My chest hollows as the room spins. I utter her name and hold her hand to my face, kiss it, my tears soaking my cheeks. Despite the heating being on full blast, the room is cold. I run my hands over her face to close her eyes.

"I'll make you proud forever," I promise her. "I'll never be a pushover to them."

I sit next to Aunt Camilla, for hours maybe, I can't be sure how long. My brain is lost in a fog. It's hard to see past this desolation, this emptiness left behind by her passing. I knew she would die soon, but that doesn't mean I was prepared for the permanence of it.

The odd glimpse I get over the waves of grief, I see a stronger me, one that Aunt Camilla would be proud of.

I put the box back in her drawer. I'll sink it in the lake once they've finished dredging it, and keep her secrets forever.

Outside, there are more splashes as the divers still search the pond, and I wonder what else they'll find in there.

Emma is a British author who now lives nowhere in particular. She has various other published works in the dystopian and thriller genre. Check out her website www.emmaellisauthor.com to discover all of her books. She can be contacted also via Facebook and Instagram. This story is a prequel to her speculative thriller duology, Be Her.

Toxic

BY RACHEL GRAHAM

Suffocated by the fake perfection of Lilypond Lane and the toxic grasp of her controlling mother, teenager Paige decides to end her life. But a sinister discovery disrupts her plan, driving a twisted pursuit for survival. Will Paige reclaim her life before the darkness of Lilypond Lane consumes her?

Tonight, I will end my life.

I've delayed it long enough. Thinking—hoping—things will get better. But they aren't, and they won't. No point delaying the inevitable.

There's a scratching, scratching in my head, like little bugs are burrowing into my brain, ever since we moved here to this so-called perfect suburbia. This picket-fence, pristine lawn, perfect garden, smiling neighbour *lie* called Lilypond Lane. Everyone is so phony, so fake. So full of desire to make their life seem perfect on the outside. Really, they are black and rotting on the inside.

Just like my mother.

It's no wonder she sought this place out. She fits right in with her fake smile and her fake happiness and her fake niceness.

The fakeness here is suffocating.

I see the way the neighbours stare. I know they plaster on smiles and enthusiastic waves, then duck away to gossip between themselves about the chunky spinster and her daughter. The Two Who Don't Belong.

Mum's so desperate to fit in. To make it look like our family life is happy—*perfect*. "*What a sweet daughter you have, Sue.*" "*I know. Isn't she a dear?*"

No, she is not a dear. Our relationship is toxic, always trying to push this false perfection. And it has eaten away at my mother, this pressure to put on a mask for the outside world. Meanwhile, she is dying inside. It finally came to a head two months ago. The cracks showed, she got fired, and tried to take the easy way out.

Only, she didn't really. She did it for attention. She knew exactly when to take the pills. She knew when I'd come home. She knew I'd find her in time.

If she really wanted to end her life, she could have. Could've taken the pills at night, and by morning she'd be dead. I would've slept through the whole thing.

But no, she did it for attention. Another sick, twisted game to manipulate me and other people into feeling sorry for her and giving her the attention she's always so desperate for. She didn't give a single thought to the fact that if I hadn't found her, she would've left me alone, orphaned.

At this point, that would've been better. Then she wouldn't have dragged me to this place. Wouldn't have separated me from my friends and life. Really, helping her was a mistake. If I hadn't called for help and saved her life, none of this would've happened.

And now, instead of *her* life ending, *mine* has. All that is left is to snuff out my body.

The bugs chitter as they scratch-scratch at my brain. I need to end this tonight.

I'll use Mum's pain meds. Only, I'll do it properly—not like her so-called "attempt."

She walks up to the lounge window and folds her pudgy arms over her bloated belly. Her presence makes my skin crawl. The bugs scratch furiously.

"We're going to have to do something about that tree," she says absently.

Her voice sends fresh anger through my veins. *Shut up. Just shut up!* I should say it out loud. Scream it at her. The look on her face would be priceless.

But, no. Then I'd have to deal with the fallout. Her whining, her crying. I cannot deal with any more of her crying. I guess there is a price to it, after all.

I cannot deal with her anymore. None of it. Her existence, the scratch-scratching in my head, this place. This place is hell.

Why did Mum have to force me to come here? She can do what she wants, but leave me out of it. She didn't have to uproot my entire life. I'm almost eighteen. I could've stayed with friends for a few months, but no. She had to make me leave. She had to drag me along on her mid-life crisis.

Why would she do that to her own flesh and blood?

I know the answer.

She wants to ruin my life. She's jealous of me and everything that I have that she doesn't. My friends, my youth. She thinks I don't see it, but I do. She's jealous and so she wants to take everything away from me. If she can't be happy, then neither can I. She sponges off me. Leeches off me. Literally sucks the life right out of me.

Well, I'll show her. She scoffed when I said moving would kill me. That I'd kill myself if she made me come. She ignored my pleas to let me go back. She even had a sort of glint in her eye, like she enjoyed my suffering.

And here I am, giving her that power over my life.

If I don't take control of my own life—my own death—then who knows what I'll end up as? What this place will make me.

That scratching, scratching in my head—it's this place. Growing like cancer inside me, making it so I cannot sleep. Cannot ever rest. Not in the almost two weeks since we got here. I don't belong, so it's going to eat at me, cut me down and destroy me. If it can't make me one of them, the fake-smiling ghouls, then it'll make me a different kind of crazy.

Scratch, scratch.

This is not living. It's time to end it.

Yes, tonight I'll show her I was serious. I'll make her pay for bringing me here.

Tonight, I will end my life.

I'm in her room. Mum is downstairs, cooking dinner. I feel oddly hopeful. Free. Now that I am taking back control. Now that my suffering will soon be over.

And with that, another feeling... glee? Yes, that's what it is. Satisfaction at the pain I will cause my mother. I'm taking away the one person she has left. The one person who is even aware of her sad, miserable excuse of a life. Soon, she will have no one. No one to cry to, no one to guilt-trip, no one to blame her depressing life on except herself.

I told her it would come to this. I gave her a chance to change it.

But she didn't believe me.

Because she doesn't know what it is like to intend to end your life. Not truly. It's freeing. I know that now.

Soon, she will pay for everything she has done to me. All the rules and scolding and lectures of "not under my roof." Now, the worst thing imaginable will happen "under her roof."

I go first to the medicine cabinet but, as suspected, Mum only has the low-key pills there. Paracetamol, ibuprofen, diclofenac... I know she has harder stuff. She gets codeine prescribed, unless she already burnt through that. I wouldn't put it past her. Self-medicating to forget her sad, lonely little life. Claiming chronic pain that no doctor can attribute to anything.

Because there *is* nothing physically wrong with her. It's all in her head, just a manifestation of her self-loathing.

I leave those pills there. I'll use them if it comes to it—enough diclofenac and ibuprofen will burn through my stomach lining, and the paracetamol will damage my liver something awful. I don't want to suffer when I do it. Hopefully she still has some codeine and even some sleeping pills so I can drift off peacefully into an endless sleep.

Finally, sleep. I smile at the thought.

I head to her dresser and pull open her drawer. I frown at the white and cream grandma-style underwear stuffed inside. Such a sad life. No romance in it at all. Of course not, who would be interested in her? She sucks the life out of anyone around her.

I rummage toward the back, grimacing that I have to touch her underwear, even if they are clean. My fingers brush against a familiar small plastic cylinder, just what I am looking for. Then, another... and another. My frown deepens and I pull the underwear away, piling them on top of each other to uncover about a dozen different pill bottles.

My eyes widen at the stash she has collected. Maybe she's planning to top herself again, properly this time.

I pull out one of the bottles. Tramadol.

In someone else's name.

I grab another. And another. Codeine... tramadol... lorazepam... zopiclone... all in other peoples' names. What is she doing with these? This is way more medication than she needs to top herself.

A chill rushes through me.

Maybe she isn't the only one she plans on giving them to. Maybe she has decided to take me with her.

The bugs dig at my brain, conjuring the image of that glint in her eye when she'd ignored my pleas to go back to my real home.

That glint... that glint was *evil*.

A second wave washes over me, but this one isn't a chill. This is a weight, lifted. Relief from the gloom and burden of repressed knowledge.

I know what it is, that blackness that hangs in the air here, thick and damp and suffocating. The shroud that is cast over Lilypond Lane that only I can see, because only I am immune.

It is a darkness—an evil—that has called my mother home. I couldn't see it until now, not fully.

That selfish cow. She is so jealous of me that she had to uproot my entire life, take me from my friends, move me to this place, just to snuff me out along with her, so no one would be around to ask questions.

Or was it all a ruse? Maybe she never intended to end her life. Maybe this was her plan all along—to end mine.

The thumping in my chest reaches my head, rattles the bugs, interrupts their digging.

My arrival to this place—that's when the scratching began. The bugs crawled in through my ears, burrowed into my brain, scratching and digging at it.

I thought they were the cancer, but now I see it clearly.

They are a warning. Warning me to beware of this place.

There is something so very wrong with this place. It has a hold of my mother. It always has. And now that she is here—now that she is home—she can finish her plan.

This is no longer about me ending my life. This is a fight for survival.

Here I was, ready to do the job for her. Take my own life. But *she* is the problem, not me. She is *my* problem. She is the cause of every bad thing in my life.

I stumble back. My legs hit the bed and I sit, processing.

I had been so close to ending it all. So close to never finding out this horrific truth. My life doesn't have to end—I just need her out of it.

I should've let her end it when she took the pills. I should never have called for help. If I hadn't, I never would've ended up here. I would've got to stay in our house—my *home*.

Not just stay there... I would have owned it. It would be *my* roof. Not hers. My roof, my rules.

As her only family, everything she owned would have gone to me.

Will go to me, if I finish the job she started. I can sell this house, and get my old one back. I can finally get the life I deserve.

My life will be far better without her.

This time will go how last time should have. This time, her "cry for help" won't get any help at all. I'll make sure she follows through, that the "suicide" is a success.

Tonight, I will end my mother's life.

I am in my usual seat, the one next to this woman whom I once called "Mum." I have to make things seem normal. I have to keep our usual levels of discomfort. If I change anything, that might tip her off, and who knows what she will do. If she planned to poison her own child… well, she might have a back-up plan.

The muscles in my neck tense. I don't have a back-up plan. *Should I?*

No, it will be okay. It will go to plan. It has to. I have crushed enough pills that once they kick in, she won't be in much of a state to retaliate.

I just need to get her to have them all.

She made dinner, so I couldn't put them in that. I had considered offering to help, but that isn't normal. It might have clued her in that I was up to something. I could've tried to slip them into the gravy while she wasn't looking, but that seemed too risky. And besides, I like gravy more than she does. She would question why I wasn't having it.

Heck, it might be poisoned already.

The bugs scratch deeper into the holes they are digging in my brain. Warning me that I am right.

I push the mashed potato around the plate, into the poisoned gravy, making it look like I am going to eat it. I glance up to check if she is watching me, to see if she is waiting for me to take a bite.

She is looking at her own plate as she carefully slices a portion of each item onto her fork. So particular with the ratios of each type of food, having to get a taste of everything on the plate in each mouthful.

So controlled, like everything else in her life. She has to control everything. Not just in her life, but mine, too. Has to control me. She resents me for taking her youth, and wants to live mine.

She is jealous of me, that's what it is. Resentful and jealous and hateful. That's what drove her to decide to poison her own daughter. I stole her youth and now she wants to steal mine.

I stab at a piece of meat and pull it off the fork with my teeth, careful to avoid getting any gravy in my mouth. My mother is eating the gravy, but that might just be because she had a separate little stash for herself, to lure me into a false sense of security, and trick me into eating it.

Scratch, scratch.

We "eat" in silence. I push the food around my plate some more, slicing off tiny pieces that haven't touched the gravy to make it look like I am eating.

When she is close to finishing, I take my own plate away and empty it into the bin before she registers how much I have left.

I have to bide my time, wait until the right moment. Wait until it is closer to bedtime, so she won't question her drowsiness. She will just go to bed, go to sleep, and never wake up.

And then my real life—the life I deserve—will begin.

"I'm gonna make a milkshake. You want one?" I ask casually, knowing she will say yes. I stand from my seat on the couch as she continues her blank stare at the television screen.

"Oh, sure, thank you," she says, not breaking eye contact with the screen. So rude. The evil has taken hold.

I head to the kitchen and prepare the two milkshakes—mine chocolate, hers lime, with an extra helping of crushed tramazezopideine, the most effective sedative she will ever take. The *last* sedative she will ever take.

I glance around and listen for movement before I pull out the small pill bottle containing the mixture I'd crushed earlier. I dump it into the milk, then shove the bottle back in my pocket. I thrust the cup under the mixer, moving quickly to reduce the risk of her coming in and questioning me.

Play it cool, I remind myself. *Act normal.*

I slow my breathing and my movements. I flick the mixer on and watch the milk, ice cream, cordial, and sedative whizz around, blending and frothing into my mother's final drink. It froths more than usual, and my heart rate rises while I plead it to dissipate. I pour the mixture into a glass, relieved to see that it looks normal.

I leave the majority of the froth in the mixing cup, then wash it thoroughly in the sink—washing away any trace of the medication. I take a cloth to the mixer and wipe that down as best I can. My heart thrums in my head as the bugs continue their endless scratching.

Breathe. It'll all be fine. No one's going to check for traces of medication on the mixer. This is a suicide, remember?

I have been practicing my mother's handwriting for years, to make all my school absence notes look legitimate. A simple, heartfelt, "I'm sorry" suicide note is all that is needed, and I have it prepped upstairs, ready to place by her bed after it is over. I will spill the remaining pills by her bed, to help paint the scene. All those pill bottles from all those different people, it will be clear that she has been planning this for a while.

Little would anyone know, it had been me she'd been planning to use them on.

I can and will play the grieving daughter, just like that girl down the street had. I will get pity and condolences, just like her. I will let it all play out until I get the house handed over and sold. Then I can leave this place and return to my real life. A better life, without her in it.

I rinse the cloth before dropping it in the sink, and carry the drinks through to the lounge.

I sip at my milkshake, pretending to watch TV. From the corner of my eye, I watch her drinking the elixir.

She scoffs it, the little piggy she is. All those pills are now sitting in her belly, just where they should be. They won't take long to work, in their crushed form.

I keep sipping at my shake, a welcome distraction for my hands and mouth, so I don't fiddle or chew my lip.

It is just after the next ads break that her face begins to crumple, and she puts her hand to her belly. By the time more ads come on, she announces with a groan:

"I'm not feeling too well. I think I'm gonna go to bed."

I nod, the glass still brought to my lips to hide any smirk that may make itself known.

"Okay, night," I say, cooly.

She stands, shakily, and puts her hand to her head. My eyes widen. Did I put too many in? Maybe she is going to collapse, right here in the lounge. That won't look good. It won't look like a suicide. I bite onto the glass.

She steadies herself and hobbles over to the stairs. She holds the handrail as she takes each step, slowly, but steadily enough, and eventually leaves my sight.

I turn back to the television, continuing to sip my milkshake. I give it until the end of the episode before I consider going to check how things are progressing.

It makes more sense to leave her until the morning, to make sure she is dead, and then stage the extra pills. But, it is probably safer to do it early, in case she spills water or something, and the pills need time to soak up. Besides, I kind of want to watch.

I peer through the narrow crack her door makes next to its frame, only slightly ajar. Just enough for me to watch her writhe in bed, curled up, grasping at her belly. I briefly consider offering her something for the pain, just for the sheer satisfaction of that irony.

I should feel something, but I don't. What does that say about me? It's not that I'm sick or heartless. She did this to herself. She was going to do the same to me. Really, this was self-defence.

She turns and vomits as she half slides off the bed, the sheets wrapping around her waist and one leg, clutching her,, not wanting to let her go. Calling her to die within them.

But gravity and her writhing win, and her other leg thumps to the ground, along with her hips, as the sheets lose their grasp.

She is face down on the floor, now, her arms pinned under her, still coughing and spluttering, chucking up bits of phlegm and vomit. She turns her head to the side and continues to cough. The heavy drops splatter across the carpet, forever bonding with the fibres. I'll have to replace the carpet when she is gone. No one will buy this house in that state. Not with the stench and stains of bodily fluids of my dying mother.

She rolls, and manages to free one arm. She scratches at the side table, like she is trying to climb it. She gurgles something that sounds like my name, and I tense. Does she know I am here? She coughs again, clearing her throat enough to say my name more clearly, though it is still just a whisper. Her voice is so weak there's no way I would've heard her if I was downstairs. I stay still, mentally reciting what I will say to the police when they ask why I didn't help her: *"I didn't know, I was asleep, if only I'd known..."*

She curls up, facing the door, and I tense again, holding my breath. Does she sense me?

She claws at the carpet with her free hand, reaching out toward the door. Toward me. Her legs swing back as she pulls her torso forward just an inch, rolling enough to free her other arm from its prison beneath her belly.

"Paige," she moans again. Adrenaline surges through my veins, but I am frozen, not breathing, not blinking. Just staring at this woman, now so pale and sickly, foaming at the mouth, vomit smeared across her chin, speckles on her cheeks, as she reaches her other hand out and rakes at the carpet.

She knows I have done this, and she is coming for me.

"Pai-" She chokes on something—probably her own vomit—and splutters.

The corners of my mouth turn up ever so slightly. She is too weak. Even if she knows I am here, even if she is coming for me, there is no way she will make it here. Her body is shutting down. Her organs are bursting and bleeding inside her.

She stretches her arm out, digging her fingers into the carpet, her knuckles white, the desperation evident through the ligaments and muscles protruding from her skin. A last attempt to get to help. To get to *me*.

Her weight and friction against the floor are too much for her dying limbs. She drops her head onto her outstretched arm and looks toward the door. She coughs up more vomit. It dribbles down the side of her mouth and cheek, onto her exposed arm, then onto the carpet. Her head tilts back, and our eyes lock, just as the life drains out of her.

I stand over my lifeless mess of a mother. This is what her jealousy—her darkness—got her. If she hadn't been so set on ruining my life, then maybe she could have made something of her own.

I place the bottles of pills belonging to strangers on her bedside table. I drop the caps onto the floor. Taking my index finger, I flick one bottle off the table, then another. The remaining pills spill onto the floor, some landing in vomit that has already seeped into the carpet.

I place the handwritten note by the bedside lamp. It is addressed to me.

I couldn't help but add an extra few words. It is simple, poetic in her final message to me.

"I'm sorry I wasn't enough."

The bugs have stopped scratching at my brain. It was her. She was the cause of my suffering.

Now that she is gone, I am free.

Tonight has changed everything.

Tonight, I have reclaimed my life.

The Daily Scoop

Teen found guilty in murder of mother

By Olivia Whitman

April 6

Two lives were ruined in a "selfish act," said Justice Avery after the jury returned a guilty verdict for the teenage girl accused of murdering her mother on May 16 last year.

Paige Turner, who poisoned her own mother and remained present at the residence while the victim slowly died, had initially entered a plea of self-defence, claiming her mother had poisoned her with the plan to end her life.

When these claims were disproven, the defence claimed not guilty by reason of insanity, employing three forensic psychiatrists to testify to this fact.

The jury ultimately sided with the psychiatrist provided by the Crown prosecution, who stated the defendant "knew exactly what she was doing." The psychiatrist agreed that the defendant may have believed that her mother was poisoning her, however she had ample opportunity to seek help.

Public opinion echoed these sentiments, with many interviewees frustrated at the repeated use of mental illness as an "excuse for bad behaviour." One mental health worker, who requested to remain anonymous, stated: "mad is not bad. They're not the same thing. [Paige] wanted her mum out of the picture, so she killed her. But I don't expect this was how she saw it turning out."

Sentencing is set for June 30, though murder incurs a mandatory sentence of life imprisonment, with a minimum non-parole period of 10 years.

The murder joins a series of horrific discoveries on the otherwise peaceful suburban street where the teen and her mother had recently moved. A neighbour, who did not want to be named, called this a "senseless tragedy."

"That girl had her whole life ahead of her. Now she'll be rotting in prison for what should've been the best years of her life."

When asked about the other occurrences in the area, the neighbour declined to comment, besides stating: "I just don't know what has happened to our lane. Things like this really make you question how well you know your neighbours."

Rachel Graham is a mental health nurse living in New Zealand with her husband and two dogs. Her inspiration is drawn from her experiences in the inpatient unit and community, and the stories of those she has worked with. Her writing is informed by her close engagement with people experiencing acute mental illness as they navigate life, relationships, and the mental health system.

Her first book, Follow Me, is available now. Follow her (no pun intended) across all social media: @rachelgrahamreads on Facebook, Instagram, TikTok, and X

Email: rachgrahamreads@gmail.com Website: rachgrahamreads.com

Let Him Rot

BY EMILY LONG

After Maisie's mom dies, she struggles to find any joy in life. Then, she meets her neighbor, Cecil. Despite her mom always hating him, Maisie thinks there's no harm in getting to know him. After all, he's just a sweet old man, right?

The front door of 7 Lilypond Lane whined on old hinges as Maisie closed it behind the last of the well-wishers. Aged wood scratched against her skin as she held her palm against it, taking a grounding breath before sliding the deadbolt into place. Only a week since her mother had passed, and it felt like an eternity. Her face ached from the forced smiles, her throat raw from the endless conversations. Neighbors she'd only glimpsed in passing had come out in droves today, offering casseroles and company, as if it would make up for the loss she had suffered.

When she was sure no stragglers lingered on her porch, she flicked off the overhead light. "Well and truly alone now," she mumbled to herself. A soft mew answered, and she cast her gaze to the fat tabby cat lounging on the sofa. She moved towards him, fingers reaching out to caress his soft fur. "Sorry, Lou. You're right. I still have you."

He stuck up his nose, as if to say, 'How could you forget?'

Maisie turned off the living room light before moving to the staircase at the back of the house. The wood creaked beneath her feet as she ascended, trying not to think about the dense silence. All she could hear was the tick of the grandfather clock at the top of the stairs. Gilded gears spun and whirred as the time sounded: 6 p.m. sharp. Summoned by the clanging of bells, a sunny-gold cuckoo bird shot out from the clockface, its cheerful demeanor so at odds with Maisie's own. The door to her mother's room, adjacent to the massive clock, was sealed shut. A sigh lifted from Maisie as she opened it and stepped inside. The heady scent of roses slammed into her, and she pressed a hand against her nose. The bed was as her mother had left it: unmade and riddled with loose tissues. An IV machine sporting a half-empty fluid bag flashed green numbers — probably notifying the user that it was disconnected. Maisie knew that particular machine would never be connected again.

It had only been six months since her mother was diagnosed with stage four pancreatic cancer. The diagnosis had come as a shock, with her mother fighting until the very end. At least, that was until three weeks ago. The doctors said there was nothing more they could do, and that she should move to hospice care. Maisie left her job in the city as soon as her mother was diagnosed. Her dad had walked out on them when she was five — they only ever had each other.

And Lou, of course.

Now that her mom was gone... she didn't know what to do. Who to turn to. Maisie sat on the unkempt bed, wincing at the smell radiating up from it. Roses and something... worse. Something almost sour. The fading sunlight bled through the gauzy curtains that adorned the window overlooking the bed. Maisie peeled a curtain back, peering down at the street below. The last of the visitors had already disappeared into their homes, taking their well-wishes with them. She was pretty sure that all of her neighbors had come tonight. A small comfort, at least.

Movement across the street caught her attention and she squinted as the front door of 12 Lilypond Lane swung open. First all Maisie could see were the wheels of the walker as they caught on the gnarled wood of the porch. Then, age-spotted hands that gripped the handles for dear life. An old man shuffled out the door before kicking it shut behind him. He hunched over the walker, his legs wobbling as he stepped gingerly down the porch steps. Only a faint glow from the sunset still graced the neighborhood landscape. He'd soon be cast in darkness.

So not every neighbor had come then.

How could she have forgotten Mr. Wallace from across the street?

The little old man who walked alone every day at sundown. The old man who her mother always called a creep, a recluse who deserved to be alone.

Maisie didn't think anyone deserved to be alone.

She couldn't help herself as she watched him shuffle along the sidewalk, wheels dodging every crack in the pavement, like he'd taken this route a thousand times. Which, of course, he had. When he reached the front of Maisie's house, he paused, lifting his gaze to the window she peered through. Maisie couldn't make out his eyes behind the thick glasses he wore, she couldn't make out his expression as he lifted a hand in greeting.

Something warmed inside of her as she lifted one back.

Days turned into weeks as Maisie got her mother's affairs in order. Every night, like clockwork, Mr. Wallace would wave to her from the street. Maisie would always wave back, looking forward to their brief interactions more than she'd like to admit. She hadn't had any real human companionship since the week of her mother's death.

Her job hunt had been unsuccessful, so she'd taken to entertaining herself with cheesy romance books and unfulfilling Tinder dates. At only 25, she thought she'd have more to live for. But with her mother dead and her friends hours away in the city, her daily wave to Mr. Wallace was the best she could get.

The oven dinged, catching her attention. She shot up from her spot on the sofa, moving into the well-loved kitchen. She pulled open the oven door, the smell of lasagna making her mouth water. An oven mitt hung on a hook just inside the cupboard, so she slipped it on before pulling the lasagna out and turning the oven off. Lou was at her feet in an instant, belly-swaying as he weaved himself between her legs.

"Stop it," she chided. "You already had your dinner!"

Lou mewed but obliged, skulking across the room.

Maisie scooped herself a portion before settling at the worn kitchen table, facing the street outside. She had officially reached the end of the casseroles. Having frozen most of them, they had done well to sustain her these past few weeks. In just a few days she would have to accept that she needed to start cooking for herself again. A hum escaped her unbidden as she took a bite, the flavor of the cheese swirling across her tongue. Her mom had always loved cooking, a trait Maisie hadn't inherited.

She instead loved to bake. Her mother had once sworn that they'd open a restaurant together — with Maisie only in charge of the desserts, of course. Tears welled in Maisie's eyes as she swallowed, grief threatening to choke her.

Just outside the window, she could see Mr. Wallace's shadow stretching across the sidewalk from the opposite end of the street. Sunset had only just begun — he seemed to be out early today. Maisie begged the tears to cease before he appeared in her line of sight. She sniffled, wiping her cheeks with the back of her hand.

She sucked in a breath, watching as the shadow edged closer and closer. Any minute now he'd appear. She begged silently for him to pass, leaving her to cry in peace. She knew she could just close the curtain, but she felt like if she did, she'd let him down. Like maybe he looked forward to their brief interaction each day just as much as she did. The shadow moved — closer, closer, closer. It jerked suddenly before stilling.

Maisie held her breath, waiting for the shadow to move. Nothing happened. She shot to her feet, dinner forgotten. Slipping on a pair of slippers by the front door, she stepped out into the diminishing sunlight. The sound of cicadas was nearly overwhelming. Mr. Wallace lay across the street, his walker beneath him. Maisie could make out his soft groans as she approached, horror overtaking her. His pageboy cap was splayed on the sidewalk. Blood coated his bushy, gray brows.

"Mr. Wallace?" Maisie whispered, afraid to startle him. Afraid of what she'd do if he didn't answer. If he couldn't answer. She stepped closer, able to make out his eyes. They were pale blue, unfocused behind skewed glasses with lenses thicker than her pinky finger. "Mr. Wallace?" she repeated, louder this time.

A shadow of recognition snapped into those blue eyes as he blinked before turning his attention to her. "Hello?" His voice was meek, the tone lighter than she had imagined. "Bethany is that you?"

Maisie crouched down beside him, reaching a tentative hand out to touch his shoulder. "Mr. Wallace, it's me. Maisie." He only looked confused, so she amended, "Your neighbor. We wave to each other every day."

"Oh. Maisie." He shifted, trying to push himself up.

Maisie flushed, ashamed that she hadn't immediately done that herself. She placed her hands on his shoulders, lifting him gingerly from the sidewalk into a sitting position. He felt breakable beneath her touch — like a frail bird. "Are you alright?" she asked, looking him over closer now. Aside from a scrape above his eyebrow and some cuts on his hands, he didn't appear to have any other injuries, though she couldn't be sure that he hadn't bumped his head.

"Yes, dear." He had more clarity in his gaze now, his eyes roaming her face. "My, what a pretty thing you are."

Maisie smiled, despite herself. "Are you okay for me to help you up the rest of the way?"

Mr. Wallace nodded, so Maisie placed her hands beneath his arms, carefully hoisting him to his feet. He was heavier than she expected. He kept a hand on her to steady himself as she bent to pick up his walker as well. His aged hands shook as they wrapped around the handles, the grip so tight his gnarled knuckles were white.

"Can I call someone for you?" Maisie asked, placing a guiding hand on his upper back as he turned back towards his house. She didn't want to force help on him — her mother had been very independent before she died, refusing any help getting around or performing tasks. The last thing she wanted was to accidentally anger him by stepping over the line.

"No, dear. I don't want to trouble you."

"It's no trouble at all, Mr. Wallace, really," Maisie promised, moving at a snail's pace beside him.

"It was just a scrape," Mr. Wallace replied, determination in his voice. He halted, those all-knowing eyes meeting hers. "Call me Cecil."

"Yes sir," Maisie said.

Mr. Wallace raised a bushy brow.

"Yes, Cecil?" Maisie corrected, her voice squeaking,

Seeming satisfied, Mr. Wallace — Cecil — nodded before resuming his pace to the house. "You hardly ever leave that house of yours," Cecil said.

Maisie felt her cheeks heat. "I've been busy," she quipped.

Cecil snorted, his feet scuffing along the pavement. "It's a shame a pretty thing like you is locked inside."

Discomfort spread like oil in Maisie's veins as she lifted her guiding hand from his back. "Oh."

"You remind me of my granddaughter. Kind of look like her, too. Same freckles," Cecil said gruffly.

Maisie released a breath, relief causing a weight to lift off her chest. Not a perv, then. Just lonely. "What's her name?"

"Bethany," Cecil grunted, taking the first step up his front porch. "Pretty little blonde thing, just like you." His gnarled hands pulled keys from his pocket. They jingled as they slid into the lock. Maisie stepped back, content to let him see himself inside. Cecil paused just over the threshold. "Can I offer you some tea as a thank you?"

Maisie shook her head. "Another time, maybe."

"I'll hold you to that, blondie," Cecil grunted before closing the door. Maisie heard the sound of at least five locks turn before she headed back across the street.

Lou was waiting just inside the door when Maisie returned home, something like concern painted across his little brown face. He huffed when she closed the door behind her before sauntering to the living room. Maisie laughed, returning to the lasagna that she knew was cold by now. Miraculously, it still sat on the kitchen table — untouched by Lou. She sat down, too lazy to reheat it. Cold lasagna would have to do.

She thought over her interaction with Cecil. In those final moments with him, he had reminded Maisie of her mother — independent. Someone not to be messed with. She supposed it was fair, given he said she reminded him of his granddaughter, Bethany.

Something about the name 'Bethany Wallace' was familiar to Maisie. She fished her phone out of her pocket, typing the name into the search engine. She doubted anything would come up, but she wouldn't be able to rest until she at least looked. To her surprise, dozens upon dozens of articles popped up. They were all dated from the '90s. She scanned the headlines: 'Missing small-town girl disappeared without a trace,' 'No leads on Bethany Wallace investigation.'

Maisie's jaw dropped as she clicked on a more recent article, this one from 2010. It was titled 'Still no body ten years on: where is Bethany Wallace?' Maisie scanned the article as she ate. "Cecil Wallace is still convinced his daughter is to blame for Bethany's disappearance," she read aloud. "There has been no trace of Bethany Wallace or her mother, Kayla. This is the latest in a string of disappearances near Lilypond Lane."

A shudder swept through her as she exited out of the article. Intrigued, she typed 'Disappearances near Lilypond Lane' into her search engine. Cold seeped through her as she scrolled through the results. Starting in the late '70s, seven girls had been reported missing: all teenagers. No bodies were ever found. Feeling sick, she closed her phone and rose from the table. She went through the motions of washing the dishes, numbness spreading through her. She hadn't realized how many disappearances there were in the neighborhood. She couldn't believe how uneducated she was about her hometown. Her gaze found Lou, who was watching her from atop his cat tower in the living room. "Good thing I have you to protect me, big man," she said.

Curiosity niggling her, Maisie opened her phone again. Article after article captivated her. She read about how distraught Cecil had been when Bethany disappeared. He detailed how he'd raised her after Bethany's mom skipped town. She never even came to inquire about her missing daughter. Maisie shuddered, her gaze landing on the greenery that made Lilypond Lane famous. Beside from the neighborhood boasting a great homeowner's association, the pond and the greenery that surrounded it caused Lilypond Lane to be a coveted place to live. Maisie never understood why. Growing up, she'd thought all the pond was good for was attracting mosquitoes and bullfrogs that wouldn't shut up in the summer months. Her mother never let her around the pond, anyways. After reading the articles, Maisie knew why.

Every missing girl was last seen near the water.

Gooseflesh remained fixed along her arms for the rest of the night. Images of the missing girls haunted her dreams. Horrific nightmares and unwelcome thoughts left her feeling restless the next day.

It was only as sundown neared that she came up with a solution to stop the horrible thoughts. Maybe her relationship with Cecil could heal him as much as it had healed her since her mother passed. Maybe he just needed an outlet for his grief. Maybe he just wanted to talk to Bethany.

Maisie laced up her shoes as soon as she saw Cecil lock his front door. She tied her hair back in a braid, blowing a kiss to Lou before heading out into the street. Cecil grinned when he noticed her, showing all his teeth. Maisie smiled back. She couldn't believe her mom had thought he was creepy — he was just a sweet old man.

"Maisie, what a lovely surprise," Cecil said as she joined his side.

"I figured fresh air could do me some good," she replied, slowing her pace to not out-walk him. "And after last night... I wondered if you wanted to talk about Bethany."

Pale blue eyes met hers. "Is that so?" His tone sharpened.

Maisie winced. "I'm sorry. I don't mean to pry. I just thought ... well, I don't know. Talking about my mom has helped me with my grief. I thought maybe it would be the same for you."

Cecil looked forward, hands tightening their grip on his walker. "She was only 18, about to go off for her first semester of college." He rolled out his shoulders, his gaze moving to the greenery off to the side. "She used to love that damned pond. Would spend evenings in the summer catching fireflies and practicing skipping stones. Then one day, she just never came home."

"I'm so sorry."

"My backyard has no fence; the porch overlooks the pond. You'd think I would've seen something."

"You shouldn't blame yourself."

"I don't, but I never stopped looking. Even if I don't get around as easily as I used to." He laughed; the sound soon interrupted by a wheezing cough. He paused his walk, hacking into his hand. When he collected himself, they continued. "And your mother?"

"Cancer," Maisie said thickly. She cleared her throat.

"That's never easy." Cecil gave her a grim smile. "Her name was Elise, wasn't it?"

"Yes. I didn't know you knew her," Maisie admitted. They began their slow return towards Cecil's home.

"Oh, not well. I don't think she liked me very much. She seemed intent on helping Bethany's mother, Kayla, get custody of her from me. They used to be friends, you know. Until Kayla skipped town. I don't think your mother even knew what happened to her."

"Really?" Maisie hadn't ever heard her mom mention Kayla. But she *did* remember her dislike of Cecil.

They reached Cecil's porch, and Maisie stopped at the bottom of the stairs. Cecil ambled up them, the wood creaking beneath his feet. Key in the lock, he looked over his shoulder at her. "Come in for tea, won't you?"

Maisie shifted on her feet, glancing back at her house across the street. "I don't know..."

"That's okay. I'm sure you wouldn't want to spend your Saturday with an old man like me." Cecil shrugged, keys jingling as he worked the lock. He pushed the door open.

"Wait," Maisie said, hopping up the steps. "I guess I have time for *one* cup." She patted her pocket, making sure she had her phone. She hadn't locked her front door before her walk, but she wouldn't be long.

The scent of stale newspaper hit her as she followed Cecil into his house. He waited until she reached the foyer before he closed the door, locking it. Maisie's brows rose. Five deadbolts lined the length of the door. Cecil chuckled at her reaction. "You can never be too careful," he said.

Walker abandoned by the front door, he hobbled past Maisie towards the kitchen. She moved slowly behind him, examining his house. Faded yellow wallpaper and busted furniture decorated the living room. Pictures in mismatched frames hung along the walls. She peered at one of the photos. It depicted a girl she could only assume to be Bethany. Cecil was right that they looked similar. Bethany's long blonde hair hung in waves, her hand was held up in a peace sign, and she had a big grin on her face. Maisie smiled, moving to the picture beside it. Another blonde woman, Kayla, maybe, and Bethany grinned in lawn chairs by the pond. The photo just below that one was of Kayla and...

Maisie blinked.

Her mother's face smiled up at her. Tears sprang to her eyes as she touched a finger to the frame. Her mother and Kayla looked like teenagers, blowing bubbles at the camera.

"The tea is ready!" Cecil called from the kitchen.

Maisie wiped her eyes and joined him. She accepted the mug he handed her and took a seat at the round dining table. The chair groaned as she settled into it. "There's a picture of my mom hanging up."

"Oh?" Cecil scratched his chin, taking a swig of his tea. "I must've forgotten."

"You really didn't know her well?"

Cecil dipped his chin. "In her youth, a bit. But after Kayla left, I tried to avoid your mother."

"Really?"

"She wasn't the kindest after Bethany's disappearance."

Maisie stared down into her tea. It was unlike her mother to be cruel to someone suffering a loss, let alone the father of her best friend. She was sure her mom had a reason.

She looked back up at Cecil. "Why?"

Cecil slurped his tea loudly, smacking his lips. "She seemed to believe I had something to do with it."

Maisie almost laughed at that. She didn't know what Cecil looked like twenty years ago, but she didn't believe the old man could hurt a fly. There were knitting needles in a basket on the counter, for Christ's sake. Just a lonely old man who missed his family.

"She was pretty stubborn," Maisie said, tasting her tea. The liquid singed her tongue. She jumped, placing the mug on the table.

"Oh, dear," Cecil said, rising to his feet. "Let me get you some milk." He wobbled as he moved, arms swinging. Before Maisie could stop him, his hand hit her teacup and sent it tumbling to the floor. The mug shattered, spraying tea and porcelain in all directions. “I’m such a klutz,” Cecil wailed.

Maisie shot to her feet. “No, it’s my fault. I shouldn’t have set it so close to the edge.”

“Could you be a dear and grab the broom from the closet across from the front door?”

“Of course.” Maisie darted from the room. She scanned the foyer for the door he’d mentioned, breathing a sigh of relief when she found it. She gripped the knob and swung it open, reaching in to grab a broom.

Except, her hand met air. The door didn’t lead to a closet, but a staircase. Leading down. A basement, maybe? Maisie scrunched her brows as she peered down the dark, musty staircase. She was about to yell out for Cecil when she felt something hard and cool meet the small of her back.

Awareness speared through her as Cecil said, “Walk.”

“Cecil,” Maisie tried, voice wavering. “It’s me, Maisie.” She didn’t know Cecil well. She didn’t know if he ever got confused. She kicked herself for following him into his house without telling anyone.

The telltale sound of a gun cocking made her flinch and cry out.

“I said, walk.”

Maisie obeyed, knees shaking. She willed her racing heart to slow. She needed to calm down to think of a way out of this. “Please, Mr. Wallace. You know me.”

Cecil laughed, the sound harsh. “I know who you are, dumb bitch.” They reached the bottom step, where a second door awaited. This one was thicker — looking like the type of door used for a safe at the bank.

Gun still pressed to her spine, Cecil maneuvered himself in front of her. Gone was the tiny, hunched man he had presented himself as. This Cecil stood half a foot taller than Maisie, with a straight spine and sure glint in his eyes. He no longer looked like a strong gust of wind could take him out. There was a dial lock on the door, which he twisted. Maisie strained her eyes, trying to make out whatever numbers he put in.

She thought she glimpsed a zero and a seven, but the last number was lost on her.

The door opened on squeaky hinges. Maisie trembled as he pushed her forward into darkness. The scent of feces and body odor slammed into her. Cecil sealed the door behind them. She gagged, pressing a hand to her mouth. Her eyes watered as he flicked on a light, illuminating the space. A row of what she could only describe as cages lined either side of the massive room.

She counted six, two of them occupied. Her bladder released unbidden as he jabbed her with the gun, careening her towards an empty cage on the far side of the room. Each cell had a threadbare bed, a toilet, and a sink. The two occupied ones caged women of various ages, both watching her with sad eyes. Maisie stumbled as Cecil shoved her roughly into a cell, landing on her knees. She cried out as he slammed it shut, locking it.

Apathy shone in his pale blue eyes as he looked her over before turning his attention to the others. "Behave yourself," he said, spittle flying.

Maisie wailed as he walked away, leaving her behind. "Mr. Wallace!" she cried. "Please. *Please.*"

He ignored her, the sound of the door closing behind him sending dread into her bones. Maisie struggled to get a breath down between her sobs. Snot dripped down her face as she pushed herself to her feet. The other women watched her with rapt attention.

"Crying is a waste of time," one said, her voice scratchy. Maisie ignored her, yanking on the door of her cell. It wouldn't budge. She let out a cry of frustration before dropping to the bed, head in her hands. "What's your name?"

Maisie looked back to the woman. She looked to be in her forties, with blonde hair that reached her waist. Freckles dotted her pale skin. "Maisie," she whispered. "And you're Bethany, aren't you?"

Bethany nodded, slowly, sadly. Jagged shoulders peeked through her threadbare top. Her thin arms wrapped around her body as she crept closer to the bars of her cage. "What year is it?" she asked.

"2024."

Bethany gasped, hand flying to her mouth.

Maisie looked to the other occupied cell. A girl, not a woman, sat on the bed, watching the exchange with wide brown eyes. "What's your name?"

The girl blinked, cocking her head. "Jolene."

She couldn't be older than ten. And so small. Tears pricked at the back of Maisie's eyes.

"My daughter," Bethany whispered.

Maisie didn't have to think very hard to understand where Jolene had come from. She gagged, rushing to the toilet in the corner of her cell. She released her stomach, wiping her mouth when she was done.

"How?" she asked. "Why?"

Bethany sat on the floor of her cell, pressed into the bars. Her fingers wrapped around them, knuckles white. "He's sick," she hissed, eyes scanning the empty cells. "They were all full when he brought me here."

Maisie thought of the missing girls. "What happened to them?"

Bethany glanced at Jolene before sighing. "They died."

"Did they… have kids too?"

Bethany nodded. "What he did with them, I don't know."

The stench of urine invaded Maisie's nose and she gagged again, looking down at her ruined pants. "He'll bring you more," Bethany assured her.

"How long does he stay away?"

"It varies," Bethany said. "Sometimes only a few hours. Sometimes it feels like days."

Maisie stood, dusting the back of her pants. Her hand skimmed over a lump in her pocket, and her heart raced. Her phone. She didn't know how she'd gotten so lucky that Cecil hadn't taken it. Hands trembling, she slipped it from her pocket and unlocked it.

Zero service.

Stomach dropping, she still dialed 911. The call failed.

She screamed as she hurled the phone to the bed. Bethany peered between the bars."What's that?"

"A phone," Maisie said, dropping to her bed in defeat.

"Did it work?"

"No." She picked it back up, opening her photos app. Pictures of Lou and her mother greeted her. And oh god, *Lou*. What would happen to him with her stuck down here? No one would be looking for her. Tears continued their journey down her cheeks as she thought of him, alone and scared. He'd think that she abandoned him. She swiped to a picture of her mom, bringing a different sort of pain.

She'd be so disappointed in her. She'd always called Cecil a creep. Maisie should've listened. She was so stupid.

The sound of the lock being turned snapped her out of her pity party and she shot to her feet, shoving her phone beneath the lumpy mattress. She plastered a smile on her face and smoothed her hair, straightening her spine. The thick door swung open, Cecil bearing a tray full of plates. He whistled as he slid one to Bethany, then Jolene, then Maisie. His nose wrinkled as he looked her over.

"Did you build all this yourself?" Maisie asked, forcing a lightness to her voice. She didn't know how well she succeeded, seeing as tears continued to leak from her eyes. "It's quite impressive."

Cecil snorted. "Flattery won't get you anywhere." He looked her over again. "I'll be back with some pants."

The sound of the door closing was heavy.

Maisie sighed, picking up the plate. Unseasoned chicken, white rice, and peas. No fork or knife to be seen. Bethany noticed her disappointment. "My mom managed to fork him when she was down here. Now we can only use our hands."

The chicken felt cool to the touch as Maisie peeled off a bite. She chewed on the meat, the blandness nearly making her gag.

The possibility of being drugged crossed her mind, but she knew she would need her strength. The basement was windowless, with another door opposite the one Cecil brought her through. More cages, maybe? Her eyes scanned the cells across from her. Bethany's was threadbare, much like her own. But Jolene's was decorated with crudely drawn pictures and a fluffy pink comforter on the bed.

"Do you still have anything to draw with?" Maisie asked.

Jolene pushed her food away as she crawled towards her bed. She lifted the edge of the comforter, reaching for a box beneath the bed. The sound of plastic squeaking on concrete sounded as she pulled it out. Prying off the lid, she tilted the box towards Maisie, showing her the contents within.

Maisie squinted before sighing. Just crayons. She supposed pencils would've been too good to be true.

The door whined open, causing Jolene to jump and send her crayons scattering across the floor. They rolled through the bars of her cage, spreading like water across the floor. "Damn it, Jolene!" Cecil barked, slamming the door shut behind him. "If you can't keep your shit together I'll revoke privileges."

Soundless tears worked their way down Jolene's cheeks as she nodded vigorously, collecting her crayons in haste. Bethany glared up at her grandfather, abhorrence shining in her eyes. "She's a child."

Cecil ignored her, instead approaching Maisie's cell. He tossed a pair of black pants towards her, nose curling with distaste as he looked her over. "Put these on. Shove the soiled ones through the bars when you're done."

He turned on his heel, leaving them alone once again. The heavy sound of the door closing behind him settled deep into Maisie's bones. Her hands shook as she peeled off her ruined trousers, shoving them through the bar into the cell adjacent like he'd instructed. The linen pants Cecil had brought her were loose as she pulled them on, threatening to fall down her body. She sat on her bed, head in her hands. Tears slipped through her fingers as she cursed herself for her own stupidity.

Ted Bundy lured his victims by pretending to be injured. John Wayne Gacy worked as a clown part-time. Tons of serial killers operated the same way. She should've *known* better than to see what Cecil had wanted her to see. She should've known better than to have ever trusted a man. Especially one her mother had loathed.

How foolish she was to assume he was lonely, to assume that he craved companionship as desperately as she did. How foolish she was to think she was making his life better. Maisie wiped her eyes with her palms before straightening.

This would not be the end of her story.

She looked again to Jolene, who had managed to collect all of her crayons. Except one.

Bethany watched Maisie with closely as she approached the bars of her cage, crouching down onto her haunches. "Jolene, do you think you could blow on that crayon so it reaches me?"

Jolene merely cocked her head.

"Do what she says, lamb," Bethany said.

Jolene pressed her face against the bars, blowing gently on the crayon. It didn't take much before it moved, gliding across the room and landing right in front of Maisie. She picked it up with trembling fingers before tucking it into her sports bra.

"What are you thinking?" Bethany asked.

"I'm thinking I don't want to die here. I'm thinking I have an angry cat I need to get home to."

"And you think a crayon is the way out?" Doubt shone in Bethany's eyes.

Maisie said nothing, only moved to lay on the bed in her cell. The mattress squeaked as she laid down, springs pressing into her spine. Her heart ricocheted in her chest as she closed her eyes, hoping and praying an idea to escape would come to her in a dream.

Maisie woke to gnarled hands making their way across her skin. She jolted, fear keeping her pressed into the bed. Cecil stood over her, his smile showing all of his yellowed teeth. "Good morning," he cooed.

Bile rose in Maisie's throat as she trembled. Her gaze met Bethany's across the room, who frowned. Cecil's fingers shook as he worked as his belt buckle, licking his lips in anticipation.

"Please don't do this," Maisie begged, tears springing to her eyes.

"It'll be better for both of us if you don't resist," Cecil said, unfastening his trousers.

Roaring in Maisie's head caused her thoughts to race, her mind to come up with something, *anything* to convince him to stop. "I'm pregnant."

Cecil froze, his lip curling. "Pregnant?" He spat on her, the wad of saliva coating her face. "Stupid whore." He pulled his pants up, tightening the belt. Maisie didn't take her eyes off him as he backed out of the cell, sealing it behind him. "Fucking slut."

He stormed out of the basement, the lock on the door clicking shut behind him.

Slowly, Maisie reached up a hand to wipe her face. Her arm was sore from his bruising grip as she sat up, bewilderment spreading through her. How had that even worked?

"He's very traditional," Bethany said. "But now he'll have to get rid of you."

Maisie's stomach dropped. "What?"

Bethany cast a glance to her sleeping daughter before looking back to Maisie. "He only takes girls he thinks are pure."

"But your mother?"

"She was an exception. She'd become a thorn in his side."

"What happened to her?"

"He eventually got rid of her, too."

Maisie sank back onto the bed, wrapping her arms around herself.

The hours ticked by as she got lost inside her own head. Distantly she could hear Bethany teaching Jolene something. Math, maybe? But her roaring thoughts drowned out any conversation from the two of them.

When would he come back?

What would he do to her?

What could *she* do to him?

She tried to think back to every true crime podcast and show she'd watched. How had victims escaped their captors? She had to be clever. She had to think of something Bethany hadn't thought of before.

She didn't know how much time had passed when she asked, "Have you ever tried to escape?"

"Once," Bethany said. "When I found out I was pregnant." She swallowed, looking at her daughter with affection. "She's the only good thing to come out of this."

"What happened?"

"My mom was still around, then. Tried to strangle him through the bars. He lost it and took her away. Told me if I ever tried that again he'd kill me. So, I never tried again."

Maisie chewed on her bottom lip. "What about any of the other girls?"

Bethany shook her head, tears shining in her eyes. "They tried everything they could. Nothing ever worked."

Maisie's eyes flew to Jolene, an idea springing in her head. "And the children?"

"What are you thinking?"

When Cecil returned, they were ready. Maisie heard the jingle of his keys before he opened the door to the basement. He carried no food or water. Only a pair of handcuffs. Maisie's mouth went dry as he approached her cage.

She opened her mouth to speak but was interrupted by Bethany wailing. "Grandpa, I've been screaming for you all day!" Bethany sobbed, voice thick. "Something's wrong. Something's wrong with Jolene!"

Cecil approached Bethany, who pointed with shaking hands towards Jolene's cell. Jolene lay in her bed, sweat beading her brow, pale skin stark against the pink bedding that cocooned her.

"Jolene!" Cecil barked. Jolene didn't move, so he stepped closer. "Jolene!"

"Please, Grandpa. She's been like this all day. She needs a doctor."

"Shut it," Cecil hissed. He gripped the bars of Jolene's cell, squinting his eyes to look at her.

Maisie's heart raced as she watched, praying he'd take the bait.

Bethany continued to wail, dropping onto her knees. "*Please,*" she begged. "She's all I have. You can't let her die."

Cecil muttered under his breath before pulling a key from his pocket. He twisted it into the lock on Jolene's cell, the door swinging open.

Bethany grasped his ankle through the bars. He turned his attention to her as he stepped inside. "*Hurry.*" She released her grip, but his attention remained on her as he picked up his pace towards the bed.

It was such a shame he didn't notice the crayons scattered across the floor. Such a shame when he stepped on them, causing them to roll beneath his feet. He cried out as the momentum swept his legs out from under him. He toppled to the floor.

Maisie winced as his skull slammed into the cement.

"Now, Jolene. *Now*," Bethany urged.

As instructed, Jolene leapt out of bed, nimbly avoiding the crayons that had taken Cecil out. She picked up the key that had flown from his hand before fishing in his pocket for the rest. Cecil moaned, reaching for Jolene. Bethany reached through her bars, grabbing his shirt. She pulled his torso towards her, slamming him into the metal.

"*Don't fucking touch her*," she seethed.

Blood dribbled down Cecil's face. Jolene didn't spare him a glance as she darted from her cell, locking him in.

"Good job, baby," Bethany said, accepting the keys from Jolene. Her fingers shook as she sorted through them, testing them for the one that would unlock her own cell.

Maisie could hear her breathe in a sigh of relief as she found the right one. Bethany took shaking steps out of the open cage and then moved quickly, freeing Maisie next.

Maisie looked to the door she'd noticed the day prior. "Should we..?"

Bethany shook her head. "He used to spend hours in there. I'd rather die than see whatever he worked so hard on."

Maisie ignored her, almost feeling a pull to open the door. Like if she didn't take a peek at the kind of monster Cecil really was, she'd never be able to stop thinking about it. She twisted the knob ever so slowly, swinging the door open to reveal a dark room. The first thing that hit her was the smell. Mothballs mixed with something more acidic scorched her nostrils. She gagged, pressing a hand to cover her nose. She felt blindly along the wall for a light switch. Finding one, she flicked it on, having to squint as fluorescent light flooded her eyes.

Bile surged up the back of her throat as she beheld what Cecil had spent hours on. Bottles of chemicals lined stainless-steel countertops, bleached bones arranged by size sat before them. In the center of the room sat a large chair that Maisie could only describe as a throne. It was constructed entirely of bones. Human bones. Beside it was a small table, also made of bones. The books sat haphazardly stacked atop it, with a small teacup that still looked full of tea. Maisie's eyes widened. No, not a teacup at all — but a tiny human skull. One that looked like it could have belonged to an infant. The bone seemed almost paper thin, sawed in half with a golden handle decorating it. Maisie strongly doubted that the liquid inside of Cecil's 'cup' was actually tea.

Her hands shook as she turned off the light and closed the door behind her, not wanting to think about who those bones had belonged to. Not wanting to think about how that could've been her. What would he have turned her into? A footrest? Had he used that room to relax in? To listen to the cries of his victims?

"Well? What's in there?" Bethany asked.

Maisie shook her head. "It's better if you don't know."

Maisie moved her attention to the thick metal door that would lead them to freedom. The metal door that Cecil had... locked. With a rotary lock. She racked her brain, trying to remember the numbers she'd seen when he'd taken.

"He put in a zero and a seven, but I don't know what else."

Bethany twisted the lock, spinning it like she'd done it a hundred times before. Maisie sucked in a breath as she heard it click open. "An eight." Her eyes met Maisie's as she glanced over her shoulder. "For July eighth. My mom's birthday."

The door heaved open.

"You can't fucking leave," Cecil roared. Maisie jumped, his voice sending a spike of fear through her. He rose to his knees, hands clutching the bars of the cage. "You can't leave me down here."

Bethany's face hardened as she looked back at him. She stepped back into the room, leaving Maisie to keep the door propped open. Bethany dangled the keys in front of Cecil's face, dropping them just out of his reach. "Get yourself out."

She didn't spare him another glance as she moved back out of the room.

Anxiety threatened to suffocate Maisie as she followed Bethany, the metal door groaned shut behind them, muffling Cecil's cries of rage. The stairs seemed endless as they climbed. Mercifully, the door at the top was unlocked.

As meek as mice, they crept out into the home. A glimpse out the window told Maisie it was sunset, the golden rays creeping between lace curtains she'd originally thought were charming. A ding of a grandfather clock broke the heavy silence, announcing the time. 6 p.m.

Maisie could only watch in awe as Bethany stepped out the back door, as her toes met the grass for the first time in over a decade. Tears streamed down Bethany's cheeks as she fell to her knees, beckoning Jolene over. Jolene didn't hesitate, looking at the grass, at the sky, with eyes full of wonder.

Maisie blinked tears out of her own eyes as she approached them. Fireflies danced over the pond the street had been named for, casting their glow into the diminishing sunlight. For the first time since her mother had died, Maisie felt at peace.

"Now what?" Maisie asked.

Bethany smiled. "We let him rot."

Emily Long is from Texas but currently resides just outside of London to attend veterinary school. When she's not busy with animals, she loves reading and finding small bookshops around London. Her goal is to one day have a career like James Herriot: both fulfilling her love of writing and working as a veterinarian. This is her first published work.

Checkmate

BY ANDREA HECKNER

Every marriage has secrets. Sometimes they are little, sometimes they are shared, but with Dr. Geoff and Lynn Alter they are deadly. One spouse is a serial killer, and the other is aware. When secrets are exposed in this game of marital cat and mouse, only one of them will survive.

GEOFF

Living on the inner circle of the Lilypond Lane community was everything that I hoped it would be. I remember the day five years ago that my friend, James Montgomery, told me about the new housing subdivision that he was developing. The next day James and I drove out to walk around the land and talk about his plans. It had been my idea to make the whole subdivision circular. The inner circle went around the lily pond with five houses, then there were four increasingly bigger circles of houses with four arterial roads creating the ways in and out of the subdivision. An aerial picture of this slice of suburbia looked like a giant windmill.

After James had gotten all the roads dug in and the lots marked, I chose the one I wanted. It was the largest lot on the inner circle and gave me the best access to the pond which was essential for my plans. I convinced James to make the lot directly across the pond from mine into a community park and had agreed to split the cost of that lot with him. This provided a large grassy park-like area that gave community access to the pond. When I drove my wife, Lynn, out to the lot and told her about my plans for the house, she seemed surprised. I suppose other men may have discussed the purchase of the lot and the building of a new house with their wives before moving forward, but I saw that as a waste of time. It wasn't like Lynn's opinion mattered to me. She knows that I am in charge because, after all, she has never financially contributed to our marriage and has always understood the nature of our relationship.

My three-story completely custom house with a walk-out basement is the largest in the subdivision. Since I didn't care, I let Lynn pick out the fixtures and finishes throughout, which had made her happy. The thing I cared about most was the room in the basement that was built just for me. The room takes up about a third of the basement's footprint and has a cement wall that separates it from the rest of the basement. The entrance to the room was from the five-car garage with a door that can only be accessed using a thumbprint scanner that is set to only my print. In addition, there was a door that opened to the backyard that was secured in the same manner as the one above it. I told James that the room was so I could clean fish and wild turkey in it, as well as to securely store my weapons. What I actually use the room for is much more sinister. After the room was complete, I had come to the construction site at night to add the sound proofing, cage, surgical table, lights and equipment.

As I stare out at the pond, I think about what my life looks like to outsiders. I am an extremely successful cardiothoracic surgeon from a long line of successful, respected doctors. My wife is beautiful and athletic, and twenty years my junior. The first time I saw Lynn working at the bar where I like to meet politicians and other connections, I knew I wanted her. When I started talking to her, it became clear that she was the perfect candidate to be my wife. Besides being young, blond and beautiful, she is not very bright, and that is just what I want in a wife. My dad had been harping on me to find someone to marry. He is all about appearances and said that me being in my forties and unmarried was not the appearance that he thought I should portray. Of course, I was attracted to Lynn physically because who would marry someone they weren't attracted to?

Lynn and I have no children, which is my choice, not hers. She is completely unaware that I had a vasectomy in my twenties and I led her to believe that she was the one with the fertility issues. The guilt that she feels for not being able to produce an heir for me is just one more way I have control over her. Lynn is involved in all kinds of charities and is terrific at hosting dinner parties, but I don't consider her to be my partner. She is in many ways a necessary piece of equipment, much like my bone saw, that allows me to pursue my only passion. Hunting, torturing and killing young women.

The first woman I ever killed was when I was in medical school. The details are so vivid that I can play the whole night back like a movie. My father and I had gotten into an argument over my future specialty. He made it clear that he expected me, his son and namesake, to become a cardiac surgeon. My father planned to have the two of us practice together and if I didn't do as he told me to, there would be no more money coming my way. After storming out of the house, I drive my Porsche 911, a gift from dear old dad, for getting into the medical school of his choice, around the metro Miami area for hours. I ended up in the seedy part of downtown, where I picked up my first victim from a street corner. She hadn't even hesitated to get into my car and was pleased when I rented a hotel room for the entire night.

Sex had become a surefire way for me to blow off steam and was always better when the only expectation from the woman was payment. I despise emotional entanglements. My first victim was exactly my type: blond, young and petite. She had been asleep on the bed when I grabbed her from behind and strangled her during a sex act. I have never felt that great of a rush of adrenaline before or after. It is the feeling I have been chasing each time that I have hunted, tortured and killed again, but has eluded me since that first victim. After killing her, I carried her lifeless body into the bathroom and thoroughly washed her. Figuring out what to do with her body was the hardest part for me and something that I struggled with for each victim until the house on Lilypond Lane.

Chuckling, I recall the night that I released the two Crocodiles into the pond. I bought them off the black market knowing they were endangered species. It was right after we moved in, before the rest of the houses were finished and went unnoticed until about a year later, when the subdivision had filled up and a few small dogs went missing. Then the neighbor next door asked me if I had noticed that there were not as many frogs in and around the pond anymore. The missing dogs and lack of frogs and turtles were the talk of the HOA meetings. No one had been sure what was going on until one of the crocodiles walked into the backyard of a house on the other side of the pond to sun itself on their slate patio.

The neighborhood erupted into hysteria within hours, with many residents asking the Homeowners' Association to have the crocodile killed. Being the president of the HOA, I stepped in and suggested we call the Department of Fish and Wildlife. The two scientists that the department sent out quickly confirmed that there was not one but two crocodiles living in the pond. They told the HOA leadership board that the crocodiles were protected by law because of being endangered, and that the pond was a good habitat for them. The crocodiles could not be moved, much less killed. The solution the scientists had proposed, and the HOA had voted to go with, was an eight-foot chain-link fence surrounding the pond and a dart gun loaded with the paralytic Succinylcholine to be used in the unlikely event one of the crocodiles ever escapes. The subject of where the gate would be located was a hot topic until I generously volunteered to have the gate on my property. Each board member of the HOA had a key to the padlock, but I am sure that I am the only one who has ever opened it. The official reason for the gate, lock and keys is access to the pond in case of emergency, but I used to make sure those two crocodiles stayed well nourished. I was also given the dart gun for safekeeping.

Twice a year since we got married, Lynn has gone to Arizona to visit her mother. I plan my hunting trips around these events so I can take my time with the prey I catch. I drove Lynn to the airport this morning, presumably in the way any attentive husband would, but really just to watch her leave with my own eyes. I know she will call me each evening for the ten days that she is gone. I have everything planned for Lynn's trip, including blocking my appointment calendar, so I am completely off work. This is, of course, another thing that my wife is unaware of. Each evening this past month, when I left my office or the hospital, I cruised through the areas where prostitutes display themselves, looking for the perfect one for me. This is like everything that I do in my life, planned down to the infinitesimal detail.

I no longer use my own car to pick up my prey, but instead buy a junker car or van in cash just before the hunting season. I have a storage unit near the hospital that I park the vehicle in until I need it and then again after I have used it but before I can dispose of it by selling it to a junkyard. This time, I picked up a gray cargo van for a thousand dollars in cash. The van is sitting alone in the storage unit until I am ready. There is nothing else in the storage unit. I don't keep trophies like most killers. I don't need to; I have a photographic memory and can recall all of my kills in vivid detail.

As the sun begins to set over the neighborhood, I prepare to leave to pick up the van, then my house guest for the next week or so. I have narrowed it down to two of the working girls I have been watching, so whichever one I see first will be my next conquest. I walk into my master bedroom, which I am well aware is no longer a politically correct way to describe it but is correct because I am the master of my domain. I remove my Apple watch and set it on the charging station along with my iPhone. After a quick shower, I don a pair of athletic shorts, a hooded sweatshirt and a pair of flip-flops. I look ridiculous and so far from my normal well dressed self that I doubt even my own office staff would recognize me if they saw me driving by.

I drove my 1964 ½ fully restored Mustang to the storage unit. The car, while not being inconspicuous, is perfect because it has no tracking type technology. If, and this is a major if, I am ever questioned regarding my activities this evening or any other evening I have hunted for the last six years, there is no digital trail of my whereabouts. It is unlikely I would ever be questioned because of my friendship with the chief of police, Rick Snyder, and my connections to every politician in town. But, like everything else in my life, I leave nothing to chance. Parking the Mustang, I open the storage unit and pull out the van, then I put the Mustang where the van has been waiting. I take a few calming breaths as the anticipation begins to build and drive towards downtown.

There she is, the one I want the most, just standing there on the corner like she does not have a care in the world. In a few scant hours, she will have many cares. Pulling up to the curb, I reach over and roll down the passenger side window as she struts up to the van. We have a brief interaction, then she opens the van door and gets in. I drive a short way to an alley that I have pulled into many times before and tell her to get in the back. I follow her into the back of the van and tell her to get naked and lay down on the sleeping bag. As she pulls her dress over her head, I inject her in the side of the neck with a hypodermic full of tranquilizer. Getting the medications I need for these missions has never been an issue for me. I sign out a little extra for every surgery I perform and split them with an anesthesiologist who has his own needs. As the hooker falls the rest of the way down, I tie her hands and feet and then roll her up in the sleeping bag. Based on her weight and the amount of medication I have given her, I have five to six hours before she will be ready to play.

I drive back to my house without a care in the world and pull into the garage stall where my Mustang usually sits. As I walk around to the back of the van, I take a moment to appreciate my fleet. The Porsche and Mazaretti sit covered in the third and fourth stalls. In the first stall is my everyday car, an Audi Q 8 Prestige and next to it is Lynn's SUV, a Cadillac Lyriq Luxury 3. Every one of the cars is black and regularly maintained and detailed, which makes the piece of crap dull gray van stand out in the harsh lights of the garage. It won't be here long, so I push down the contempt I feel for it ruining the aesthetics of my garage. Before grabbing my cargo, I open the door to the basement room and flip on the overhead lights.

After I drop the hooker unceremoniously into the cage and lock it, I take out the first of the tools I plan to use, laying everything out like my scrub nurse does for me at the hospital. I leave the lights on as I depart the basement room so that when my guest wakes up, she can fully see her surroundings. I stroll into the house, mix a drink at the bar next to the kitchen, and head upstairs. I will take a four-hour power nap before I head back down to start my fun. Since moving here, I have come to relish the time I can spend with each of my victims. I glance at my phone and see a missed call from Lynn. She didn't leave a message because I have taught her not to. If she is safely at her destination and I don't answer her call, she knows that the missed call notification is all the contact that I need.

Falling off to sleep, I know I will not dream because my next few days will be better than any dream my mind can create. My last thought is that I may need to talk Lynn into visiting her mom more often.

Lynn

Watching Geoff pull the gray cargo van into his garage, I marvel at how much time, energy and money he puts into each of these projects. I know that by the time I return from supposedly going to see my mother, all traces of the van and whoever he has in the back of it will be gone. Geoff thinks I am totally clueless about so many things, but he is the one who is clueless. You see, I have always known that Geoff is a killer because he is the one who killed my sister seven years ago.

Evie, my older sister by two years, was a sweet girl who, unlike me, really was clueless. She became a drug addict while in beauty school. Within a year or so of the first time she did cocaine at a party, she was selling her body on the streets to keep up with her addiction. My mom cut her off after Evie stole from her a few times, but I never gave up on Evie. We met twice a month so that I could be sure she was alive. We always met at a hotel that was close to downtown. It was not a place she went with men but rather the cheap kind of place that down on their luck people stayed some times. I paid for a room for two nights, and Evie and I slept there. Twice a month she took a break from the streets, took a shower, ate junk food, played chess with me, which we have done since we were kids, and laughed until our stomachs hurt. That is until she did not show up seven years ago.

I sat in that hotel room for two straight days praying that she was just running late, then I drove around the areas that she hung out. Finally, I talked to the other prostitutes that I knew she was friendly with. I had met them a few times when I had given Evie a ride. All of them told me she got in a high end sports car a few days before and had not been back. None of them had been worried until I showed up because they told me they thought she was with me. Evie was never seen again and her body has never been found.

I filed a missing persons report with the police, but they told me that my sister was a drug addicted prostitute and therefore just off partying somewhere. They never even searched for Evie, but I became obsessed with figuring out what happened to my sister. The other working girls she hung out with told me that Evie was not the first of them to simply disappear, but it was hard to say what happened to any of them. Some women move on to other places, some go to rehab and get clean and some overdose and are buried in the pauper's graveyard. I checked every bus route and train, so I was reasonably sure that Evie never left town. I checked all the rehabs, the hospitals and the morgue. There was no sign of my sister.

About six months after she disappeared, I went out to the corner she used to frequent to see if anyone had heard anything. I was talking with Evie's friend Monique when a silver Maserati pulled up to the curb about two blocks in front of us. We watched as a petite, blond girl who was likely only fifteen or sixteen got into the car. As that car pulled away, I took a picture of the back end, including the license plate. Since Evie vanished, I have been taking pictures of the high end cars the men who picked up girls on this street drove. Then I handed Monique a prepaid calling card with my phone number written in marker on the back. She promised to call if she heard or saw anything that would help me find Evie. I left thinking that I would never hear from Monique, but I had to keep trying to find my sister.

The next night, or actually the early morning two days later, I was walking out of my job as a bartender when my phone rang. It was a number that I did not know, but that didn't stop me from answering the call. Monique was calling, but it wasn't about Evie, well at least not directly about her. The girl we had watched get into the Maserati had not been back, and Monique talked with her friends. It seemed the girl went by the name Sunny and crashed in a flophouse with several of the girls that Monique talked to. Sunny had never returned to the flophouse and her friends were worried because she left all her stuff behind. They said she never would have left without the photos she kept under her sleeping bag.

Once I got back to my apartment, I pulled up the picture I had taken and typed the license plate number into a search engine. It cost thirty dollars but was worth it because I not only had the name of the owner, but his address as well. In no time at all, I learned that Geoff Alter was a doctor and lived in a swanky condo in the part of downtown that had been gentrified. There were plenty of pictures of the good doctor and he was not bad looking. I also learned that I was certainly his type, young, fit, and blond, based on the various women on his arm at local charity events. That was when I came up with my plan, I was going to meet Dr. Geoff Alter Jr and make him mine. Then I would set out to prove that not only had he killed Evie, but that he was a serial killer.

After watching Geoff for a few months, I knew that he frequented a bar in a high end hotel near the hospital he worked at. Every bar I have ever known of is perpetually short of bartenders, so getting a job there was the easiest part of my plan. Within a few months of my starting at the bar, Geoff was aggressively hitting on me. I feared that if I was alone with him, he might murder me as well, but honestly, he was a perfect gentleman while we dated. He asked me to marry him with a great deal of fanfare at the mayor's annual Christmas party with the who's who of the city looking on. Our wedding would make many starry-eyed women envious, and my mother thought I was the luckiest woman in the world. I beamed that day but not from love but because my plan was going so incredibly smoothly.

We were married about a year when Geoff brought up having a baby. I almost laughed in his face because I would never be willing to have his child. Who would want to have a child with a monster? I continued to take my birth control pills, making sure that I kept them hidden and took them while he was at work. That was until I found out he had a vasectomy in his twenties. This is another fact that he believes I don't know, but at least this is one secret that I appreciate. After we failed to conceive, we went to a fertility specialist together. I am not sure how Geoff faked his sperm count test, but I for one sent a woman I paid to the lab to have her blood drawn. I remember looking at the results and thinking gosh; she is healthy as can be. The specialist declared that there was no known cause for our infertility and suggested In Vitro Fertilization. Geoff pretended to play along but quickly laid out for me all the reasons we should not go down that road. I seemingly acquiesced to what he wanted, and the subject of a baby was dropped. Well, at least between Geoff and I it was dropped. I am well aware that his father suggested on more than one occasion that Geoff divorce me since I was barren. His word, not mine. Geoff always put his dad off with talk of loyalty, but really I believe he no more wanted a child than I did.

The first few years we were married, we lived in Geoff's condo and there was little opportunity for me to figure out if he was still murdering. When he took me out to see the lot he had bought where his house now sits, I immediately knew he was up to something. I have never considered this to be our house. Yes, I live here, but it is not my home. From my count, he has killed eight women in this house since we moved in and tonight he plans to kill another. When I first started this, I planned to gather evidence to prove Geoff was a serial killer. Unfortunately, in the last six and a half years, I have come to understand that he is way too well connected for me to get anyone in authority to take me seriously. The only way this ends is for me to kill Geoff or for him to kill me. When I realized that I would have to take matters into my own hands, I began planning. I often wish I could have saved all eight of the women he has murdered on Lilypond Lane, but I needed to have everything in place first.

The couple across the street from us, Marge and Trey Anderson, are snow birds and within a few months of moving into their new home, mentioned looking for a house sitter. They intended to spend the summer months back in Wisconsin, where they had lived prior to moving here. I offered to be their house sitter and the access to their home provides me with the perfect place to plan and hideout from Geoff. I keep my laptop that I use for research at Anderson's house. Figuring out how to get into his basement room was the biggest hurdle. Luckily for me, Geoff supplied me with seemingly endless funds and rarely asked questions about my spending. The internet taught me how to collect Geoff's fingerprints from around his house. Using those fingerprints, I created a negative in Photoshop, printed that image, and then put wood glue on top of the imitated fingerprint. After the glue set, I molded the backside of each of his fingerprints to my corresponding fingers. When Geoff was at work, I tried each of the fingers on the scanner. When I pressed the thumb to the scanner, the lock clicked, and I opened the door for the first time.

Thinking back, I should have been scared out of my mind to go down those stairs, but I just kept thinking about Evie. I also should have been shocked by the room I walked into, but at that point nothing compared to the images I had created in my mind. The room was sterile as an operating room and resembled one in every way except for the cage. There was a locked cabinet which also opened by scanning the glue thumbprint. One side of the cabinet contained surgical instruments and the other vials of medications and syringes. I walked to the backdoor, noted that the dart gun for the crocodiles was leaning next to it, and opened it to the backyard. The gate to the pond was directly in line with the door. That was no coincidence.

When I visited my mom after gaining access to Geoff's lair, I picked a fight with her. I knew bringing up Evie would cause her to get upset, and I did it anyway. Reminding her she gave up on her daughter, but I never have was like ripping a scab off her broken heart. We have not spoken since, so she would never ask why I didn't come for my bi-annual visit. I feel bad about making her upset and leaving it like this for so many months. After I wrap up this situation with Geoff, I have to make it up to her. I hope that I am the one that survives because I would hate to die with this rift between mom and I. I wrote her a letter and it is sitting on the Anderson's kitchen counter. If I am the victor, I will shred the letter and, if not, the Andersons will find it when they return and hopefully mail it to her.

I never told Geoff about the fight with my mom, nor the fact that I would not see her this week. He drove me to the airport this morning, which he always does, though I have never really understood why. After he drove away, I got an Uber to the Andersons. I watch as the lights of the house go out and I know that Geoff will probably be asleep for a few hours. Walking to the back door of his house, I press the glue thumbprint to the scanner and let myself in. There is a young teen girl, passed out in the cage. Part of me is screaming to let her out, but I need to see my plan through to the end. Grabbing the dart gun, I tuck myself into a dark corner of the room and wait. My favorite game is chess and I feel like I just moved my queen into position. Game on!

Geoff

I don't need an alarm for these encounters, exactly four hours later, I wake up. I put the athletic shorts and flip-flops I wore earlier back on but nothing else. Clothes are not really an essential part of the next few days. The lights in the hallway, stairs, and most of the first floor are on motion sensors, so I do not need to waste my time with turning them on or off. I make my way through the house and down to my basement room. The hooker is sitting in the cage, crying, and begins to scream when I walk in. Like all the ones before her, I will make promises not to kill her if she lets me do what I want and at times she will actually believe me. There is no chance she will live, but I love to give them hope until I snatch it away. Her hands and feet are still bound, so the best she can do is slink back on her butt when I open the door to the cage. She is naked and shaking, probably from both fear and the cold of the basement. I drag her towards me and out of the cage.

Strapping her onto the operating table, I tell her that the less she screams, the nicer I will be to her. I wonder if she believes me because I know I don't. I reach to pull my shorts down when a movement behind me stops me. As I turn, I feel a sharp pain in my left foot and look down to see a dart sticking out. Looking up, I see Lynn standing a few feet from me with the dart gun raised. Pitching forward towards the table, I am able to get out the word why. Lynn's answer makes no sense to me. I would swear she said checkmate. She shot me with the Succinylcholine so I can hear what is going on around me but can't move a muscle. What the hell is she planning to do to me? How did she even get down here?

Lynn

It worked. He is paralyzed. I had been aiming for the side of his chest, but hitting his foot worked. Laying down the dart gun, I push him off the poor girl who he captured and ask her to help me. She seems to be still dazed but nods her head. I strip off my t-shirt and hand it to her. It is not much, but it is better than nothing. I open the backdoor and grab the Anderson's wheelbarrow that I left there a few hours ago. Together, we load Geoff into the wheelbarrow and I pick the dart gun back up. I unlocked the padlock before I went into the room tonight, so I just have to pull the lock out of the latch and swing the gate open. It is dark, and I mean dark. One thing the HOA did was ban people from having lights that illuminate the pond. It was Geoff's suggestion to not attract the crocodiles anymore, or at least that is what he convinced them the reason was. I am sure he just did not want some insomniac neighbor viewing his disposals.

I tell the girl to wait outside the gate and push the wheelbarrow towards the pond. Despite the cool night air, I am dripping in sweat. The two most risky parts of this plan were confronting Geoff, which went perfectly and walking into the crocodile enclosure. As soon as the ground softens and I feel the mud, I dump the wheelbarrow forward and Geoff out of it. I hear his body hit the water; I drop the dart gun and turn, running as fast as I can, pushing a wheelbarrow. As I come through the gate, the girl slams it shut and speaks for the first time.

"What is in there?"

"Crocodiles and my serial killer husband. Let's get out of here."

Geoff

As soon as that conniving wench put me in the wheelbarrow, I knew what she was going to do. I am shocked that she had the guts to confront me and now to walk through the darkness into the pond area. If you had asked me earlier today what would end my killing of women, never in a million years would I have said my wife Lynn would murder me. How did I miss the fact that she was on to me?

I feel the water splash as she dumped me out, and I know those crocodiles will be on me quickly. There is nothing I can do.

Lynn

I push the wheelbarrow into the garage of the house that I occupied with Geoff. The girl, whose name is Desiree, and I go into the house. I got her some clothes as we are the same size. I offered her the van as we passed it on the way in and she wanted it. Dropping me off at Geoff's storage unit, she drives away with a van. I hope that narrowly escaping a serial killer will be what she needs to get off the streets, but I know that I will never know for sure.

Two Years Later

Lynn

I wake up to the sounds of my mom in the kitchen. Laying in my bed in the primary bedroom, I think back over the last two years. I called Chief Snyder two days after I left Geoff with his crocodiles. The chief was patronizing to me when I told him Geoff was missing. It wasn't until seven days later, when he failed to show up for a scheduled surgery, that the police took Geoff's disappearance seriously. When a dozen officers, two detectives, and Chief Snyder showed up at the house, I played the ditzy, worried wife to a tee. The officers split up with half looking around the house and the other half outside. The detectives and chief were talking to me with the chief, starting by asking me why I didn't go visit my mom as planned. I marveled at the fact that he knew I was supposed to be gone and told him about the fight, not wanting Geoff to know and staying at the Andersons. I was about to explain how I began to worry about Geoff when he didn't leave for work, when all three of their cell phones began ringing. I watched as all of them and the officers in the house ran down to the gate to the pond. Standing on the deck, I could hear snippets of the conversations, they could see the dart gun and what looked like black fabric near the edge of the pond. The padlock was open and sitting on the ground to the side of the gate.

Animal control came out, and the crocodiles were temporarily moved to the local zoo while the police looked for evidence. When the police located a hip bone, it was tested and found to be Geoff's. There were distinct markings on the bone that could only have been made by a crocodile's teeth. The conclusion was that for unknown reasons, Geoff had entered the enclosure and that the crocodiles had overpowered him. My husband was declared dead.

I spent the next six months taking apart and disposing of his killing room, then listed the house for sale. Geoff had never sold the condo, so I moved in there. I told anyone who asked that I couldn't stand to look at the pond and think about what had happened to my husband. My mother had come for Geoff's funeral and we had spent the last two years growing closer than ever.

Today was a day of lasts and firsts for me. The last day I would be Mrs. Altar and the first day I would be Mrs. Rodriquez. I met Manny Rodriquez a year ago at the park where we both played chess. We went from competitors to friends and slowly to a romantic relationship. Manny is the opposite of Geoff in so many ways. He is from a large working class family and is proud to be the regional produce manager for a grocery chain. Sweet and soft-spoken, he treats me like the most precious person in the world. Our wedding this afternoon will be a small, intimate event on the beach because, after all, it is my second marriage. Oh, and I am four months pregnant with a little girl we will name Evie.

Andrea Heckner lives in Wisconsin (United States) with her husband, David. She has three grown sons and three grandchildren. When she is not writing, you will find her spending time with her family or reading. As a child, Andrea often made up stories to entertain her friends and siblings, and this continued when she had her children. Her stories have evolved over the years as she has refined her style and found a genre that intrigues her: Crime Thrillers.

As a public school teacher for twenty-plus years, Andrea loved to teach others to read and write as a way to experience the world as well as to express themselves. After telling students for many years to just write and let their stories flow, she took her own advice and began writing her novel. The Farm was released in August 2023, and she has since written three more books in the series and plans for at least two more.

To find out about Andrea's next releases, visit her website https://andreahecknerauthor.com/and her socials: Andrea Heckner Author Facebook PageAndrea Heckner Author Instagram

Metamorphosis

BY CAITLIN MAZUR

After a horrific accident leaves her orphaned, Carmen puts her faith in an unconventional wellness retreat that promises to heal her trauma. But when the retreat members begin getting sick and the leader's methods get progressively stranger, Carmen begins to lose her grip on reality. Now she's not even sure she'll make it out alive.

Carmen stands barefoot at the pond's edge and wonders if baptisms wash blood from your hands.

It's not a real baptism, of course. At least, she doesn't think so. Rona, the leader of the Metamorphosis retreat, looks just about as far away from a holy figure as one can get. The older woman wades through the pond water, her gray hair frizzing in the summer heat. Her brightly colored clothing hangs loose on her thin limbs which are adorned with clanging jewelry. A line of women follow her into the green water, Carmen at the end, her best friend, Isabelle, ahead of her.

The pond on Lilypond Lane has been a staple in Carmen's life since she can remember. Her parents bought a house here long before she was born. This place represented her childhood and adolescence. She moved back right before college graduation, anticipating this place to be part of her adulthood, too.

And then she killed her parents.

Large, detached homes encircle the pond and Carmen gets the distinct feeling someone is watching them. Let them. If this is the thing that helps her move past her trauma, she'll happily take the neighbors' whispers and judgments. The Metamorphosis retreat promises a shedding of old ways. A new outlook on life. And, most importantly, the ability to heal minds from deep trauma.

Isabelle convinced her to do this, and Carmen is desperate for it to work. After two months of inconsistent attendance, her job fired her. Her friends have grown weary of her grief. If she's honest, she's tired of herself. There is nothing she wants more than to forget the accident. Even if it requires being dunked in dirty pond water.

The line moves quickly and soon Rona is gathering Isabelle in her arms like she's holding a small child. She instructs Carmen's friend to cross her arms over her chest and then bends down, shoving Isabelle's tall frame beneath the water. Her long blonde ponytail floats, the only visible part of her.

"Without water, nothing can grow," Rona says for the eighth time that day. "I baptize you in the name of our Highest Power, who will bless you with a new spiritual life. Depart from her, superficial conditioning, painful judgments, and all things that no longer serve her mind, body, and spirit."

There's a struggle beneath the water. Isabelle pushes against the strength of Rona's grip. But the older woman does not budge. "You are born again through this water. Let this baptism strengthen, enlighten, and allow you to open your heart to receive the gifts bestowed upon you these next few weeks."

Isabelle's legs come up, writhing, kicking against the stagnant water. Carmen looks to Rona, whose eyes are closed, chin tilted toward the sky as if she's unaware of the struggle in her hands. Icy fear slides down her spine and she freezes. Isabelle is drowning. What's gone wrong? It wasn't like this with the others.

This was a mistake. How could she have been so stupid? Her limbs are slow and it's a moment before she moves forward, ready to pull her friend free from the older woman's grip.

But just as quickly as it began, it's over, and Isabelle shoots up from the water, clothes stuck to her curves, spluttering water, wiping moisture from her face. She laughs sheepishly as she catches her breath, looking at the group of women gathered by the edge of the pond. She flashes Carmen a reassuring smile before joining the others.

Carmen's heartbeat slows in relief. Silly. A trauma response, most likely. Hopeful once more, she edges forward and awkwardly allows Rona to take her in her arms. The water makes her almost weightless.

"Relax," says Rona.

Carmen inhales, trying to let tension slide away from her limbs and remind herself why she's here. It's difficult. The water smells musty and is unpleasantly warm. But she crosses her arms over her chest and holds her breath before Rona dunks her underwater.

Carmen focuses on the older woman's muffled voice, trying to make out distinct words to no avail. Instead, she studies her body, the pressure of the air trapped in her lungs, and the way the water feels around her. She wants to feel at peace like this moment is the beginning of something new — the precipice of a new Carmen. It's no use. She feels slimy. Her chest begins to burn. She lets a few bubbles out through her nose and tries not to panic as her lungs tighten.

I want to be free, she thinks. She begs. Prays. Manifests.

And now she can't help but wonder how long it's been. It can't be much longer now, can it? Rona's hands tighten around her body, holding her in place. Her eyes open, but everything is a murky shade of green.

The rest of the air leaves her lungs. Her teeth clench together, head begins to spin. She'll need to inhale soon. No. Not soon — now. Right now. She opens her mouth to scream just as Rona releases her. At the mercy of gravity, she flails, accidentally sucking water up her nose.

She hacks a cough and finds her footing. Regains her breath. Forces a smile, then a laugh. Rona guides her from the water and she scolds herself for thinking the leader would let them drown. If anything, this shows just how badly she needs Rona's help.

Carmen reminds herself that nothing worth having comes easy.

Isabelle promised great things from this highly unconventional wellness retreat. Rona's accolades speak for themselves: 2021 Leading Woman in Wellness, 2022 Leader of Advocating for Mental Wellness, and a 2023 award for being a Leader in Wellness Innovation for the Metamorphosis retreat.

It's a highly sought-after event. Rona never reveals where or when it will happen and you must be personally invited by Rona herself or an invitee. Isabelle has been on the list for nearly a year. Carmen was a last-minute addition — the benefit of offering up her dead parents' house for two weeks as the retreat location.

Carmen feels guilt for a moment, allowing strangers into her childhood home. She watches as the women carry their bags, pillows, and toiletries through the hardwood foyer and up the carpeted stairs. She splits nine of them evenly between three bedrooms. Rona insists on sleeping on the couch downstairs.

Isabelle and Carmen decide to share a bed. The third to their room is Rachel, a woman with fair skin and freckles, her wavy brown hair tied up in a wet bun. She places her things beside the air mattress.

"What an afternoon, huh?" Rachel comments, shaking out her hair. She digs through her bag and pulls out a brush.

"A little much, if you ask me." Carmen picks at her cuticles.

"All part of the experience," Isabelle reassures them. "No matter how silly it feels."

"It did feel pretty silly." Rachel laughs. Isabelle joins her. Carmen lets the tension in her shoulders fade, at ease with their new roommate.

After a rest, the women convene outside. Carmen's mouth waters at the smell of meat on the grill. Rona has set two long tables with white linen, candles, and bottles of wine. Drinks are poured, dinner is served, and the women tuck in. The group is of varying ages and each has a different reason for being here. Rona leads a short meditation before they eat, reminding them of their two-week commitment inside Carmen's home, where they will cocoon and re-emerge as new souls.

Carmen scolds the giggle that grows in her chest.

Soon the sky darkens to a star-spotted indigo. The table is littered with empty bottles and plates, the tablecloth stained with red rings and mustard. Cigarette smoke fills the air, and the women are laughing, their eyelids heavy, sharing their deepest secrets. Carmen feels light — lighter than she has in ages — and tells anyone still listening how much she misses her parents.

The next thing she remembers is Isabelle tucking her into bed. She's thankful the alcohol will suppress her nightmares.

Carmen's head throbs as she rolls over on the mattress. Her tongue feels like sandpaper and she can smell the wine she's sweated onto her pillow. She groans, reaching for the bottle of water someone left on the nightstand. At breakfast, she's not the only one hungover. Two women at the other end of the table rub their temples and nibble their toast, no doubt wishing they'd stopped after their third glass of wine. The morning's work of yoga and meditation passes at an excruciating pace.

Now, Rona stands before the fake stone fireplace in Carmen's living room, her arms lifted and her eyes closed.

"This afternoon, we begin our shedding workshop," she says, blinking her eyes open as she studies their eager faces. "A forewarning, this process will not be simple. It will not be pleasant. And it will not be without pain." Carmen feels Rachel tense beside her. Rona inhales deeply through her nose. "But in order for us to live as our most authentic selves, we must wade through the deepest, darkest parts of our minds. Yes?"

"Yes, Rona," the room echoes.

The exercise begins with the women finding a comfortable place in the room. Carmen chooses her father's old leather recliner. It squeaks as she climbs into the worn cushion, smelling of pipe tobacco and teakwood. She can almost hear his booming laugh as she nestles her head against the leather.

Rona leads them into what she calls a hypnosis but Carmen struggles to focus on her words and not the remnants of her hangover. But the faint throb grounds her somehow, the dull ache reminding her no action is without consequence.

"Dig deep," Rona says. "Beneath the blankness. The darkness. Dig below your subconscious and unearth your traumas. Where does your hatred lie? Your guilt? Your shame?"

Carmen knows. She doesn't want to go there, but isn't that what this is all about? Isn't that why she's here? So she allows Rona's words in and wades through the last three months of survivor's guilt and suicidal ideations. She remembers things backward. The first time she laughed again. The first time she went to the shops again. The first time she visited their graves.

Before that, she remembers returning to this house after the funeral, showering with her black clothes on. She remembers the viewing, the way the embalmment made her mother and father's lips look stretched and unnatural. She remembers the hospital, the chaos, and the hot iron smell of blood. And, despite having pushed it away for so long, she remembers that night, the last time she'd felt happy, the blinding lights of the oncoming car, and the smell of burning tires and flesh.

"Imagine yourself in a cleansing body of water, a waterfall roaring overhead. Dip yourself in it. Feel your traumas slide away," says Rona, somewhere far away. "Watch how simply they disappear. Watch your shame, your guilt, your hatred wash away. Watch how —"

It's the last thing Carmen hears.

Watch how.

Watchhow.

Watchow.

Watchout.

WATCH OUT, CARMEN!

Someone is screaming. A hand grips her shoulder. She startles, her eyes open, and she can't close her mouth.

It's her.

She's screaming.

❧ ❧ ❧ ❧

Carmen lies beside Isabelle in the queen bed, watching the rise and fall of her friend's chest as she slumbers. Shame floods her body. Isabelle invited her here. She has things of her own she wants to heal. She shouldn't have to keep putting Carmen to bed like a child.

I will fix this, she promises herself. *I will do better.*

The sky outside is dark and the red analog clock reads 4:03 a.m.. Her stomach grumbles. She hasn't eaten since lunch.

Carefully, she peels herself out of bed, padding barefoot down the stairs and into the kitchen. The house looks different in the dark. Shadows stretch and spiral in the corners, making the familiar layout feel eerie. She half-expects her mom to be sitting at the kitchen island, looking up at her over her reading glasses, the silver chain glittering around her neck.

But the chairs are empty. Her mom is dead. There are Saran-wrapped cookies on the counter and Carmen takes three — enough to hold her over until breakfast. As she climbs back up the stairs, she sees a light on at the end of the hall.

Curious, she approaches the door, peering into the spare room that once stored workout equipment and plastic totes. The light is on. Rona kneels beside an inflatable mattress, hunched over a thrashing figure. Carmen leans into the door jamb and strains her ears.

"— and flush this sickness from her mind," Rona says, hands outstretched, like she's conducting an orchestra.

"The house!" the woman in bed urgently whispers. "Rona, the house!"

"Be free from these troubling thoughts," Rona continues, rising on her feet. Carmen can see the figure sitting in bed, a woman named Michelle. She clutches the covers in her hands, knuckles white, face flushed. Her brown hair clings to her forehead with sweat.

"The house is on fire, Rona!" she croaks, eyes bulging from her head. "Please!" She brings her hands to her head, wincing in pain, before falling backward onto the mattress. "We're all going to die in here!"

Carmen's heart is beating so loud that she knows they'll hear her, and something tells her to back away before they do. Rona will take care of this. Rona will fix whatever is happening to Michelle. She warned them all at the beginning that this process would not be easy. The woman must be having an adverse reaction to Metamorphosis, just like Carmen did earlier that afternoon. This is normal. That's why Rona isn't panicking.

Carmen convinces herself nothing is wrong.

At breakfast the next morning, neither Michelle nor her roommate, Kayra, are there. They do not reappear during their morning prayer, yoga, or the next workshop, in which Rona has them write down their best and worst traits.

Carmen's head hurts as she writes down, *Sad*, then tries to think of something good to balance her list. She can't. In fact, Carmen can't focus at all. Michelle's troubling behavior lingers and she can't continue to ignore her absence. Carmen excuses herself to use the bathroom.

Once she loses Rona's gaze, she tiptoes up the stairs, down the hall, and back to the guest room where she pushes open the door. The room is stiflingly hot, thick with the smell of sweat. Carmen tucks her nose into her shirt.

Two women lie on blow-up mattresses on the floor. Kayra shivers on one in the far corner, wrapped in a thick blanket. Michelle lies on the other from last night, a sheet around her ankles. She wears matching gray pajamas she's sweated through.

"Michelle," Carmen whispers, kneeling by the bed. "Are you okay?" Even as she asks the question, she knows it's foolish. Michelle's eyes are as red as cherries, staring up at the ceiling. It's as if she hasn't noticed Carmen at all. She puts her hand beneath her nose to ensure she's still breathing. She is, but barely. And her breath is scalding hot.

"Michelle?"

The woman blinks, her dark pupils shifting to focus on Carmen. The movement frightens her and she recoils.

"The house is on fire," Michelle says. "Don't you feel it?"

"We're fine," Carmen soothes, looking around the room. "Everything is fine. You're just — " She searches for the right word. "— having trouble adjusting."

Michelle blinks again. Her lips are chapped and her tongue comes out to wet them. "I'm ill," she says, seemingly in a moment of clarity. "Rona won't let me out of here."

"What?" Carmen's heart begins to race again. She's not sure she's heard her correctly. "What did you say, Michelle?"

But she's back to staring and there are footsteps in the hall. Carmen gets to her feet but it's too late. Rona stands in the doorway with a disapproving frown. Her bracelets clink together as she crosses her arms.

"Carmen," she says, and even though her voice is gentle, Carmen knows she's full of anger. "What are you doing in here?"

"Michelle and Kayra are ill. We should take them to the hospital."

"Michelle and Kayra are fine," Rona answers, shaking her head. "They are having difficulty processing their trauma. Come back downstairs, please. This is not your concern."

Rona's voice coaxes her out of the room, but despite the older woman's certainty, her doubt hovers. Rona turns to her as she leads her down the stairs. "This is all normal," she promises. "Reactions like this are why this retreat works."

Carmen believes her.

The next day, it's Rachel who feels strange. She struggles to get out of bed and vomits up her breakfast. Rona brings her upstairs to sleep. Neither Michelle nor Kayra have returned.

"Do you think they're sick?" Carmen whispers over her orange juice to Isabelle.

"I've heard your body might have physical reactions to the healing process," Isabelle says with a shrug. "If Rona says they're alright, then I believe her."

But Carmen is worried for the rest of the day and by the time she sits to eat dinner, her neck is stiff and there's a dull ache in her temple. She feels warm but convinces herself it is all in her head. Isabelle said they were fine. Rona said they were fine. Who is she to say they aren't?

Rachel is still sleeping by the time Carmen and Isabelle come up to go to sleep that evening. The analog clock reads 8:36 p.m.

Carmen is asleep before her head hits the pillow.

Rachel's bed is empty. Her bags are gone. There's not a trace of her left in the bedroom. Carmen shakes Isabelle awake and worries as she watches her friend's eyes blink open. They're red. As red as cherries.

"Rachel's gone," Carmen says.

Isabelle rolls over to look at the empty bed, then sits up. "Maybe she's downstairs with Rona."

But she's not downstairs and neither are Michelle or Kayra. Rona sits in the recliner near the window, sipping tea.

"Where are they?" Carmen asks, her voice trembling with worry. "Rachel, Michelle, and Kayra?"

"They've been sent to the hospital," Rona says, without looking at them. "But there is no need to worry." She puts the cup on the saucer, placing it on the windowsill. She catches Carmen's eyes and her smile grows wide. Too wide. Her lips stretch over the lower part of her face, spreading outward like her lipstick is bleeding into her wrinkled skin.

Carmen blinks. Rona's smile is normal. She tilts her head, as if concerned.

"Oh," Carmen says, surprised. "Okay, well ... good."

The women eat breakfast before Rona leads them in rui-katsu — crying therapy. The group watches parts of sad films, meant to evoke tears, before Rona encourages them to think of personal experiences that might prompt the same emotion.

"Group crying is a healing practice," she explains. "We are detoxing our minds with our tears."

Carmen sits back on the couch, clutching her notebook and pen and squeezing her eyes closed. She goes back to the accident, back to the aftermath, the moments just after the crash.

She sits behind the steering wheel. It feels like an elephant is sitting on her chest. The airbag hisses. A yellow light blinks in the distance. The radio is playing a commercial for the mattress sale at Bob's Discount Furniture.

Her head swims. To her right, she sees a hand. It lays limp on the center console, a gold bracelet around the wrist. She follows it to a forearm, a bicep, to a shoulder belonging to a woman with dark, bloody hair. Carmen knows her.

Some part of her feels urgent. Panicky. Guilty. But she can't figure out why. There are red and blue lights, flashing so brightly and quickly that Carmen's brain can't keep up. Someone lifts the weight from her chest. And then she's upside down, or right side up, looking back at a hunk of twisted metal.

"They're gone," someone says, and when she looks around, she's in a white box filled with bright light. Gloved hands roam her body, poking and prodding and asking if it hurts. Someone shines a light in her eyes and she's trying not to cry but the tears come anyway.

"Who's gone?" she yells. "Who's gone?"

She knows who. She's sure of it. But she can't remember even though she should.

And then her eyes are open and she's staring at a group of women staring back at her. A gray-haired woman with loose-fitting clothing and clanging jewelry kneels on the floor, looking up at her.

"Who's gone?" she hears herself ask. "Who's gone?"

Carmen wakes up on the back porch in her pajamas. The air is thick with humidity and she's drenched in sweat. Her limbs feel weighted, heavier than normal, and her mouth is so dry she could drink the ocean.

How did I get out here?

She turns to the house, walking through the quiet kitchen. The oven clock reads 2:12 a.m.

She blinks.

The oven clock reads 4:52 a.m.

Her head is going to split open. The pain is unlike anything she's ever felt before and she can hear herself moan as she rolls her forehead into the warm pillow.

"Carmen?"

It's Isabelle's voice, but when she lifts her head, she sees Rachel, with her wavy brown hair and freckles. Deep, black holes sit where her eyes should be, and blood runs from the sockets like tears. Tenderly, the eyeless woman touches her cheek.

"Are you okay?"

Carmen screams.

Isabelle recoils, brown waves turning blonde, eyes blinking back to blue. She looks worried. Carmen's heart feels like it might explode from her chest.

"I'm going to get Rona," Isabelle tells her. "You'll be okay."

She turns on the mattress, staring upward. Clouds roll in over the painted white ceiling — gray, angry, and pregnant with rain. The heavens open and cold water splashes across her face. She struggles to open her eyes, but when she does she's no longer in bed, but in the shower tub.

How did I get here?

Rona stands over her with the detachable shower head.

"You have a fever. This will cool you down. It is all part of the process," Rona reminds her. "Your body is shedding all of your trauma. My goodness, is it a lot."

❧ ❧ ❧ ❧

"You must eat," says her mother. She lays a tray on her legs, fluffs the pillows behind Carmen, and helps her sit upright. A bowl of soup rests on the tray — chicken noodle, her favorite.

Her mother is as she remembers her when she was small. There is no silver hair weaved between the black, no sun spots on her forehead, and the laugh lines on her cheeks are barely there. Yet Carmen knows how her mother will age. She knows how her mother will die.

"I love you, *mija*," Mami says and slides her hand into her daughter's.

Her mother's hand feels frail and as Carmen traces her thumb across her skin, it moves unnaturally. She can mold it into place and so she presses harder, hard enough to make the skin peel away from the muscle and bone.

The skin around her knuckles mottles, then turns gray, becoming moist between her fingers. Carmen looks up at her mother's corpse as her skin sags from its skull. She can see every tooth inside her jaw, the sinewy, sagging cheek muscles working up and down as she speaks.

"Eat up, *mija*." Her voice rattles, like gravel beneath tires.

Carmen looks down at her soup, at the small maggots wiggling in the broth as they drown in it. There is bile in her throat and she feels her stomach contract.

"Carmen!" The voice belongs to Rona, who kneels on the floor beside her bed, mopping up the spilled soup with a towel. "You must eat," she says, shooting her a disapproving look.

She isn't sure if she answers, because the next thing she knows she's outside in the dark. The night is cloudy and the humidity has lifted, sending a chill across her fever-ridden body. Her father sits on the porch steps beside her, his neck twisted at an impossible angle. When he turns his head, she can see his spine protruding from his back.

"You must eat," he tells her.

She nods, gets up, and goes into the house, knowing she should feel fear. Her belly cramps with hunger and she grabs the first thing she sees when she opens the refrigerator — the tin foil-covered soup Rona has left for her.

She doesn't know what day it is or how long she's been in bed, but Carmen has a sudden moment of clarity. Her head still throbs and her voice is so weak it seems impossible she is even able to call Rona's name.

Rona appears at her bedside, and Carmen briefly wonders where Isabelle has gone.

"Please, Rona," she begs. "I need to get to the hospital. Something is not right."

"Shh," Rona hushes, placing a hand on her chest. She leans her back against the pillow. "An ambulance is on its way."

"Thank you." It comes out as a whisper, carried away in the wind that brushes her face as she sinks back into darkness.

* * * *

She is wrapped tightly in a cotton blanket, her arms tucked into her sides, legs confined in a pleasant warmth. She nuzzles into the blanket. Dim light illuminates beige walls and the room's adornments — a small flat-screen television, a wooden bedside rolling table, and a green plastic chair in the corner. A curtain hangs on a track from the ceiling and Carmen sighs in relief. Rona kept her promise.

Grateful for her moment of clarity, she looks for her cell phone or some indication that someone has been here. She'd like to get in touch with Isabelle, and let her know she's okay. She's curious about Rachel, Michelle, and Kayra. She wants to make sure her parents' house is left in good condition.

But the table beside her bed is empty, so she waits for someone to come. The blinds are pulled closed over the window and she wishes she could see outside, just to know what time of day it is.

There are no clocks in this room, no way to distinguish night from day.

It feels strange to her, but she lets it pass.

Finally, the door opens and someone enters. A tall woman wearing a nurse cap enters, her gray hair tied neatly back in a bun. Carmen squints, but no matter how hard she tries, she can't see any of her features.

"Hello?" tries Carmen.

The nurse does not respond. She is busy in the corner of the room, fiddling with something. And when she turns, Carmen sees a large syringe in her hands, filled with something red.

But that's not what makes her scream.

The nurse comes into view, standing over Carmen. Her features are somehow distorted, upside down, and all wrong. Wide lips stretch over the upper part of her face, or is it the bottom? It doesn't really matter, does it? Because the nurse is Rona.

It can't be. Carmen knows this. How could Rona be here, in the hospital, when she is meant to be back on Lilypond Lane, looking after the girls? Looking after her dead parents' house?

The woman hovers over her, with the needle in her hand. Carmen freezes, unable to turn her head. She wants to scream, to call for help, but her body and brain refuse to work together. She's helpless as she watches Rona jab it straight between her eyes, right into her brain, the pain so sharp she's convinced Rona is sawing her in half. She's screaming. Or at least she thinks she's screaming.

The world falls silent.

Everything shifts, the walls, curtains, and bed. But she can't move, as badly as she tries. Disoriented, she shakes her throbbing head, trying to find clarity. The room is dark and her head is heavy. As she shifts her body, she swings.

Details settle into place piece by piece. She sees her body, wrapped up tightly in a white blanket. It hangs from the rafters in her parent's garage. Her feet are held tight together over her head. Her forehead is at least three feet off the ground.

Carmen is not alone. She hangs beside other bodies, wrapped up the same way. Beside her swings Rachel, her brown hair dangling in loose waves, nearly touching the ground. Her eyes are lifeless, white, and cloudy. But still, her head turns.

"Carmen," the dead girl calls.

Carmen is crying. She can feel her tears rolling over her forehead, down into her hair.

"Carmen," Rachel tries again.

"Please stop," she begs.

"Go get help," Rachel says. "You must get down from here and go get us help."

And so she tries. She writhes and wiggles, shimmying her body in the tight prison. Once she gets herself swinging enough she thinks she can loosen the blanket's knot up on the rafter, but whatever sickness is inside her body tires her before she can get too far. It's useless.

She cries out for help. Wails. Calls for Rona, Isabelle, and the other women. She calls for her neighbors, friends, and dead parents.

Nobody comes.

Her voice is strained, and she's exhausted. The blood rushing to her already sensitive head makes her see stars. She can taste blood in her mouth. She can smell it.

And then, Rona appears. She eases herself out into the garage, barefoot and untroubled. The old woman gazes at each of the bodies. Carmen counts six in total.

"Your transformation is nearly complete," Rona says to them. "Your sickness is the physical response to your mind shedding your trauma. The more you fear it, the more you reject it, the harder your healing will be." She scans the room, the smile bright on her face. "You are now in your cocoon. This is the last stage of your Metamorphosis. You must trust yourself, your mind, and your body to break free from this environment. Just like the larvae work to become a butterfly, you must let go of your past. Only then will you truly know what you can endure."

Rona closes her eyes and breathes in the stench of decay. Then she raises her hands in the air and begins to sing.

The song is pleasant. Alluring. Her voice is soft and delicate, soothing Carmen into a soft slumber. Perhaps Rona is right. Perhaps Carmen has been fighting her trauma for too long. Perhaps it is time to let go.

There is clarity in the thought. Carmen signs in relief.

I am finally free.

Stephen Barnes sits in a sterile lab, staring at the most recent test results his underqualified assistant just handed him. Four weeks into the investigation and the local police department is still at a loss as to how every woman strung up in the garage had bilateral brain lesions.

The answer lies in front of him, and it makes his stomach churn.

"Naegleria fowleri," he says.

"God bless you," says his assistant.

Stephen shakes his head and points to the stack of papers he holds. "Bacteria," he says. "That's what was in the water, in that pond near the house. It infects the brain and destroys brain tissue. After symptoms start, most patients die within five days." He sighs. "There have been survivors, but only when they were diagnosed early. Still, whoever hung those women up took away any chance at survival they had."

He places the papers on the table and stands from his seat. Why would anyone go into that dirty pond? And how did they ingest water? Did somebody know a deadly bacteria was lurking beneath the surface? Stephen leaves the cool lab interior, removing his gloves as he fishes a cell phone from his pocket to call Detective Larson.

This is now, officially, a homicide investigation.

❧ ❧ ❧ ❧

Caitlin Mazur is a multi-genre author whose works span science fiction, speculative fiction, and horror. As a transracial adoptee, her work often touches on themes of found family and self-discovery. She is currently writing a five-party dystopian thriller series. Follow Caitlin: https://linktr.ee/caitwritesstuff

The League

BY DANI STEVENS

Tonight, on Aimee's eighteenth birthday, she'll sacrifice her date and complete her initiation to join the prestigious secret society: the League. But Theo has secrets of his own and is no helpless victim. By the end of the night, everyone's truth will air, and not everyone will survive.

AIMEE

A little princess, ditsy, well-trained, tame. That's what they all see in me. The League, my brothers, my parents. Even Theo, and he was supposed to be my future boyfriend. The sports and academic trophies pass judgement down from my bedroom shelves, just like Mother does. Tonight, once I kill my date, everything changes. They'll say I'm an assassin, ruthless, powerful, and that I belong to the League: the upper class, exclusive web of matriarch-led families.

Belong. Such a dirty word. The League needs new blood running it. Mine.

I pin another auburn curl behind my ear, then let it flop back beside my chin. I undo the gold hairpin, and my curls cascade down my back. The cool of the pin's metal brings my jumpiness down a notch.

I'm being a *dramatic teenager.* Like when I asked Theo to be my date. No one cares that it's all an act. I'm scrabbling for the slightest bit of control over my evening. It's all a distraction from the real issue of the night. How I plan to shed myself of their perceptions and reveal my own position within the League. No more *'just the Baines girl'* after tonight.

A soft knock at the door stalls my daydreaming.

I sigh and straighten my posture. "Come in, Ethan."

"Never could fool you," my oldest brother chuckles as he steps inside, shutting the door behind him. "You look stunning."

"No one else bothers to knock." I run my gaze up his tailored suit and slick, dark hair. "So do you. You must have all the girls fawning over you in the city."

"You know you're the only girl in my life," he says with a wink. These jokes are allowed only between us. If Mother were to find out about his taste in men, she'd disown him in a heartbeat, let alone the consequences from the League. Another reason it needs new blood leading it.

"Don't you ever get tired of hiding?" I pat the white ledge next to me, and he settles down with a groan, looking out over the lake.

"Aims, we've been over this. The League —"

"The League is outdated and cruel, and run by stuffy, middle-aged, white women. Maybe it's a good thing someone's killing them off in the city. They should allow you to be who you are."

"— is too powerful, and too vast to have one person change all the rules," he finishes with a breathy laugh. "But who knows? Maybe one day you'll rule them all. Just be careful. You know how quickly these initiations can go askew."

I bubble with pride at his words. "If I ever get out from under Mother's thumb. I heard her this morning. She doesn't think I'm ready. She called me fickle, Ethan. I'm never going to earn her respect, no matter what I do."

"So, what will you do?"

My grip tightens around my hairpin. "Luc gets aggressive and competitive against us —"

"Typical middle child."

"— and Mother wrinkles her nose at him. I have to be subtle. Smarter."

I'll tear them apart from the inside.

He chuckles. "If it's worth anything, I think you'd make a great matriarch. Better than Mother."

"Thanks. I'm glad you're home. Can't you stay longer?"

"You know Lilypond Lane isn't my home anymore. I'm sure by tomorrow there will be much for me to catch up on in the city. Always lots of paperwork after an initiation. Plus, with the families being murdered in the city, they need me there." His eyes droop as he looks away, taking him away to more exciting lands than this suffocating cul-de-sac. "Theo's here. It's time."

My heart patters high in my throat, and I smooth out my dress. This is it. Everything I've trained for, and planned in secret, is about to come to light. After tonight, everything will be different.

THEO

Staff welcome me through the house with a warm grin, take my suit coat, and hand me a glass of champagne. I let it sit untouched in my hand, aware of the social faux pas it causes. I leave my blazer on. No need for them to know what gifts I've brought for the Baines family.

Out the back, on the dark, stained decking, the air nips at my ears, now that I've cut my hair short.

The younger son, Lucian, swings a baseball bat at a distance on the lawn. His shouts travel across the open fields surrounding the house and into the distant woodlands.

Lucian Baines. Twenty-two. Unemployed. Dyed salt and pepper hair.

I wonder if he'll wield the bat tonight, or if they'll let Aimee hunt alone. My muscles ache at the thought. I address the stately woman beside the fire pit. The current matriarch. "Mrs. Baines."

Piercing hazel eyes, styled with neat black hair and a Prada suit, stare me down with a whisper of curiosity. "Theo Hartman. It's nice to finally meet you. Weeks living next door, and you haven't come to visit us. Please, call me Emilia." Her voice, melodic and low, sends chills up my arms, and I calm myself as I shake her hand.

Lucian joins us, and he sculls two glasses of champagne before pointing to the house. "Princess is here."

Ethan leads her out with her arm linked with his. With his navy-blue suit, he looks just like the domestic royalty he belongs to.

Ethan Baines. Twenty-eight. Accountant. Heterochromia.

I nod to him, following their customs, and then turn to Aimee.

Aimee Baines. Seventeen. Personification of the bored rich white girl.

She pays her family no attention, instead her hazel eyes — just like her mother's — rest solely on me. Ravishing in a deep plum dress, she almost skips away from Ethan in her haste to join my side. Her white teeth dazzle in the lowering light.

"Hi, Theo." Her words come out rushed and breathless. The nervous energy coming off her vibrates the air around us.

"Happy Birthday, Aimee." Pulling a silver envelope from my blazer pocket, I hand it over with a small bow.

She swells, and the gold lights above us catch in her eyes as she beams at me. "Thank you. You didn't need to bring me anything. Just being here is gift enough."

You have no idea.

Her family gathers around us. Even Lucian shivers with excitement, and this is only his second time on a night like this. I keep my breathing slow, controlled. Aimee won't like my palms too sweaty.

"Speech!" Lucian calls out, already slurring his words.

The others repeat his request, and heat burns Aimee's cheeks. "All right. Calm down."

She glimpses a peek at me. The girl has so much potential, and tonight she may lose it all if she doesn't play her role.

She's not at fault. It's not her doing. She's not the one you've come back for.

I can't hold the smile, but I do my best for her.

Emilia clears her throat and Aimee jumps. "I guess I should say thank you first. Thank you for tonight. I've been thinking about it for a long time."

Ethan's lip twitches.

"Everyone here has turned eighteen at some stage, and I know it must feel silly for me to get emotional. But I am really appreciative of this chance to become who I'm meant to be. I want to prove how valuable I am to this family and the legacy we're part of." She entwines her fingers with mine and gives me a genuine smile. As though tonight is nothing but a party to celebrate her birthday.

"First," Lucian declares, "A game of baseball."

Out of the corner of my eye, he swings the bat. There's a whoosh of air beside my ear, and a blinding white *crack*.

The world spins. Then, nothing.

❧ ❧ ❧ ❧

The voices blur together.

"Oh, he's waking up. That didn't take long. I was worried I'd be bored."

"Bianca took *forever* to wake up."

"Hush, boys. This is Aimee's night. You need to step back."

"Theo? Theo, are you okay?"

Amongst the swimming lights behind my lids and the thumping within my skull, I cling to my name.

Aimee's tone betrays her barely restrained panic. Warm hands cup my cheeks. "I was getting worried."

"Aimee, get up."

"Yes, Mother."

The hands leave me, and icy air bites at my skin. It brings life back into my body, and I manage to open my eyes. Only for a moment, before nausea swirls the room around me. Twisted behind my back, my wrists sting from the too-tight cuffs keeping me in the dining chair. I wouldn't have anywhere to run, even if I got loose. I groan and let my head droop, processing my location.

Wooden walls. Rugs moved to the side. Plastic sheeting taped to the floor. Each of the Baines are present. I'm horrendously outnumbered.

My blazer presses into my spine when I lean against the chair, forcing my eyes open despite the spinning. No doubt Ethan would've searched me before tying me up. The notebook is still in my hidden back pocket. Emilia will know who I am. What I've done in the city. They let me keep the book as a taunt. Tonight, I die at Aimee's hand, or I kill them. There is no third option.

The energy of everyone in the room floods my system, making it hard to think.

Emilia speaks now, voice strong. "Are you ready, Aimee?"

Ready to kill me. It sends cold, sharp pains through my body, waking me further. I will the adrenaline down to my limbs, my hands, my feet. I won't have time to recover.

"Yes, Mother."

She nods to Ethan. "Release him."

Something small and hard slides into my back pants pocket. Then the cuffs click open. Ethan helps me to my feet, patting my back in an almost jovial fashion. "Have fun, brother. While it lasts."

When he moves away, removing my support, I stumble in a slow circle.

Four exits. One to outside. One in the direction of the front door.

I must have imagined the panic in her voice. Aimee has her eagle stare on me, unwavering in her body language. Feet light and fingers curled: she's primed for a kill.

"The game is simple, Theo." Emilia lifts her palms. "Do your best to survive. We will not interfere. May the strongest win."

I act first, putting my strength into my punch. Aimee's fast, but I manage to swipe the side of her jaw as she dodges.

She grins as she resets her pose, wiping her mouth. Blood coats the back of her hand. "Good hit. Keep them coming."

I glance at the others. Ethan has his arms crossed and fists tight. They won't meddle; it's Aimee's initiation. She's a couple of years younger, and I've got half a foot over her in height. I could hurt her.

What will the others do if I win?

I step forward and throw another punch, and she slips left. As she does, her fingers encircle my wrist, and next thing I know, I'm on my back on the floor.

Lucian bursts into laughter and slaps his palms to his thighs. "Get up, brother. She has a mean thunder kick."

Which she goes to demonstrate, and I barely roll away and to my feet in time. The room spins. As my stance widens to accommodate for my dizziness, so does her grin. I can't figure her out. Have the weeks of flirting really been an act? Is she prepared to kill me, after all?

I stop holding back. Innocent or not, she can't win this fight if I'm going to exact my revenge.

We dance for a few minutes, landing blows on each other until we both sport cuts guaranteed to end in bruises. Lucian shouts encouragement and taunts. With each second, my vision clears and my hearing calms.

She's tiring — I may not be as strong as Lucian or Ethan, but I'm no civilian — but her punches and claws leave my skin burning. I can't land more than a half-fist. Her smaller size and weight work against me. But when she kicks, she avoids muscles that would impact my ability to run.

The longer we fight, the more my strength returns, and my theories falter. If Aimee wanted to kill me, she would have in the first twenty seconds. She's toying with me. The others don't see, because they never saw Aimee for the person she is, only what they believed her to be. Incapable of winning. Emilia half-watches with the disinterest of attending a horse race. Lucian wanders from the room. Only Ethan remains focused on the fight.

As Ethan glances down at his watch, Aimee darts around me and slams into him, knocking them both to the ground. She screams back at me, "Theo, run!"

I hesitate on the balls of my feet. Is this a trap?

Emilia's brows furrow, and she reaches for her back pocket.

Ethan grunts underneath her. "What are you doing?"

Never mind if it is; this is my chance. I sprint for the door, out into the blackness. Clouds cover the full moon. The trees sit half a kilometre away, but even with the shadows veiling my possible escapes, I recall exactly where they are.

AIMEE

I glimpse a peek at Theo. He has a ghost of a smile on his face, contradicting the sorrow in his azure eyes.

We crouch under the window in the corner of the staff house bathroom, on the other side of the tree line. In the distance, Luc taunts us with his calls. Wolves hunt in the dark, and Theo and I are the prey.

I hold his hand, and he pulls me in close. "I'm sorry for fighting you. I wanted to give you enough time to recover from being whacked with the bat before making you run and hide."

"I don't understand what's happening." His eyes hold an inferno even in the dark. "Why go through all this? Why not just leave?"

"It's not that simple. They'd find me. Their pride won't let them stop, not without killing you first."

"That's not going to happen."

"No. I won't let them kill you. But I need to stop them. I have to go back out there."

"How would they find you if you left Lilypond Lane?" He peers down at me, concern pulling at his mouth. His calm tugs at my heartstrings.

I've picked the best person to help me stop my family. Most other boys would've run screaming for the police by now; that's why they wouldn't have survived the evening. Weeks of flirting through windows have paid off — he wants to save me.

"It's called the League. We've gone back generations. My great-grandmother was the most powerful woman in the area. She funded Lilypond Lane. Gave our house what it needed." She knew how to get jobs done.

"The League tells you what to do?" I can't tell if he's pale or flushed, but it doesn't matter. He's alive. We've made it past the first hurdle.

"I'm meant to kill you tonight. That's what my initiation is. Murder." Fire licks at my chest, bringing tears to my eyes. I gesture to his muscles. "I'm so sorry. I chose you because, well, you seemed to know how to handle yourself. You'd survive for sure. I didn't want it to be anyone else. But I never wanted you to die. That was never *my* plan. I need to stop them. If I'm going to prove myself to the League, I need to take control of my family."

"And what will you do to make that happen? Your family isn't weak. They're out there, hunting us."

"Whatever it takes."

THEO

Darkness keeps me in a chokehold. Tonight, I break free of it.

"Let me come with you."

I want to watch the light dissolve from their eyes as I take it back.

Aimee shakes her head, panic stiffening her joints. "No. You can't. I held back before, because I didn't want to hurt you, but you shouldn't see us fight. We... don't play nice. It'll get messy. I may not even walk away from it. You don't know what they've —"

"I do." From my blazer, I pull out my tattered notebook, held together with duct tape and rubber bands. "I'm more prepared than you think. I'm well aware of the death that haunts Lilypond Lane."

Her face falls. "What is this? What are you, a cop?" Her eyes widen, and she leans back as she considers her future if she's caught. It's in her expression; how could she have missed that? I look too young to be a cop. I work at a café.

I pull her back in. Her presence calms me. "No. I guess I should share my secret too. This isn't my first time living here."

The open page shows photos of Aimee's family. Photos of her parents — my main targets. Without them, and Ethan, my parents would still be alive. Aimee would never have forgotten me. "What do you know of Ethan's initiation?"

She shrugs. "Not much. I remember... it didn't go as planned. I had a friend, a boy a little older than me. Most young families don't stay long here, and another child always stands out. He got me in trouble, and they all moved away after. For months, I begged Ethan to tell me about his initiation, but all he said was *I got to have two*. Guess he was always the favourite," she grumbles.

Splinters pierce my heart. The blackness crushes around me, pushing the frozen air from my lungs.

It's not her fault. She wants to be better.

"They didn't move away."

"What?" She leans in close, struggling to hear my strained whisper.

I can barely force the words out. "The family didn't move. The boy was sent away after his parents were murdered."

The understanding creeps along her face. One muscle slackens at a time until she gapes at me. Her gaze flickers around my body, my face. Calculating my age, her age, my appearance. The beard can't hide it all. "You."

"Theo is my middle name. You used to call me Liam."

She pulls back, brows scrunching together. Her eyes dart around my face, faster and faster, searching for an answer I can't give her. "The boy next door."

"It wasn't your fault. When you showed me the ledgers, you had no way of knowing what they were. I barely understood it myself. But my father did, and he died for that knowledge."

"Ethan got two," she whispers.

"Two victims."

“My brother killed your parents.”

“Under the instruction of your parents.”

The emotions pinwheel across her face. Her chest heaves as she processes it.

I squeeze her hand, sending what comfort I can. “We can end this. Together.”

The shine in her eyes reflects the moonlight’s glow when it peeks between the clouds. “I’m so sorry. All these years, you’ve been trapped by my family, too.” She grabs my hand. She doesn’t suppress her strength now, and I hold back the wince. “Let’s be free. We can fly away, never to be hurt again. Take me to the city.”

I lick the roof of my mouth when it dries. “I can’t return there.”

“Then the ocean. Hawaii. Rome. Take me away. I want to be free of my family.”

“What about the League?”

Her eyes flash, and she sets her jaw. “Screw those old asshats. I’ll be the new League.”

AIMEE

As the full moon blazes through the window, Luc finds us.

“Let me fight,” Theo insists.

Luc smirks and gestures for me to stay back. I do.

They exchange blows, and I hover on my toes, ready to help. Within seconds, both have hair ripped from their scalps and blood splattered on their shirts. Each time someone slams into the wall, the noise echoes through the cramped space.

Theo puts up a good fight against my brother, having prepared for this for years. Even stabs Luc in the shoulder with my hairpin that he pulls from his back pocket. He's calculated. Controlled.

But he's no match for Luc's ferocity. When Theo ends up pinned to the tiles, I leap into action. Landing strikes on Luc, stopping him from cutting off Theo's airway. Until firm arms circle around my torso and restrain my arms against my sides. Ethan murmurs in my ear, but my screams block him out.

When I won't stop thrashing, Ethan throws me to the ground, and my face smashes against the vanity. Despite years of training, I'm not prepared for the pounding it causes in my skull.

They drag a barely conscious Theo away after Ethan cuffs my wrist to the claw foot tub. I writhe on the floor, slipping on spilled blood. Ethan leans on the vanity with his hands behind his back for a moment, studying my ferity in silence. When he leaves, Mother's silhouette enters and stands in the doorway.

"Such a disappointment."

I've lost.

I break down, sobbing into the side of the tub. "Mother, please. I'm sorry."

She flicks on the light, blinding me for a moment. She bends down and slaps me across the face.

I flinch from the sting. My cheek already smarted from my fight with Theo.

"Why all this for a boy?"

"Not him." I spit at her. It sprays my chest with bright red blood. "To stop you."

She stands with disgust in her eyes. "I always knew you'd be our biggest mistake. You're too clever for your own good." She stomps the three steps to the window and kicks Theo's notebook in my direction. With a raised brow, she waits for me to clutch it to my chest. "Help yourself."

"He's not the monster here," I snap. "He's doing this because of your mistake. There are rules for a reason. You stuffed up Ethan's initiation, and you married outside of the League. Father tainted our line, and you let him. Luc is a straight up future serial killer, not a League member. You're so *messy*. You don't deserve to be matriarch. At least great-grandmother led with her brain."

Her eye twitches and breaks her composure for a second. Then a smirk plays on her lips. "Open the notebook, Aimee."

I follow her command, unable to resist as always.

While I flick through the pages, the ones Theo didn't show me, a bile-inducing knot forms in my stomach. Each page peels away a layer of my heart, shrivelling it.

Her smirk grows.

When I reach the end, I climb to my knees, unable to stand with my wrist cuffed. "You think I wanted to marry him, like you fell for Father?"

Her smile falters. "How does it feel to care for a man who murdered all those families in the League? Ethan may have killed his parents, but he's butchered entire families."

I glance around the room at our privilege. At how Mother has failed our future because of one error ten years ago. Ethan's pistol, silencer attached, sits on the vanity — tucked under the hand towel, only visible from my kneeling position. I don't care how it came to be here. It will serve me fine.

I wiggle back on my knees, away from the monster that raised me.

"You know what, Mother?"

I whip out a hand and snatch the pistol. I can just reach it. The bullet nicks her in the side of the neck. She doesn't have time to scream before she collapses. I shoot the cuff while she gags on the tiles. Blood spurts across the window and wall.

"The League was right. Marriage from the outside is dangerous. But I know better than you did. I'll use what you taught me." I rotate my wrist, working out the stiffness. Then I point the gun at her chest. "Don't worry, Mother. I'll take good care of the family line."

My family never needed to explain how it felt to kill. They couldn't have described the black *nothing* that swells inside me. It craves more.

I pull the trigger again.

THEO

I'm back in the goddamn chair. My muscles strain under the bindings to my arms and ankles. The men hovering in front of me have no intention of releasing me this time, despite Ethan's false promises. Every joint has been twisted, every limb attacked with fists and the bloody bat. The hairpin sticks out of my thigh. Without Aimee, I'll die in this chair.

Ethan steps back, wiping his brow. "Luc," he pants. "Let's slow it down. No need to kill him so quickly."

Lucian glances up with a savage grin. "You getting tired? You always were the weakest." He slams a fist into my side, and I wheeze in a breath. Stars dot my vision, and his face blurs inches from my own. I want to rip more hair from his scalp. "It's fun. You just got to work out more," he adds with another punch, making the room spin around me.

Aimee's cries stopped a minute ago. Has she succeeded in fighting off her own mother?

My left eye swells shut when Lucian drives an elbow against my face. Sounds fade when he shouts something and there's a crunch in my foot.

From my half-open right eye, I glimpse movement in the doorway, followed by a feminine screech. The blows stop, leaving thumping pain behind. My head lolls to the side, throwing the room off balance. Aimee — covered in blood — braces herself against the doorframe, pistol in her outstretched hand, fire in her eyes.

Lucian drops first. He staggers to his knees, clutching his blooming chest. By the time his head thumps to the stone, his cries have stopped.

Ethan is next, but he moves quick.

She hasn't shot him, not yet. He reaches her shoulders, fingers splayed and curved into talons, when her gun touches his forehead. "Don't," she warns. "Let go, big brother."

He releases her, hands falling limp at his sides. "Mother?"

She stays in the doorway, gun pressed to his face. "Dead."

"Why?"

She lifts her chin. "You know why. The League must be fixed."

"And you think you're the one to do it." An eel-like smile spreads across his face.

She juts her chin out. "I know I am. If not me, then who?"

He grins and gestures to me. "I'm glad you feel that way. Go to him."

"What?" Her eyes flick between us.

Ethan just chuckles. "I know you want to."

Her grip tightens on the gun, but she hesitates. "I will shoot you, you big lump of —"

"Aimee." I reassure her through my busted jaw and swollen tongue. I want her to blow his brains out. "Breathe. You're in control. You can end this."

She backs over to me and holds me steady. She buries her hand in my hair, careful to avoid the worst of my injuries, while Ethan explains.

"The League wasn't impressed with how our parents handled the Starling situation."

"Theo's parents." She glances at me. "You two know each other?"

"Yes," he says. "When I left for the city, I discovered how deep our parents' error went against our code. While preparing for your initiation, the League assigned me to adjust how our family is run. By that point, I was already well aware of Theo's activities in the city. I made some calls, organised for him to buy the house next door. He's the catalyst to bring down our family."

I hold back my laughter, and the beating-induced pain helps me focus. Ethan thought I'd forgive him once he got me out of the city, away from the League's looming consequences for slaughtering their families. When Aimee's fingers caress my head, my thudding heartbeat calms at how easy it was to gain not only her trust, but access to her whole family.

Aimee weaves the story together. "You wanted Mother dead, too."

"Maybe not as much as you, but a reset always requires some bloodshed."

"You planned everything? None of it was me?" Agony explodes across her face, bringing a tremor out in her hand as it rests on me.

"I wouldn't go that far. You had your role to play, and your ideas were brilliant. The League sees your potential. It's time for you to become the matriarch here. Work with me."

"I'd still be under your control?"

Ethan screws up his face, scratching his head. "Control is a harsh word. Consider it a management deal. You'd have far more freedom than you have been given up to now."

Aimee glances at me, brows furrowing. Let Ethan try to control her. Let her think she has no other option. Her eyes shine as the tears build.

"The next steps are easy. We blame Theo for Mother and Luc's deaths. You kill Theo, we go to the League, and we'll be hailed heroes for stopping a murderer. Just follow me."

We've been playing each other for months. Only he hasn't taken into account that Aimee is, above all else, a seventeen-year-old girl. Does he think I've wasted my time getting to know her? How controlled she feels by her family?

He thinks she respects him more than she cares for me.

Tears drip from her lashes. For the first time since I moved back, I see her chin tremble in *real* pain. "I love you, big brother."

Ethan doesn't see the change in her eyes. He's not even looking at her face. He gazes into the near distance, likely imagining the future of his rule. The arrogance that got his family killed will kill him, too.

"But a matriarch doesn't take orders." She lifts the gun and pulls the trigger.

He doesn't respond at first. It takes three heavy breaths before he stares down at the red spreading from his chest, then looks back up at her.

She steels her expression and waits for him to collapse before she puts down the gun. He dies without a word.

It's over. Shame I wasn't the one to do it.

That pain is still in her eyes, although the tears have stopped. Free or not, she will grieve for the loss of her family.

I squeeze her hand when she unties me. "I can't tell you how long the pain will last. But it fades. Slowly, over time."

"It's over now. Just like that. It feels... strange."

It hurts like a bitch to talk. But I keep her talking, to stop her slipping away into her grief. "All this time, you've been waiting for me to save you, like a prince. And it's you that's saved me. You know I want nothing to do with the League. We can leave now. You've given me a way to find peace."

"Peace. That sounds nice." Her eyes melt, swimming in unshed tears. "You know, all my life, I just wanted a friend. I had one in you all along. How I wish that night ten years ago ended differently. We could've been together properly, without all this nonsense. I've spent months dreaming about how this would go, and I don't even care that the League tried to orchestrate the ending."

She smiles up at me. "I won. The little Baines girl won. No more Ethan. No more Mother."

She gives me the bat to bite down on and eases the hairpin from my thigh. "Now, the League will bow to me." She opens her arms and holds me, gentle with my injuries.

I close my eyes. Chanel perfume tickles my nose, mixing with the metallic blood in her hair. She was the only one who deserved to survive. My job is done.

My eyes fly open as a sharp pain shoots up my neck, and my hands crash to my sides against the chair. I can't lift them; they're nothing but dead weights.

Aimee stands and leans over me with a rigid smile, holding me upright when I can't keep myself steady. "Mother gave me one last birthday gift before I killed her. She gave me the truth you tried to hide. You think you're different from Ethan, from us, from everyone on this damn street. You believe your revenge trip is noble."

I try to talk, but nothing comes out but garbled croaks. Air won't enter my lungs. I can't move. When her hands cup my cheeks, they're empty.

"So many bodies, Liam Starling. Far more than my parents. When I realised how far you're willing to go for straight up revenge, I realised something. We can't be together, my love."

Dark spots flood my vision, blocking out the room around us. Her serene expression fills my field of view.

"I want to shape the League. You want to destroy it. Why would you stop with my family? It's not like we're the only killers on this street, but we can cohabitate because of discretion. Let's be honest, if Ethan didn't kill your parents, someone else would have, eventually. Some have been killing longer than I've been alive. No matter how you act around me, regardless of what I do next, we will never fully trust each other. I really am my mother's daughter, and it was only a matter of time before you knew that."

She kisses my forehead with a tenderness, as my heart beat slows in my ears, then thumps one last time.

"Fly free, Liam Starling."

❧ ❧ ❧ ❧

Dani is from sunny Perth, Australia, and now lives in regional Victoria where it rains nearly half the year. The League is her second published short story, and she dreams of publishing a variety of novels one day.

Bird Nest

BY HEATHER CURLEE NOVAK

Colette and Megan are not singing in harmony, as all is not well in their birds' nest. The promising new home on Lilypond Lane may be the last straw.

I bit my lip, wondering if I could stay in the sleek, red car and refuse this new future. The two-story house was expansive and glorious, but the sterile yard surrounding it had short grass that looked uninviting. The houses on Lilypond Lane boasted beautiful gardens ushering guests up expensive front walks into magazine-worthy homes. This house seemed to fall a bit short of the others. The house belonged to my wife's father. Now, I supposed, it belonged to my wife.

I knew very little about Megan's father. Once my beloved had whispered her horrible secret to me, I never asked about it again. We never went to see him. No one sent cards or made phone calls. Megan's mother died when she was in middle school, and the horrible secret meant she was truly alone until she escaped the house.

This house. This fine, green, two-story in a nice neighborhood on an even nicer street. Could I just not go in?

"Babe?" Megan was beautiful, even when she was impatient, like now. Her black curls were neatly picked out around her brown eyes in a soft, round, golden-brown face. I was so easily aroused by my wife, even when the rest of our relationship was dicey.

"Babe." Megan's sharp voice made me jump.

"Yup. Sorry!" I scrambled out of the passenger side of the Camaro and joined Megan on the sidewalk. *I hope she isn't mad at me again. Not today.*

Megan put on a bright smile and took her hand. She laced their fingers together, squeezing just a little too hard for it to be romantic. She was probably nervous. I tried not to notice the pain. We went up the front walk, Megan jingling the keys in her other hand. At the front door, she turned to me and I saw the childlike fear in her brown eyes for a moment. It was gone just as fast. I squeezed and released Megan's hand to allow her freedom to open the heavy door with unfamiliar keys.

The door swung open, and I inhaled with wonder. The home was so much grander than our tiny, cramped apartment of three years. Even from the front door, the possibilities thrummed. Though the inside had not been updated or well-cared for, the bones of the house were close to perfect.

I turned to my wife. "Are you okay?"

Megan nodded and took a moment before saying more. "I haven't been here in almost twenty years. It looks...weird."

I nodded as Megan moved in front of me, looking around. Her face was blank, but a tear snuck down her cheek. I reached to caress her back, missing her as she moved through the space. Instead, she crossed her arms, and looked around. The foyer swept up to a second-floor chandelier with several lights burned out. The floors were covered in a nasty, dusty, rust-colored carpet, and I wondered if it might just have hardwood flooring underneath. Built-ins flanked a grand fireplace of large river stones. I imagined filling the floor-to-ceiling shelves with books. I could arrange them in the ROYGBIV rainbow colors I admired on social media feeds.

"Oh, gawd! C'mere." Megan's voice beckoned from another room.

I shook myself from the decorating daydream and moved quickly toward the voice. Megan stood in a dining room with a formal dining set, including a huge china cabinet and something I thought was called a buffet.

"He just didn't do anything." Megan gestured towards the newspapers piled on the grand table. Some were still in the plastic sleeves, others appeared to have been read and were open, sprawled in layers across the table. Dust coated every surface.

"Wow. I'm a little scared to see the kitchen."

Megan nodded as we exchanged anxious faces. The house was so big that walking to the kitchen took some time. How many steps? Was the dining room twenty feet wide? I tried to peer out dingy windows as we walked. I heard the muffled sounds of birds outside, a kid yelling, and street traffic. The house was cool, the thermostat kept at a severe sixty-four degrees year round. There were no open windows. They probably hadn't been opened for decades. Every room smelled stale and stuffy despite the cool temperature.

"It's so big, Meg. Maybe we could be happy here?" I hoped my words sounded more enthusiastic than I felt. Just because I got out of the car didn't mean I had to stay. I didn't have to live here with Megan. I could leave. I could ask for a divorce.

"Wait til you see the upstairs, my Little One!"

My entire body tightened, as I didn't enjoy the nickname Megan used. I said nothing as Megan chattered on like a museum docent.

"There is a gigantic bathroom with a huge glassed-in shower and a two-person jacuzzi tub. Of course, it might not work anymore."

We reached the kitchen. There were some dirty dishes in the sink, just coffee mugs and small plates. A dusting of fruit fly carcasses littered the sink near the drain. It smelled musty and old in the kitchen. No one had lived here for months now. The counters were lightly cluttered with quick box meals and a few clean plates. Perhaps the elderly man lived there without cooking at all and instead of putting the dishes away, he left whatever he used out on the counter.

Megan stood by the yellow Formica table in the corner of the kitchen. The four chairs were tucked in and the tabletop was clean.

"I guess he still sat here." Megan ran her fingers over a chair back. "He sat over there and I sat right here."

I tentatively stepped closer. I couldn't read my mate at this moment. Megan's round cheeks lost their flushed pink, but her face remained smooth and luminous. I was afraid to disrupt her reverie and remained quiet.

"He would sit down with me at meals while my mother served him like a fucking Sultan. She would talk back to him, so I don't think she feared him. She didn't know that he often put his hand on my knee under the table. It was his sick way of..." She stopped talking.

The room felt airless. My pulse pounded in my ears as I pictured Megan as a small girl, likely to be voluptuous even then.

"Hey. Could you show me that bathroom, babe?"

She shifted focus, leaned toward me, and nodded, relieved. We held hands as I tugged her towards the towering staircase. It had a faded rust-colored carpet runner over dusty wood stairs. We giggled breathlessly as we ran upstairs. She paused at the top, looking both ways before turning right and heading for an open door.

The bathroom looked like marble and was slightly smaller than our entire apartment. Megan made great money at the bank, and I did okay as a server when I used to work. She preferred I stay home, so I did. Even without having children of our own, Megan wanted me to take care of our home, and her. Our small place was downtown in the city, so that was where our money went: good food, home decor, clothes, and her fancy car. I didn't need a car, so when mine broke down, we never bought another one.

This bathroom could be why I remained married. It had the most incredible space. The huge shower was a room of its own with several different water sources. The jacuzzi tub was full of random crap, but I would campaign hard to get it in working order. I could see myself in this house, if she could.

We toured the rest of the house giddily. Megan had a hard time in her old room, so we decided it could become my office, library, or guest room. We would tear the master bedroom apart, changing everything about it before we moved in. Since I didn't work outside the home and loved decorating, this would be my project. I felt proud Megan believed in my skills and abilities.

I should have known it was too good to be true.

We gathered the tools for my work to begin, and Megan dropped me off a few days later before she went to work.

"Try not to spend all my money, okay?"

I grit my teeth to keep from saying something I would regret. I had not even begun the project, and she was already critical.

Megan must have read my face and instantly changed her tone. "I'm just kidding, Little One. You'll do great. I know there is all kinds of crap in the basement. Try to use paint and stuff we already have there first, okay?"

I nodded sullenly, but if she noticed, she didn't react. I watched from the expansive front picture window and chewed the inside of my cheek as she drove away. All the comebacks I couldn't think of when she was there flooded my mind as I watched her leave. I stood and back talked through the window to the empty Lilypond Lane in front of the house.

"You aren't the only adult here, Megan." I grinned and waved my finger in the air at my absent mate. *"Why don't you go make that money, since you are worthless at hard work?"* That was a good one. I'd like to see her do any hard work at all.

"I'm thinking about leaving your bitchy ass almost every day lately, so don't push your luck, Big One!"

I kept up my too-late tirade until a brown blur and a *thunk!* sounded and broke my focus. I stood there for a moment, trying to think what could have made the sound. My mind moved slowly and I shook myself into going outside.

Beneath the picture window on the cropped grass was a dead sparrow. I bent down to inspect the poor thing, looking for any signs of life, hoping it was merely stunned. Its poor little neck was twisted at a very much dead angle. Tears pricked my eyes as I looked down at its feathered body. I stood up, trying to shake off the surprising sorrow over such a minor event. I wiped at my tears with the back of my hand before returning to work in our new house.

I spent the rest of the morning and half the afternoon clearing crap out of the master bedroom. Everything smelled stale, and I struggled to open the windows. After so many decades, most were sealed shut. I scraped and fought one of the bedroom windows open, and the fresh air helped clear the space. I stood looking out at the enormous backyard from the second floor. Like the front yard, it was sterile, with no flower beds or cheer. It merely met the expectations of the neighborhood. I would love to plant herb beds, roses, and wildflowers. I'd hang some birdfeeders and put a patio set out back. This house could be a place of love and life again. Could Megan and I be happier here, despite our challenges and her rough childhood in this house?

I pulled myself out of my daydream and back to work. I began washing the bedroom walls to paint them. Remembering Megan's request to be frugal, I dutifully headed to the basement workroom to check out the paint cans we saw when we toured the house. We almost fought down there in the basement over the paint shelves. It was a dumb fight. I knew Megan would like a home gym and I'd said if we moved the paint shelves to another area, she could use the space for a gym.

"No. The shelves belong there."

I remember thinking her voice was suddenly sharp, and I thought she was being awfully prickly over where we put old paint cans. I'd backed up the conversation and even said she could just make a workout room in one of the other bedrooms if she'd rather. That seemed to mollify her, and we continued the tour.

I shook off the memory and faced the heavy metal shelf stocked with dozens of old paint cans. *I seriously doubt any of this is usable.* I began to shift cans and looked for splotches of old paint on the lids to see if there was anything bright and happy in the ancient leftovers. Most of it was beige or brown. I reached to the back of the shelf, bumping my fingers over something that felt like a picture frame. I groped around, trying to figure out what I was feeling when I heard the front door open.

"Colette?"

I felt like I was caught doing something naughty. I hustled upstairs to greet my wife and saw she had a few bags in her arms. I smelled good food as I stepped to take some of the load.

"Sorry, I was working. What is all of this?"

She grinned, leading me towards the kitchen again. I strained to keep up with her. She was already unloading bags when I entered the kitchen and joined her at the table. She unpacked a luxurious body wash and two plush-looking bath sheets in a rose color we both loved.

"I thought after all that hard work today, we could enjoy the big girl shower tonight?"

I nod, very pleased at the idea of a hot shower with this sexy woman. She took out a big rose-scented candle, a wand lighter, and a bathmat I recognized from our apartment. I laughed.

"Couldn't break the bank completely, right?" She laughed beautifully.

I unloaded the rotisserie chicken, microwave veggies with sauce, and a bottle of red wine."Do you think he had a bottle opener?"

"Drawer to the left of the dishwasher." She didn't even turn to look at me. I went to find the opener but felt uncertain. We should have eaten while the chicken was still warm, but I was dirty and wanted to shower.

"Um, what do you want to do first, Megan?" I checked her face, and she was studying me.

"What would you like, Little One? What does my Colette want?"

I appreciated her handing me the options, but it felt like a trap. I didn't want to do anything that made her good mood disappear. I smiled and tentatively began to offer my preferences when she interrupted me.

"I think you need to shower. You...kind of smell." She laughed and poked me playfully, but her long, sharp nails stung. I swatted her hand away, and she got *That Look*. I grabbed the towels and ran for the stairs. She laughed like a gauntlet had been thrown and followed closely behind. She let me win the race and soon we were kissing inside the vast bathroom.

I stripped off my filthy shirt, jeans, underwear, and sports bra. She gingerly undressed from her tailored work clothes. She hung her pants on a hook, followed by the blazer and blouse. Underneath, Megan has on black lacy briefs and a bra. She was a four-hook bra kind of woman, weighing twice what I did and curvy in all the right places. She turned away from me, wordlessly expecting me to unhook it for her. I did.

I was in awe of her breasts. I was in the thrall of her large, goddess body as it was uncovered before me. I began to feel aroused and traced the curve of a heavy breast with my hands.

"I wish you would wear prettier things." Her voice sounded sweet, but the words cut me.

"I was–I'm working in the house." I released her breast and stepped back slightly.

"Yes, but you wear sports bras all the time, and they aren't sexy." She chucked me under the chin and turned away, swaying her hips seductively as she headed to turn on the shower.

We both knew I would follow her. We both knew I would always try to make up, even when the hurt wasn't mine to correct.

Megan was the first woman I had ever been with. From the beginning of our courtship, she made me feel so alive with sexual pleasure that she barely got to propose before I was kissing her everywhere with my head over heels in love "Yes!"

I'd thought about that morning proposal so many times. I wished I had taken a day or two to consider what it would mean. Neither of us had a supportive family. We didn't share any friends, and once I started dating Megan, I let many old friends drop out of my life so I could see her more.

"Are you coming?" Megan's silky voice was almost a command. I saw the steam already building against the shower's glass walls. I felt the ache in my muscles from my efforts today and moved quickly into the too-hot shower with my woman.

We couldn't stay at the house yet, so the next day Megan once again dropped me off at our new front door. I waved as she drove away, then glanced at the grass under the picture window. The poor sparrow from yesterday was gone. I fitted the key into the front door properly on my third try. It still didn't feel like home, with the outdated furniture, ugly rust carpet, and airless rooms, but I could make it better. I put down the new supplies I had with me. I wanted to deep clean the bathroom. It was a great night last night, but the bathroom was pretty grotty. I wanted it to sparkle for our next shower, or hopefully, jacuzzi bath.

I dropped everything in the bathroom and checked on the master bedroom only to see I left the window open last night. No matter, the weather was fair and the room smelled better. I wandered back through the other rooms upstairs, thinking about furniture and things we might like. Our place was so small, I couldn't wait to have all of this space. It will be good for our marriage, to be able to get away from each other a little. I could breathe with a room of my own for my books and silly art Megan hates.

Megan hired movers to remove anything we didn't want to keep, and then two days later, after the carpets were steam cleaned, our things were delivered. I wished we could rip up the carpet. There could be hardwood underneath. Megan said we might later on. She wanted me to pack up our house and prepare this one but I didn't know if I could do all of that inside one week. I'd asked her to make it two or even three weeks, but she just shook her head. That head shake was law in our house. I just had to work harder. My body was sore, and I had a few new callouses, but I was eager to see what I could do with this huge house.

I headed back to the basement to continue my paint hunt. When I was once again facing the heavy metal shelves, I remembered the feeling of the strange frame under my fingers. I'd been so engrossed in Megan and the shower I'd forgotten. I reached past the shelves and ran my hands against the wall, catching cobwebs and grit that made me shriek. I had been holding my breath and the holler helped calm my tension. How on Earth was I going to clean this house and pack our house within the same week? I was angry with Megan but excited about the house... so I stepped on my feelings. Who knew I just needed to be freaked out by some cobwebs to see that situation better?

I grabbed an old paint stirrer and used it to swipe the back wall for any other cobwebs, then found the little raised space on the wall that caught my attention yesterday. I peered through the shelves to the back wall but didn't see anything. I ran my fingers back over it and felt a small ridge again. The basement was dim and even the overhead fluorescent lights didn't help. I pulled out my cell phone, turned on the flashlight, and shone it on the back wall.

There seemed to be some sort of line on the wall, and my fingers sliding over it told me it continued above my head and below the shelf. I couldn't see it even with my flashlight, but I felt like there was a panel of some sort. Curiosity buzzed in my brain as I tried reaching behind the shelves to explore the panel. My hair and face caught more cobwebs. I shrieked, flailing to get them off my face, and then laughed at myself. I didn't have time for this Nancy Drew shit. I needed to get to work.

I selected two of the heaviest paint cans in what looked like a grayish-white. It wasn't ideal for our bedroom, but it would be a nice starting coat for something more fun later. I ignored the extra paint tools abandoned and covered in dust in the basement. I did take the ceiling extension, since I could use that with the new rollers and handle we bought. I headed upstairs stepping heavily under the weight of the two cans. The wire handle cut into my fingers as I thought ahead to my work.

It took me longer to stir the paint into submission than it did for me to paint the first coat on the bedroom walls. The brighter color changed the whole look of the room. It was mid-afternoon when I finished the second coat and I was grinning to myself as I started feeling excited about moving our bedroom set in here, and looking out on the backyard when we woke up in the mornings.

I was cleaning up from painting when Megan arrived. I sucked in my breath, anxious about what her mood might be. I blew that same breath out and went to meet her. There were no grocery bags this time, but we had new rose towels hanging in the now-clean bathroom. She came into the house and called for me. I stood at the top of the staircase and greeted her.

"Welcome home, baby! Come upstairs and see what I did today!"

Megan smiled at me as she started climbing the stairs, her steps muffled on the rust-colored carpet runner. I went to give her a kiss and she stepped back gesticulating at my messy paint clothes. I laughed self-consciously and blew her a kiss. She didn't notice as she headed to the bedroom and I followed a few steps behind.

"White? Honey, it is so sterile. What about some color?" Megan walked through the room like I was a hired contractor.

I felt dejected. My shoulders dropped and I stopped following her. I'd been feeling so good about the clean bathroom and freshly painted walls, now I was awash with other feelings.

"You asked me to use what was already here..." My voice sounded very small.

Megan didn't turn to me but continued through into the master bathroom. She smiled and nodded, so at least she approved of my work in this area of the house.

"You are usually such a magician with spaces, I guess I thought–well I don't know what I thought." She turned to me then with soft eyes.

I watched her rearrange her face to look more loving and kind. I hated it when she did that. It was like she went from my manager to my lover and thought I wouldn't notice.

"Thank you for doing all this work, Little One. It looks great!" Megan turned away from me and headed back downstairs to the front door.

Once again I found myself standing at the top of the stairs confused.

"Are we going already?" I sounded like a child. Megan looked up at me with annoyance passing over her beautiful features.

"Uh, yeah. This place certainly isn't ready to live in yet. I know you want to get packing and I thought I could pick up dinner for us while you pack at home." She looked at her watch like I was some kind of client who needed hurrying along. I dutifully came downstairs, grabbed the stuff I wanted to take home with me, and followed her out the door. When we approached the car, she paused, looking me over.

"You don't have any wet paint on you, do you?"

I felt like a little kid even though she was only six years older than me. I wanted to bite back, but instead, I shook my head. Just in case, she made me sit on plastic bags we kept in the glove box. I didn't feel like a wife. I didn't feel like a partner. I felt like a servant and not the sexy kind. I was so tired from my efforts and so drained from her reaction I didn't know how I'd possibly pack tonight. All I wanted to do was take a hot shower and fall into bed.

It was two more days before I went back to the house on Lilypond Lane. Packing up even our tiny apartment took care and attention, and with the movers coming within days, that became my priority. When everything outside of necessities was neatly boxed and packaged for movers, I was once again dropped off at our new home to continue cleaning and preparing.

Megan came in with me this time and we went through each room by room putting sticky notes on things we didn't want to keep. The movers would be here later to remove the unwanted items. I suggested we have a yard sale or an estate sale, but Megan didn't want people coming into our home and she certainly didn't think it was the kind of neighborhood where you would put things on the front lawn for strangers to gawk at. I called a local thrift store and arranged the donation of anything we cast off.

Megan left after about an hour to go to work at the bank. I began emptying drawers of the pieces we were not keeping. Almost everything was junk, but some things were interesting. In a drawer of the master bedroom nightstand, I found a journal. I didn't say anything to Megan because I was pretty sure she wouldn't want to know about it or read it. Besides, I wanted to look it over first. I was a little angry with her still and as I flipped through the journal I realized it was not from her father's diary. It's not her mother's either, as the dates were after her death.

The diary seemed like a daily log of food, exercise, and visits. The early entries were so faded it was difficult to read. The diary ended halfway through the pages. The more recent entries were in pen. As I flipped through it, puzzling over what it was, I realized the handwriting changed. The faint, early pencil was a very shaky hand and small letters. Then there was some space without anything written. The pencil entries began again, but this time it was stronger, blocky letters with very different handwriting than the first. The contents were the same: a date, diet notes, exercise notes, and occasionally notes about a visit. Then there were the pen entries, and they were more of a cursive style. I tossed it into a box and continued emptying drawers.

After several hours, I emptied the drawers and cleared the spaces for the movers. They were due any time in the next few hours. I had a headache and my stomach cramped. It was almost four o'clock and I'd forgotten to eat lunch. I got out my sandwich and chips, grabbed a soda from the fridge, and sat down at the yellow Formica kitchen table to eat. As I ate, I inventoried the work I'd accomplished and felt quite proud of myself. My mind drifted to the paint shelf, to the strange panel, and since I had a little time before the movers were expected, I tossed my trash into the garbage can and headed down to the basement.

The paint shelves were just as I'd left them. The house felt more like mine now, since I'd spent almost every day cleaning and painting and packing it up. I shone my cell phone flashlight on the wall behind the shelves again and ran my hands over the groove that felt like a picture frame. It was strange that I could feel it, but couldn't see it. I tried to push against the paint shelves to move them away from the wall to give me more room to work, but they were so heavy and large they would not budge.

This is ridiculous. You are being ridiculous.

I shook my head at my folly in the solemn quiet of the basement. I quickly began unloading paint cans from the metal shelves onto the floor. The shelving was in pieces, and I only needed to move the section of shelving in front of the wall panel. The wire of the paint cans cut into my hands as I lifted them from the shelf to set them on the floor a small distance away. I began to sweat and noticed my body odor as I wiped my face on my shirt and continued to work. I felt almost manic in my curiosity, but I needed to work quickly as the movers were due anytime and I would have to work with them. This was my chance to explore and solve this silly little mystery.

Once I unloaded the shelf, I expected it to be easy to move away from the wall. It wasn't. I pushed and shoved and pulled until finally it scraped with an eerie *screech* against the basement floor. I only had to move it out a few feet to see what had eluded me every time before. There was a panel on the wall. It was the size of a door.

The picture frame piece I could feel but not see was some sort of latch with a metal loop at the top.

I stood panting and sweating. What was behind the panel? Maybe some sort of storm cellar, or storage? The house was so vast, it certainly wouldn't need a little pocket like this. It wasn't old enough to have some sort of canning jar storage. I pulled at the latch, digging my fingers underneath it into a space I couldn't see with my eyes. To my surprise, the entire panel made a scraping sound and pulled free without much effort at all.

As I shone my phone flashlight into the space beyond the panel — which was actually a door — a room came into view. My brain mercifully checked out for a moment. The smell in the space was awful, and I wondered if some kind of animal had died back here. As I was better able to take in what I was looking at, I realized it was maybe some kind of bomb shelter. There was a bed to one side. I swept my light through the space and I realized it was actually a room. There was a small TV tray table, a cracked plastic lawn chair, and some boxes on the floor.

A chill inched along my spine as I stood gawking at this hidden room. When I turned to look at the entrance behind me, I saw marks on the wall and the door. The cement brick was scratched at my shoulder height and along the flat metal panel door, there were rust-colored streaks and scratches against the metal like something had been trying to get out of this room. My stomach plummeted and bile rose in my throat. This wasn't a place to seek safety, this was some kind of prison.

I was reminded of the journal upstairs, the diary with the entries of food and exercise and visits. The three different sets of handwriting. How strange Megan had been when I suggested we rearranged the basement–including these very shelves. These shelves that blocked this hidden, horrible room.

What exactly had happened here?

What was this room for?

Against my better judgment and my screaming nerves, I stepped closer to the boxes, not touching them, but shining my light in them. There were some remnants of food boxes, mouse droppings, a tattered dusty, old magazine, and some kind of novel. I didn't touch any of it.

I moved to the bucket and while its contents were desiccated and covered with dust, I would have bet my life had been used as a toilet. That must be where the bad smell came from. I thought back to the journal, my mind racing. I wanted to look at it again. What had happened here? Did Megan know about this room? Dear God, was Megan ever in this room?

Tears fell from my eyes and I wanted to curl up on the floor and sob. I also very much wanted to get the hell away from whatever this was. Was this her father's doing? What had happened here? My mind screamed to run. I couldn't live in this house. I couldn't stay here a moment longer. I began to back out of the room when I was startled by Megan's low voice behind me.

"What the fuck are you doing in this room?"

My blood froze and my insides clenched.

"What the fuck are you doing in here?" She repeated. Her anger bit through the words, and something else I could not process in my terror.

I turned slowly, dirt and tears still streaking my sweaty face. I did not meet her eyes, staring at the floor as my brain tried to come up with a response, a reality where I could speak again. Moments passed, years, maybe, and Megan stepped toward me slowly, blocking my escape from this horrible room.

"I never wanted you to see this." Her voice broke, and she took a deep breath. When she exhaled, I felt it on my face. Minty. She chewed gum in the car on her drive home, usually a sign she was in a good mood. But not now.

She took my chin in her hand, gently, and lifted my face to hers. I saw sorrow, fear, and unraveling in her brown eyes. Not what I expected. She continued to speak after releasing my chin. I managed to keep my eyes on hers, hoping she could explain this room.

"My father would send me here when I was bad, or when I ate too much, or when I fought him off of me." She paused when I gasped. My throat felt tight and my eyes burned and I was still overwhelmed by the stench of the room. "Sometimes it was for a short time, once it was for several days."

I watched her look around the room, taking it in. I shifted sideways, hoping to slip beside her, past her, out of this room. She didn't move. Her face appeared dead, and the light in her eyes flattened as she looked over my shoulder.

"He made me write down whatever food I'd eaten, made me do a list of exercises..." She trailed off.

I suddenly understood the weird diary. Fresh tears came to my eyes. Was this why she was the way she was? This poor, beautiful, broken soul! I reached for her with my tears wetting her clothing. She felt stiff as I tried to take her into my arms to hold her.

"I saw the journal. It's upstairs."

She pulled away from me, absently pushing me back farther into the room again.

"What?"

She looked embarrassed and something else, hidden to me.

"Yeah, I...I didn't know what it was." I wiped my nose. I wished I could have been anywhere else. I needed to get out of this room, away from this house.

"Well, now you do, huh?" She kept looking at the room but didn't move out of the doorway.

"There were several different sets of entries, different handwriting —" I trailed off, hoping she would answer my unasked question. She looked surprised and confused. We stared at each other until finally, she said something scarier than this room.

"There must have been others, then."

I covered my mouth and closed my eyes, reeling. Overwhelming anxiety clawed up my chest and into my throat. My imagination was no worse than the truth. I never met her father, and I was very glad he was dead.

I inhaled, raising the energy to speak again. "Megan, we cannot live in this house." I slid toward the opening out of the room, hoping she would see it as me moving towards her, closer, as if we were on the same team here. She blocked my escape, slid her arm around my waist, and pressed me against the doorframe.

"Yes, yes we can. We can block the room up again. I told you the shelving was staying here. I never meant for you to know about this." She changed her face, trying to look endearing. It didn't quite work and she looked terrifying.

I wanted to shove my way out of the room, to run out of this house, and away from her. My terror kept my limbs locked as I desperately tried to guess what she was thinking, what to do, what to say to make this all stop. Anger bubbled up under my fear, sending adrenaline thrumming through my muscles. I stood straighter and locked eyes with her.

"I am not living in this house." My voice sounded strained but strong. My blood rushed in my ears and my stomach threatened to reverse its contents. Megan gawked at me for a moment, her reassuring face sliding away as she realized what I was saying. She looked like she'd lost her mind completely.

"Of course you will, Colette. You might need some time to think it over, that's all. You certainly aren't leaving me? Are you?" Her voice slid between us, a coiled snake.

I was terrified of her and the horrible little room. My lips pressed tightly together to keep the truth from coming out. She saw all of this plain on my face, placed her soft hand in between my breasts, shoved me backward into the room, and slid the door closed.

Heather Curlee Novak is a woman who knows red lipstick and glitter are meant for more than special occasions. She has lived a lot of life – some of it messy, most of it meaningful – and she is eager to help other folks find energy, engagement, and excitement in their own stories.

For the latest news on Heather's next releases, follow her on Threads, Facebook, and Instagram.

Potluck

BY EMMA ELLIS

Sandra detests the new neighbours before she's even spoken to them. They're young, ambitious, not her sort at all. But Sandra is used to dealing with such nuisance neighbours, and she has a very effective method of getting rid of them.

I'm careful when I pull back the curtain. There's an art to watching the neighbours. No sudden tug, lights off in the house, nothing that would catch their eye. I even remove my watch at certain times of day, so it doesn't catch the sunlight. No need right now though. From the living room bay window, we are in shade since the sun is behind the overgrown poplars. The new couple that moved into that house never spared the time to tend their garden. They've left now, of course. No one ever lasts.

I wonder what makes them all move out in such haste. The lack of phone reception here, or the sound of screaming at night. Perhaps it's when they hear about all the missing people. The woods behind Lilypond Lane are rumoured to horde souls. It never says that on the property listing, of course.

The truck that caught my attention trundles down the little street and all the way around the central grassy area with the lily-pond. It's a removal truck. Again. More people moving in. I just hope that this time they're the right sort.

The man gets out first, a stout thing, dressed like he's about to play a game of football instead of concerned about making a good impression on his new neighbours. And, oh dear. He has a beard. It makes my face itch just looking at it. A terrible, wiry thing that looks like it's made of terrier fur. We had a dog with fur like that once. He was a cute thing but he always stank.

A woman follows. She looks like she's expecting another, her stomach protruding from her shiny top. I assume it's his wife, though I can't make out a wedding ring from here. The last thing we need is more unmarried couples creating scandals. Not since the last time.

I can still hear their shouting. Such anger. Such hatred. Such fear.

The sight of the mistress sitting on the patio like some harlot, the clothes being thrown out of the top floor window, confirmed everything I thought about such people.

The wife's funeral was well-attended at least. The husband's, well, they never found him, so I suppose he's still merely classed as missing.

"You going to tell me what they're like, Sandra?" My husband calls from his special chair on the other side of the living room.

He can barely raise his voice above a whisper these days. If I don't strain to listen, sometimes I don't even notice he's here.

"Just wait, Paul."

"Well, I want to know."

I peer a little closer to the window and squint. My glasses need to be a bit stronger but the opticians in town have gone all up-market. Like everything.

"Young," I say.

"Pah. Typical."

"With a child." I say this through my teeth.

"Oh no. Not again."

I purse my lips as I watch the adults unpack swings and slides for the garden as the child runs around like it's feral. No doubt that little brat will ruin the grass area around the lilypond.

When I first moved into Lilypond Lane, the houses were small. Modest, we called them. Then people wanted bigger houses for their bigger families. The one across the street had an extension all the way round, clad in some gaudy wood. Awful. Not in keeping at all. I put a stop to it where I can. Some weeks, I spend hours writing to the council to contest planning permission that promises to turn these houses into monstrosities.

The new family hug on the front lawn for a moment, and I sense that emotion they share. The man thinks nothing is good enough for him and his brat. Ambition. Desire to inflate his house along with his ego.

Over my dead body.

That house backs directly onto the woods. Those woods will terrify them and, with any luck, they'll be long gone by the time their plans for an extension are drawn up.

I scrunch my nose at the sight of them. The child, I can't tell if it's a boy or a girl. Parents like to keep it ambiguous these days. I see it all the time around town: little girls in sporty shirts and little boys with long hair, then they tut when we get it wrong. On top of that, they call them names like River and Grassy Meadow or whatever and expect everyone to understand what their child is.

Hipsters. That's what the press calls them. Gentrifying hipsters, putting us traditional people out to pasture.

I'll bet this new family are the sort to go to the vegan bakery that's opened up. It used to be a lovely butcher, but now you can sit in, have a hugely overpriced coffee, and the tea is terrible. I couldn't believe it when we went there once. I had to ask the server to repeat the price three times. A month's gas bill on a couple of coffees and a piece of cake, just because they make a swirly pattern in the milk foam.

There used to be a very reasonably priced greengrocer. Now, it's all organic mumbo jumbo. It's hard for me to get to the bigger supermarket sometimes. Leaving Paul isn't always an option for that long, so many times I have to hobble along to that local shop and wince through the checkout as the cashier tells me the price. It's the same cashier who worked in the greengrocers. She looks no happier. I wear a scarf and sunglasses to hide my face, so she doesn't feel bad when my dismay is evident. It's not her fault the prices are so ridiculous, so it wouldn't be fair to make her feel guilty.

The new family go inside their house now, the child running ahead, the parents holding hands. I lick my lips.

As much as Paul and I try to put a stop to this madness, the young people keep coming with their big ideas.

And we keep having to get rid of them.

When they have children though, it's difficult. I draw the line there. Their meat never tastes as good.

I pondered once if it was my cooking method. Perhaps the young meat needs a lower temperature, or longer to brown, perhaps. Maybe a slosh more sherry in the sauce. But it's no good. However many methods I have tried cooking young meat, it never comes out tender. It's always a bit chewy and dry.

At my age, I can't just dig a hole big enough to dispose of the child. So it's a conundrum when there are children. One that I have been pondering a solution for just in case the need arises again. Paul used to be so useful but as I gaze at him now, he's a sorry sight. Pale and hunched, his breathing ragged with emphysema. It's hard to get him to eat enough these days and his once broad body has withered into almost nothing. It'll be our fiftieth wedding anniversary this year. But it's clear he'll never be of any use again. Still, it's nice to have his company.

There's a knock at the door and I release the curtain and make my face all smiles. Such a wide smile my lines dig deeply around my eyes. I open the door and throw my hands up as if a gift has been presented to me.

"Oh, my! Hello!"

"Hi," the man with the beard says. I know this from the way his hair moved and not because I can see his mouth under that doormat of a facial feature. I could clean my wellington boots on that beard. "We're your new neighbours. Just came round to introduce ourselves. I'm Caleb, my wife Darleen, and this is little Tony."

Darleen looks like she's coloured her eyebrows in with a marker pen. I have to force my eyes away from them to stop me from staring. I gaze upon the child instead, all grass-stains and messy hair.

So the child is a boy then. "Nice to meet you, Tony."

"Tonia," the child says.

"Excuse me?"

"My name is Tonia," it says, folding its arms.

Is that a girl's name or boy's? I've no idea. The clothes are too boyish, jeans and a muddy T-shirt. It's a hooligan. That's all we need.

"How precious," I say, keeping my smile lifted. "And how lovely to have some young people in the street. I simply adore the sound of children laughing."

"Well, we were thinking of having a potluck on Saturday, picnic style, out on the green," the beard says.

I hold my hands to my chest, as if the messiah himself is talking. "What a marvellous idea. I make a wonderful pie. I'll bring some along. And welcome to the neighbourhood!"

I close the door and relax my face. That smile was beginning to ache.

"What did they want?" Paul calls from the living room and I walk through.

"They're inviting us to a potluck lunch on the green on Saturday."

He grunts and wheezes a laugh before responding. "Might as well fatten them up a bit."

My lips curl as I laugh along with him. "Of course, dear. Of course."

The large chest freezer is in the garage, and I walk out there to inspect what I have. Despite the warm day we've had, the garage is always cold and I tighten my cardigan around me. Paul always planned on insulating it, but never got around to it.

My hip gives me some grief on the way, a twinge that is playing up more and more. I'd go to the doctor, but getting an appointment is near impossible. All their time is taken up with babies and expectant mothers. No one has any time for us oldies. I worked all my life, as did Paul, and this is how we are repaid in our old age. At least I'm doing something about it now. Poor George who lived in number six was booted out of his home by his family. House prices were too good to pass up the opportunity, they told him, before carting him off to a nursing home where he gave up on life and succumbed six months later.

The couple who moved into his old house though, they didn't last much longer. I lick my lips as I think of them. They were quite delicious.

I open the freezer door and the blast of cold air chills my bones. The cold mist clears and I gaze upon my wares. I have several pies already made: meat and carrot, meat and peas, meat and cream, though I've quite forgotten what meat is in each one. I should write an age on the label, since I don't want to share my best but also not my worst. There was that couple who moved in a few months back, late thirties they were, the best age for a tender pie. And they were a large couple. They went quite a long way. I could share their spoils, but not the rump. Not the best cut. Maybe some cheek or breast meat. I shift around the pies until I locate what I am sure are the right ones, and my stomach growls. There's three left, and I choose one for our dinner tonight.

As I lift it, the frost sends shooting pain down my arm, and almost drop it. My damned neuralgia. I rest the pie on the shelf and shake out my arm, take some deep breaths and it passes quickly.

With poor George gone, and Paul of no use, disposing of the new family is going to be very tricky. Adjacent to the freezer, the shelves are filled with all manner of saws and chisels. I run my hands over them, a little tingle spreading through my body, and my stomach grumbles even more.

Where there's a will, there's a way, Sandra, I tell myself.

I walk back to the kitchen and leave the pie on the side to defrost. This kitchen was fitted thirty years ago and every time I come in here, my chest still swells with pride at how lovely it is. Peach cabinets and green tiles. All the new kitchens I see on TV adverts are white or plain wood. Like people don't want any colour these days.

I take a slice of yesterday's dish out of the fridge and put it in the microwave for ten minutes before returning to the living room to find Paul dosing. I sit on the chair next to his and change the channel. He prefers the news or documentaries, but I enjoy a soap opera or mystery. *Midsummer Murders* is on at the moment, and that seems quite fitting.

The smell from the kitchen wafts through, and when the microwave pings I can hardly wait. This was a particularly good pie. Rump cuts from a thirty-year-old. The best. I sit at the kitchen table to tuck in, enjoying every mouthful of the filling and oozing sauce. The pastry is never as good when recooked, but it is moist and crumbly enough.

Human meat wasn't always on the menu. If these damned youngsters hadn't made every corner shop and cafe so damned fancy and forced out the traditional shops, we'd still have a butcher. If these youngsters didn't bleat on about every political decision, worrying about the environment so much, farmed meat would still be affordable. How are we meant to survive on our pensions?

There are too many people anyway. They're building another new housing development on the green belt, would you believe it? That area is supposed to be left undeveloped, but with demand so high, they don't give a hoot about conservation laws.

Family homes, they're saying they'll be.

Well, we just need to stop there being any families demanding homes.

Just as I am eating my last mouthful, there is another knock at the door. I push myself up with a sigh, my knees protesting as I do. What do I have to do to get some peace around here?

I fashion that same smile and open the door. "Caleb. What a lovely surprise again!"

His hands are pressed together in front of his chest as if in prayer, and now I notice the lack of wedding ring.

"Meant to say," he says, "it'll be a vegetarian potluck, we decided. Since over half the street are vegetarian."

"Of course. I assumed as much. Ever since my granddaughter went vegan, I decided to be vegetarian myself. I actually make my own meat substitute. It's quite tasty."

"I look forward to trying that!"

I smile even wider. "I guarantee you've never had anything like this before."

Despite my aches and pains, I make the most of the fine weather the next day, keeping the privet neat and tidy, the clematis nicely attached to the trellis. Paul appreciates a tidy view outside from his chair, even though he doesn't really get outside to enjoy it now.

I choose my time carefully. Nine-thirty. The young neighbours — the ones left — should be at work then, the brat at school. It's a Thursday so this is my time to enjoy the street.

I don't have one of those noisy lawn mowers. It's an old manual one and pushing it down the garden keeps my arms strong. Today is a good day. Despite my aches yesterday, today I am relatively pain-free. I glance over at the woods. I'm going to have to go there before Saturday to set the snares. Perhaps, given my lack of aches, today would be a good opportunity.

My father taught me how to snare, although he used to hunt rabbits. The idea is the same though, although with humans you have to be a bit quicker. And make sure they are inebriated enough.

Perhaps I can get rid of these latest without the need. My freezer is full enough. I can cope without their offerings for a while.

Paul used to deal with the sound effects from the woods, with a little help from George. Even that Spanish woman who lived at the house opposite mine wasn't opposed to scaring off the odd new resident we didn't think was the right sort. Of course, she didn't know we took things a little further.

Just as I am finishing up with the clematis, standing on a little stool to reach the top, he comes running out of his house.

"Sandra, let me help you with that."

"Caleb. Oh, how kind." I step off the stool and stand as upright as I can. I am not frail and certainly don't need help for such a simple task.

"Feel free to ask if you ever need any help. I used to care for my grandparents, so I know how tricky some things can be."

I do my best to hide my offence behind a smile. "You not at work today?"

"Working from home."

I clench my teeth, which aggravates my neuralgia in my jaw. Working from home indeed! A new invention designed specifically to intrude on us older people, I'm sure. This means there's no chance I'll get to the woods today. "How wonderful," I say. "You all settled in?"

"Getting there. Tonia is making herself right at home. She likes the woods out the back."

She? It is a girl then. "Her bedroom is the back one, I suppose?"

"Yep. Squirrels galore at her window!"

"Precious," I say. Perhaps I can figure out the speakers on my own. That little boy/girl overlooking the woods is perfect. There's something so evil about children, like they think they've got you all figured out. But they scare easily. A brat terrified of a nightmare is one of the few pleasures in life.

"Oh, just to let you know, we've got the broadband people coming round today," he says.

"You're in a band?"

"No. Broadband. Internet. They may have to dig up a bit of the street but should just be an afternoon's job. It'll be done and filled in today."

Digging up the street for the internet! Dear god. "Well, needs must, I suppose."

I go inside and tell Paul what I just heard. He is so disgruntled, when he nods off, he curses in his sleep.

The band people come, their noise shaking the widows as they jackhammer the tarmac over. When they're done, a blacker streak remains, mismatched with the rest of the road. It's gaudy and stands out like anything like some eyesore.

I heat the pie I took out of the freezer yesterday. They take a day to defrost. It's chewy, sinewy ends get stuck between my teeth. Six years old at the most, must have been that little boy who kicked his football against my window. That memory makes it taste better.

* * * *

The good thing about my pies is none of these neighbours would have tried this flavour meat before, so I can easily say it's one of those fake brands. Human meat is less rich and a grainier texture than livestock meat and in any case, with enough seasoning, everything tastes like chicken. Once they're a little sozzled on whatever it is young people drink these days, they'll happily demolish the lot. It's my bit of vengeance, the fact that they won't even know. And it clears some space in my freezer for the bounty to come.

When Friday arrives, I can't wait any longer. I must go to the woods. I spend half the morning peering out of my living room window, ensuring the neighbours aren't out and about. The new one's car is still on the drive, so it's a fair bet one of them is in. If they see me go into the woods, I'll just have to say I'm blackberry picking or something.

In my wellies, gardening clothes and gloves, I make my way across the street. With the dark clouds collecting, rain is likely this afternoon so the soft youngsters should stay indoors. The way young people are all so adverse to bad weather these days makes me wonder if they're made of flour.

I have barely made it across the street when Caleb comes running over. I mute my sigh and plaster on my smiling face once again, sure it's going to give me a headache soon.

"Sandra, hi."

"Good morning."

"Just wanted to remind you about the potluck tomorrow. Everyone is looking forward to your pies!"

I bet they are! "I don't need reminding. My memory is quite good, thank you."

"Oh, I didn't mean to imply — "

I wave off his concern. "No offence taken."

"You off to the woods?"

He has a smell about him. Paint, I think. Along with some pungent aftershave. He'll need a great deal of scrubbing before he's edible. "I want to see how the blackberries are coming along," I say.

"We heard stories about the woods." He looks over that way and his shirt lifts a little, revealing some paunch. I chew on the inside of my cheek as I imagine taking a bite. "Some daft rumours," he continues. "Darleen was quite concerned about them, but it sounded like such a load of old nonsense."

"People do say the daftest things. I've lived here forty years and visit the woods frequently."

"I'll let Darleen know. That will certainly put her mind at ease."

"Well, I best get to it."

As I walk away, I lick my molars. Perhaps I'll order a second freezer. Just so nothing goes to waste.

It takes all afternoon to check my snares. I'm using bear traps this time. They are so difficult to open, especially today since my arms are tired after all my gardening. After considerable effort and twinging my back, I prize open four of them and place some bags of brightly coloured sweeties in each. That should attract the brat, and these traps will snap her in half. That will save me some of the effort of sawing through her and make her much easier to dispose of. I know exactly where I've left them all, memorising the knots and branches of the trees. Then, my can of pepper spray will disable the parents long enough for me to do away with them.

I glance up at the speakers hidden among the foliage. It's such a shame Paul can't help with that anymore, but it really is beyond me. Those times he helped were so wonderful. Such theatre. The ghostly sounds, the whispers, the cries of help. He had voices of little children singing, a haunting sound. I think the flavour of the meat is so much better when they have been terrified at the end, like the adrenaline tenderises the flesh. Perhaps it's just my joy that adds to the taste.

My mouth waters. The pies smell delicious. I opted for three in the end, no livestock were killed in the making of the pies. "Completely pig, cow, chicken and lamb free," I say with a hearty laugh as I put the dishes on the table.

It's a lovely day, a little too much sun for my liking, but I have my large hat. Some of the residents have laid out chairs on the grassy bank, which I ignore. I may be the eldest here, but I am quite capable of standing.

"Sandra," Caleb says. "Take a seat."

I ignore his patronising gesture. By the looks of his wife, she is in far greater need of a chair than me. "Sorry Paul couldn't make it," I say.

"Oh, not at all. How are you?" the wife says, I've forgotten her name already. I swear she's drawn on even bigger eyebrows than last time.

"As well as always, I suppose."

I know she wants to sit down. She shuffles on her feet and her ankles look swollen, yet she stays standing next to me like some passive aggressive show of fitness.

"It's a big house to maintain by yourself," she says.

"It's my home. I am quite content."

I take the knife and slice pieces of pie, the lovely sauce oozing out. I worry that they'll come across a tell-tale sign, a fingernail or something, though I meticulously picked those out.

"Caleb was saying you've lived there forty years?"

I nod and place some pie on a plate and cut another slice.

"He's already drawing up plans to extend," she continues, and I start cutting through the pie crust with more vigour. "He applied before we even moved in, but that was rejected. The new plans are being drawn up now. Yours will be the smallest on the street then. You ever thought about extending? It could add a lot of value."

I shove the plate towards her, forcing her to take hold of it. "As I said, I am quite content."

The brat comes running over, a football in her hands and mud down her front. It's still hard to believe it's a girl.

"Have you explored the woods yet, my dear?" I ask.

"Daddy says I'm not allowed on my own and they've been so busy moving in."

"Well, maybe we can go over a little later?"

She grins, showing me all the gaps where her teeth haven't yet come through.

I watch the family as they chew on the first slice of pie, making all those agreeable noises to show how delicious it is. Perfect.

The sun is setting behind the poplars and, besides the pregnant woman, all the residents have had far too much to drink. Loudly chatting and swaying, spilling their sticky beer onto the grass, a bottle even ends up in the pond. So disrespectful.

I shiver and tighten my cardigan around me as dusk creeps over Lilypond Lane.

"Perhaps it's time we called it a day. Time to get the little one off to bed," Caleb says.

"Oh, but she was wanting to see the woods," I protest. "I promised her I'd show her around. You know, I think I've seen fairies in there!"

The brat does a gleeful jump, and Caleb does a slow exhale, his beard flapping a little as he does. "Very well. Ten minutes."

The brat takes my hand. "This way, Sandra, I think I see the fairies!"

It's dark in the woods and my eyesight isn't what it used to be. I know where the traps are though, and I hobble along behind the child, my hips giving me plenty of grief, popping and creaking with each step. I've been on my feet most of the day, so it's hardly surprising.

"Look out for the sweeties they leave behind!" I say.

She's so close to that knotted oak now. It's easy to recognise. It looks just how a child would draw a tree. There's even a little loose bit of bark at the bottom that looks like a fairy door. Like all the idiot children, she runs straight to it.

I wait for the snap.

She stops running and turns to face me, then puts her hands either side of her mouth and whispers, "Come a little closer, here. I think I see them."

She steps a little further away from me as I approach. She's inches away. Just one more step... Then —

Snap!

The pain hits me instantly, and I cry out. My whole body instantly drained of strength. Looking down, the bear trap's teeth are so deep in my leg, it might have gone right through.

"Oh, my god! Oh, my god!"

The little girl is a blur in front of me as my eyes water so much the world turns to a smudge. There's something brightly coloured in her hands, sweeties, I think. She steps closer. I can smell the sugar as the world spins.

I hear Paul's voice, calling me, shouting my name. I can't hear him from here, not all the way from our house. I search the foliage for the speakers, then the woods for him. He couldn't walk this far, but there it is again, breathy, certain.

"Sandra."

"Paul!" I cry out, or at least I try to, my diaphragm weakening with the rest of me. I look at the speakers, someone must be playing his voice.

The little brat is in front of me, sticky blobs from the sweeties all around her horrible mouth. It must be her. Children have the most vile imaginations. She's playing his voice! She made me step in the trap!

Tingling sensation ripples all over my head and neck. The woods tinge yellowy green and swirl around me. My eyes slow in their blinking.

"I saw you from my bedroom window. I saw you put it by the tree, so I moved it. Silly lady. That could have hurt the fairies!" She laughs, a little haunting, girlish giggle that travels through the woods on a breeze, and I collapse to the floor.

Paul's voice calls for me again and again. I assume I will die here, and wonder how Paul will cope without me.

There's no pain when I wake. God only knows what medication they have me on, but I feel quite wonderful, all considering. Then I peek under the blanket, and notice half my right leg is no longer there. My stomach caves in, and I cry out.

"Sandra!" Caleb is here. To gloat, probably. His beard looks even more overgrown. It must smell like a doormat. "We've been so worried about you. You've been out for days since the operation. Are you in any pain?"

Days? I search the room. It's bleak and grey, not like my home. "No. No pain. Paul. I need Paul."

The woman with the eyebrows is here now, holding hands with the brat. "She's confused," she says, not to me, but to that ragged beard. Now she looks at me, those drawn-on brows all knitted together. "Caleb found all sorts of awful old things in those woods. It was such a hazard in there. It's such bad luck they got you. We are so grateful Tonia was okay. That could have been her leg in there. You really saved her."

"Paul!" I cry out again. "I need Paul!"

I don't want those people near me. I don't want to hear about that brat!

"Sandra," the beard says, and puts his hand on my shoulder. "Paul died a year ago, remember?"

I pull my head back. What nonsense do they speak? "No. He's alive. He's sick, but he's alive. He's at our house." *That brat had his voice!* They look at each other with pitiful faces. "Don't you pity me like that," I snap. "I know exactly what's going on here. You're trying to get me sent away!"

Eyebrows leans in this time. "Social services —"

"I don't need the damned social services! I need to get home to Paul!"

It's the beard's turn to get too close to me now. I want to rip that monstrosity off his chin. "It must be so hard, to lose your husband of so long. His ashes are on your mantle, with his pictures. It must feel like he's still here with you."

The woman makes that pitiful smile again. "The other neighbours all say you've been a bit confused since."

"Don't you patronise me, bitch." If I had a little more strength, I'd punch her.

"I am a social worker," Ms eyebrows says. "And, well, we've had you booked into that home for a while."

No! "You can't do that! Going behind my back. I have rights, missy. I'll write to the council."

The beard tuts and shakes his head. I push myself back into the bed as I'm sure I see lice crawl out of that thing. "I think you've written plenty of letters to the council, don't you? Sixteen letters to the council objecting to planning permission." The beard shakes his head again. "As head of planning at the council, I alerted social services a while ago. Such action is clearly a cry for help."

I raise my arm to slap him, but they must have sedated me. My arm is feeble, like I'm swatting away dust.

"Darleen's got you into a lovely care home," the treacherous beard says. "And the price your home will sell for, it's affordable for you."

Words don't come this time. I search my brain, but it's like wading through treacle and the room starts to blur.

"The extra painkillers must be kicking in," a voice says as my eyes start to close. I don't know that voice, maybe a nurse.

"They even cater for vegetarians," that's eyebrows' voice now. All haughty and shrill, and I bare my teeth at her. "We've given them a heads-up, so they know to have plenty of vegetarian meals prepared for you. Those pies were lovely, by the way."

I smile then, and allow sleep to come. I'll dream about those pies, about the sight of them eating them with no idea as to what they contained. My only solace. I hope they have a bit of toenail stuck in their teeth.

Emma is a British author who now lives nowhere in particular. She has various other published works in the dystopian and thriller genre. Check out her website www.emmaellisauthor.com to discover all of her books. She can be contacted also via Facebook and Instagram. Her story, See Her, is a prequel to her speculative thriller duology, Be Her.

Perfection

BY MANUELA LEHMANN-BILLINGSLEY

To her husband's annoyance, Abby might have more than just a touch of OCD. So what better place to live for her than the perfect neighborhood, Lilypond Lane? She has no desire to ever leave, but her husband has other plans.

Suddenly Abby finds herself confronted with an important decision; one she ponders while tending to her beloved garden. Maybe the answer lies among the flower beds...

Snip. I smile with relief as the wilted blossom falls to the ground on which I'm kneeling. It's hard to say what causes this rush of endorphins in my veins: that the garden pruning scissors make me feel powerful or that my flower now looks perfect. It matters to me. Maybe more than it should. But I love things to be just right. I need them to be just right. That feeling I get when something is crooked or uneven or just doesn't match... It's almost impossible to describe. Imagine a terrible rash, but on the inside. Picture your brain yelling at you to fix it, over and over again - until you do. Sometimes I pause, count to seven, and swallow three times, before I am able to continue what I was doing, because these are my special numbers. There is a name for it: magical thinking. It's not uncommon for people like me. People with OCD. Most people don't like to be labeled, but I find comfort in knowing that I'm obviously not the only one. Having Obsessive Compulsive Disorder can be isolating. I've known that I have it for most of my life now. Ever since the triggering car accident I was in that killed my parents when I was eleven. They found me in the wreck mostly unscathed. At least on the outside. Spending hours trapped in a wreck with the dead bodies of your parents will do things to you. I might not have died that day, but the old me did.

"Abby!" His voice pulls me out of my stupor. It used to be the most beautiful sound in the world to me, but now it's like fingernails on a chalk board. At least he's not using my real name today, unlike most days when he's annoyed with me. I go by Abby, because all the letters are in alphabetical order and there's an even number of them. Just thinking about it makes my body relax, and a little smile forms.

"Of course you are in your stupid garden again!" He shakes his head at me as he steps into my little backyard paradise.

I'm never more relaxed than here among the buzzing bees, explosion of colors, and ethereal smells - Plus I get to wear gloves and none of the neighbors would ever wonder why. They don't know about me. This neighborhood and everyone in it is so perfect, so immaculate. That's what I love about Lilypond Lane. Not a hedge untrimmed, not a hair out of place. It's almost too good to be true.

"Hey! Earth to Abby!" He snaps his fingers right in front of my face and drops of spit land on my hot skin. He hates when I zone out. I hate when he brings me back. Back to him. Despite the scorching sun above his head, I look him in the eyes, because if I don't, he will grab my chin and make me. And he won't be gentle. I know from experience. There's triumph in his eyes. He has trained me well. "What the fuck are you doing?"

"I'm pruning the roses. If I don't, it will stunt their growth. I want them to look even more beautiful next year," I respond shyly.

"Whatever for?" He throws his hands in the air in disbelief. "You know where you'll be next year? Not here, that's where. We've talked about this. I'm putting the house on the market. Sonya said it's the perfect time to sell. I'll sign the paperwork later today. You should start packing up instead of wasting your time in the dirt. The next owner is probably gonna pull out the flowers and whatever else you got here, and lay down fake grass. Or even better: I will. I'm sure Sonya would approve. Curbside appeal and all."

The blood drains from my face and dizziness sets in. I can't let him see how much he is hurting me. A cruel smile forms in the corners of his mouth, and I know he can still see my pain. He feeds on it.

I have known about his plans for a while. He started talking about moving and about how much he hated this neighborhood shortly after a conversation I overheard when tending to my lilies. I was crouched down, so they couldn't see me. Him and Gemma, one of our neighbors. Gemma, an uneven number of letters all out of order. I should have known she was trouble. That and the endless legs she likes to show off.

"I want you to leave me alone!" she hissed. "Me and my family! Or I'll get a restraining order against you and my husband will make sure you'll be persona non grata wherever you go in this town."

I guess I should have been upset, but I couldn't help but grin. She just showed *him*. *Thwack*. I smack a bug off of one of the leaves of my most perfect lily. You won't harm her. Not on my watch.

Smack! This time a blow to my head brings me back to him.

"What the fuck is wrong with you, you crazy bitch?" he yells.

I pray none of the neighbors can hear him. *He* might not care anymore, but *I* do. Because *I* am not leaving.

I knew it was getting serious as soon as I heard him talk to a real estate agent. And when I saw her, I knew how serious it was getting. Sonya. Another name that makes me cringe. One of three things I liked about her were her signature pearls. Perfectly round and shiny—and exactly forty. I know because I counted them more than once while she was sitting on our couch, her long legs crossed as ladylike as her mini skirt would let her. Every once in a while one of her perfectly manicured hands (you've guessed it, that was the second thing I liked about her) would land on his shoulder, followed by a high-pitched laughter that revealed stunningly white and even teeth (and there's number three).

They've been calling each other quite a bit. So she is either the most dedicated agent I have ever seen, or she is his next victim. He can be very charming and persuasive. I remember. Sometimes I wonder if I was the first one. Or what happened to the ones before me. The lucky ones that got away.

Everything seemed perfect in the beginning. How did I miss the signs? I never miss a detail. That's the only reason I am able to work despite my condition. I proofread what others write. No mistake makes it past me. My boss knows that, so she is willing to let me work entirely from home. She tolerates that I need a little bit longer than others, because I get hung up on a word or a sentence and I need to reread it over and over again - until it feels right. It's like I have to wait until my brain opens the gate and lets me continue.

I'm a freak, I know. Maybe that's what made me so attractive to him at first. That and the fact that I have no family to protect me. I couldn't believe my luck that somebody like him would be interested in me. He dangled that promise of a normal life full of love in front of me. How could I not grab it without looking at it more closely? I was the perfect prey. I didn't see the spider until I was so tangled up in his web that I knew it was over. Every one of her movements shaking me to the core and taking me closer to my inevitable end.

I know he's not planning on taking me with him, no matter where he goes from here. The other day I was rearranging a messy pile of papers after I had not been able to stop thinking about it. The weight lifted off my shoulders with every move I made to arrange the papers in a neat pile according to size. That's when I saw it. The glossy brochure with smiling people in white coats. "Serenity Meadows". A fancy loony bin for people like me.

I froze in shock. Not only would he take me away from here, not only would I lose my garden, but he would lock me away. Disposed of at a place where all hope of a normal happy life goes to die. I'm only in my thirties. What if I never got out again? What if they pumped me full of medication until I wasn't me anymore?

With trembling hands I put the brochure back, when my eyes landed on a box with numbers in the right hand corner of it. Tears filled my eyes and my sight blurred, so it took me a moment until I could see clearly enough to make out what the numbers were. Rates. Shockingly high ones. That's when I knew I would not end up there. He would have me locked up in a low-cost dump for the mentally ill instead. One that would make "Serenity Meadows" seem like paradise.

Or so I thought until this morning, when I found another document among his messy desk drawers: A life insurance policy over 1 million dollars he had taken out for me with him as sole beneficiary. That's when I knew I wasn't going anywhere alive. I just don't know when or how he'll do it. But I'm certain he won't do it here on the property. Who wants to buy a house that somebody died in? No, he will take me somewhere and I will not return.

My chin quivers and a lump forms in my throat. I want to see my newest plants grow and bloom again even prettier next year. I don't want to die. And knowing him, it won't be pain-free. *1, 2, 3, 4, 5, 6, 7. Swallow. Swallow. Swallow.* I cannot let my anxiety win. Not this time. I need to get out of my feelings and into my brain. It might not be working perfectly, but I need to be smarter than him this one time.

As if looking for comfort, I look around my flower beds. Big shoe prints among them mark where he had carelessly stepped on my flowers as he stormed back inside. With tears in my eyes I softly pick up the ones that now lie crushed on the ground. *This will not be me.*

Furiously, I grab the pruning scissors that had fallen out of my hand during the latest blow. My grip is so hard that my knuckles turn white. The metal blades shine in the sunlight. I might be able to attack him with them, but he is awfully strong. What if he overpowers me? I would have to attack him from behind, but if I only get one shot, I need to stab him in a deadly spot—his neck, maybe. Or his thigh. Maybe I can figure out where the aorta or the femoral artery are. But then what? He will probably scream and draw attention to me. He might be saved and able to tell the authorities what I've done. If he bleeds out, what am I going to do with all the blood and the body before somebody sees him?

This plan has too many unknowns. It's barely a plan at all. I need something that will make me feel calm. I need a perfect plan, because my life depends on it. For once, my sense for detail and my obsession to think everything through repeatedly will not just make me feel safe. It will *actually* keep me safe.

"For crying out loud, Abby! Get your ass in here, wash up, and get in the car! Sonya just called. We both need to sign the papers for the sale." He slams the sliding door shut behind him.

My whole body is shaking now. This is it. This is how I'll die, if he gets his way. And he always does.

I slowly stand up. *1, 2, 3, 4, 5, 6, 7. Swallow. Swallow. Swallow. Damn it, Abby. Not now.*

I let my eyes wander over my perfect piece of heaven one more time. Once I'm dead he will kill my babies, too. Before I turn around to open the sliding door, my gaze falls on the blueberry bush that is full of perfectly round juicy berries this time of year. It is not foolproof, but it is all I've got left. I grab a handful of berries and keep them in my gloved fist. Then, I carefully add some berries from another one of my plants. They, too, are round and dark, but they are smaller and not blue. And that will make all the difference.

He is already waiting for me by the front door. His car is parked right in front of it on the street. I have only one room that separates me from my fate. I inch closer to the kitchen counter that divides the living room from the kitchen sink. The blender. I have to put the berries in the blender before I take off my glove. That is vital, in case I have any abrasions or cuts. I wriggle my left hand out of its glove and use it to open the blender. Quickly I dump the berries in and use my left hand to put the lid back on. Then I push the start button. *CRRRRRRRRRRRRR*. This has to work. The berries mix together into an inseparable and indefinable mash. I quickly take off the other glove and make my way over to the spotless kitchen sink, using my right arm to turn on the faucet. The water is scorching hot. Just the way I like it. I use the back of my hand to get several pumps of antibacterial soap from the dispenser and start scrubbing. This ritual calms me down immediately. I was hoping it would. It was either that or an even longer handwashing procedure fueled by my anxiety, which was through the roof until a few seconds ago. What if I didn't get enough of the black berries? No, not me. I know there were ten. What if it doesn't work with milk? No, I would have heard or read that somewhere.

"Jesus Christ, Abby! Sonya's office is one town over. Let's gooooooo!"

One town over. That means it's about an hour away at this time of day. He won't do it on the way over there. He still needs my signature on those papers first. Let's say the meeting takes about thirty minutes. That means I need to stall him here for just a little bit longer. I can't have it set in at her office. She would call an ambulance. But the symptoms take about two hours to show. Two hours until I'm either free to live here for as long as I want, or never to return.

"I need to change real quick", I say. "I got dirt on my pants. I can't let Sonya see me like that and I'm sure you don't want dirt in your car either."

He sighs, but I know my arguments were convincing enough. On my way to the bedroom door,Quickly, I turn to him. "Can you please add milk to the mixer and turn it on again? Once the smoothie is done, please put it in my to-go cup. That way we won't lose more time."

Another sigh from the front door, but I hear him walk over to the kitchen counter and open the fridge. He will do it. And once he's made it, he will drink from it. He won't be able to stop himself. He loves blueberries, and it is hot today.

I slowly change out of my gardening clothes and into some nicer ones. He knocks on the door so hard it shakes.

"Coming," I respond in my best singsong voice.

As soon as I open the door, he grabs me by the arm and pulls me across the room towards the door. His other hand is holding my cup. I can see it is not full and I pray to God it really is a touch of bluish milk mustache I see above his upper lip.

He always thinks of everything he wants as his. Today is no different. This will be the last time he will force me to do anything. Soon, the way he looks at me will change. I can picture it. The triumph in his eyes once I've signed the papers. His hand on Sonya's ass as we exit her fancy office. - His smug grin when he takes me back to the car to finish what he started. And then his look of shock, disbelief, horror, when his heart starts racing faster and faster until it stops beating completely.

This time I won't make it look like an accident. They might still find traces of Belladonna in his bloodstream, and once they start looking, they will find it in the cup, the blender, my garden, my search history.

No, once he is incapacitated, I will take over the wheel until I can park the car somewhere in the woods. I will switch seats with him and once it gets dark, I will drag his body into the house. *My* house. My signature on those papers will be no good, because I will have signed them with Abby. Like I said, not my real name, but those two lovebirds will not pay attention to detail. I will drag him into the bathtub on the bottom floor. I will have that room remodelled after waiting a decent amount of time. Because the next step will likely ruin the coating on the tub. As a gardener, I always have bags of lime handy. Once I'll have emptied the contents into the tub with his body, I will open the faucet and watch the magic happen. Quick lime will leave me with nothing but bones after a few days. It helps that all the books I proofread are science books. Good thing I have lots of gloves here, and plenty of flowers that need nourishment. They truly will bloom even more next year.

Deep down I know I can do it, because I have defeated a monster before. My father. That fateful day in the car he had yelled at me once too often and I knew if we made it home, I'd surely feel his belt again. And my mother would do nothing. As usual. So only I made it home that day. Just like I will today. And I will live here in peace and tend to my garden, where I will continue to exterminate what threatens my babies. Everything will be just right. The way I like it. It will be perfection. I told you my brain won't stop yelling at me until I have fixed what is not right.

1, 2, 3, 4, 5, 6, 7. Swallow. Swallow. Swallow.

Manuela Lehmann-Billingsley (M.L. Billingsley) is originally from Germany, where she was published in magazines. She now lives in Washington with her husband, where she teaches, works for an exchange program, and sells real estate. When she is not busy working, she enjoys reading, writing, going for walks, taking pictures of nature, and watching murder mystery shows. She is currently working on her first book.

You can find Manuela on Instagram: mlehmannbillingsley and Facebook: Manuela Lehmann-Billingsley and get in touch via her email: mlehmannbillingsley@gmail.com

How Lucky Are We?

BY JENNIFER CYR

What is your breaking point? How much can you take before you blow your whole world apart? The incessant tickle of a stray hair? A sliver you can't remove? Would that do you in? How about a headache or a paper cut? Will they get you over the edge of madness or does it take more, so much more...? And when you get to that point, what do you do? How do you react to what irks you and makes you crazy?

❀ ❀ ❀ ❀

ME

You know that annoying feeling when you can't get a song out of your head? You hear it somewhere, maybe from a car passing by, or a jingle in a commercial...and you only remember the chorus. And you hum it and sing it and hum it and sing it and you cannot for the life of you remember the rest of the song.

Well, that is how it starts. But how it ends, well, let's just say I prefer the damn song.

RISSA

"Would you just look at this place? Can you believe that it's all ours?" I know I am directing my comments to my daughter, but she is clearly focused on anything other than the sound of my voice.

At least Buddy is listening, his tail is wagging, and his ears are alert. I guess that's what you get when you "tear apart" her family and "ruin everything"...well, at least if you are a mom who is finally putting herself first. And did I mention that my daughter is thirteen and full of resentment and confusion? Oh, and anger, we cannot forget the anger.

I wish I could say it's a unique story filled with drama and revelations, maybe even sex and scandal. It isn't that kind of story, though it would be so much easier if I could give her a concrete and clear reason for all of this. I met her father when I was young, and at the time he was everything I ever wanted. The trouble was that I continued to learn and grow and explore, and he was content to keep things the same. I found myself feeling like the marriage no longer fit me, like a comfy old sweater. You love it because you've had it forever and you wear it all the time because it feels so familiar and cozy. And then you see the sweater your friend is wearing, and you wonder what it might be like to have a different sweater, a new sweater that you get to pick out for yourself. And it will be your present self, the self you are now that might like brighter bolder colors, or finer softer yarn, and you would choose some beautiful and intricate stitching.

Anyway, when your kid wants to know all the details, you give them what you can, what you think they can handle, what you think they need to know. Well, she didn't like my sweater metaphor, not even a little. She has decided to focus all of her confusion and anger in my direction. I'm grateful she hasn't taken it out on Buddy, at least. She still cozies up with him at night and sometimes, when it's really quiet, I can hear her talking to him.

And I'm okay with that. After all, what choice do I have? I love my daughter, and there isn't a damn thing that will change that.

Besides, I'm the only parent she has left now after her father has moved away. And yes, I'm sure she is madder at him than me, but since he isn't here, well, you get the idea. So, I will take all her indignation and hostility as she works her way through all the feelings that reveal themselves into her tone of voice, her facial expressions, her actions.

She scowls at me now, and I'm pleased because at least she acknowledges my presence. I'll take what I can get, and I will wait patiently for her to come around. I keep my face frozen for fear she will startle and turn away, like a frightened bunny or a shy deer.

Then she says something I am surprised to hear, "I don't completely hate this house, but it better have WiFi."

❦ ❦ ❦ ❦

Me

An eyelash gets caught on your eyeball, making your eye itch and you rub, and you rub, and it just feels grainy and hot. Finally, your eye tears up and you pull your fingers across toward your ear and you know you've got it. And then you see that your hands are covered in dirt, and you've left some behind, in the eye you thought you just relieved.

❦ ❦ ❦ ❦

Rissa

I unlock the door to our new home and usher her inside, with Buddy following close behind. We had to move to a smaller house now that I am the sole provider, which means Periwin, or Peri as I call her, might have had to go to a new school. Thankfully, I was able to find this wonderful house in the same district. This will help fortify her from the stress of other changes stemming from the divorce. That's the hope anyway. There is a front porch with a sweet swing on one end and a built-in bench on the other. When you open the front door, you are faced with going right to the dining area, left to the living room, or straight ahead up the stairs. The kitchen, pantry, laundry room and bathroom are around the back side of the stairs. It is all quite spacious considering my newly shrunken budget. I don't know how we got so lucky, but the seller took my offer right away even though it was way under the asking price.

Peri walks up the stairs, and they creak. I once again must hide my joy. This means it will be more difficult for my teenager to sneak out, because you know how teenagers can be.

"Mom, which room is mine? I want the bigger one."

I saw that coming, and I smile and tell her she can have the larger bedroom. Eventually, she will figure out that they are the same size, but in this moment, she wants that sense of control and power that has been beyond her reach. The room she walks into is a soothing lavender with a shiny hardwood floor. It extends into what feels like half the house. That leaves me with the soft green room that reminds me of new moss. The bathroom between the two rooms is lavish and bright with a beautiful clawfoot tub, gilded mirrors and white marble everywhere. I really lucked out with this house, and I am so pleased with myself that I don't notice the stain in the hallway that sits at the top of the stairs.

Of course, Peri spies the stain, crinkles up her nose, and moans, "Ewww, gross...Mom you have got to rip up this floor and get that out of here."

Buddy barks his agreement and paws at the floor. I love how loyal he is, echoing his best friends' emotions. Wondering what could be that bad, I take a look. At first, it appears to be nothing more than a blotch on the floor, nothing sinister or nefarious. As I look closer, I can see why she wants it gone so badly. It is a small sketch of a penis, and while not very skillfully drawn, it is quite obviously a penis.

"There must've been an angry teenager living here at some point who wanted to make a statement. Don't get any ideas, young lady. We can sand it down and refinish it, and in the meantime, we can cover it with a carpet."

ME

You wake up laying on your side and your ear feels wet inside the canal. You try to wiggle the ear to help the fluid move around and work its way out. It just feels so wet in there, so you get a cotton swab, and you try to clean it out. It still feels gooey and wet, and the more you try to wipe it clean, the more wax seems to flow into the canal. And you just cannot make it stop tickling.

That's how this is going so far. And I just can't stand it.

Rissa

The movers have come and gone, and we have been unpacking like crazy. Of course, Peri unpacks and sets up her own room, and then she calls it a day. She and Buddy are snuggling up together on her bed while she scrolls through her phone. Meanwhile, I have the rest of the house to make our own. I'm happy to do it really, though. I never really lived alone before and it's kind of fun to be the only opinion, the only critic, the only spectator. The fatigue sets in though, and I find myself sitting on the porch swing drinking a glass of water. My arms and legs feel heavy, so heavy that it's a challenge to sway back and forth. I have overdone it, overexerted myself, and I am exhausted. Yes, that's it, it must be. And then my water glass falls from my hand shattering on the floor. I know I didn't let go, why would I do that? I'm thirsty and I wasn't finished with it. I sit frozen, unable to move for a moment, just a brief moment. It is the strangest thing. Am I having a stroke or something? What is wrong with me?

And just as quickly as my limbs began to feel like cement, sensation returns, and my fingers attempt to close around the glass that they think is still there. My feet move the swing back and forth and I yawn as if waking from a nap. Okay, that was weird. Just then, Peri comes down from her room and stands just inside the doorway.

"What are you doing out there? You're embarrassing me. People will think you're a drunk, Mom."

My face flushes as I realize that she is right, that anyone who saw me like this might make assumptions. But no, I don't care what other people think. I was tired, and I sat down on my lovely porch swing for a break. I didn't do anything wrong. I was taking a moment to myself, something I have not done nearly enough of since becoming a mother, and I will not feel embarrassed or ashamed about how this looks.

And then I notice a sound, a low growl, one that I haven't heard before. Buddy is at the top of the stairs. The German shepherd is poised for defense, teeth bared and muscles tense. The growl becomes louder and erupts in a cacophony of ferocious barks. Peri and I are stunned. And as quick as it began, it's over. Strange. We both stand in silence for a moment, unsure of what happened just now. And like a spell has broken, Buddy comes bounding down the stairs and jumps onto Peri, lavishing her with kisses.

I ask her to grab the broom and dustpan for me and with an attitudinal eye roll, she complies. Buddy follows happily. After the glass is cleaned up, I order some pizza, delivery since I am so tired, and Peri and I eat in our dining room together. I catch her face seeming peaceful and serene for a moment, almost happy, but not quite. She isn't ready to allow herself to feel that yet, or for me to know about the possibility, so I just eat my pizza. I can taste the spicy tomato sauce, the rich cheese, and the sautéed veggies are cooked just right. I hate it when you order a pizza with veggies, and they just take a cheese pizza and throw them on top. I like the toppings cooked along with the cheese so that as the cheese melts, the toppings sink into the cheese a bit. I am enjoying my pizza so well that I don't notice that the room is now empty, and the sky outside is dark. How long have I been sitting here? Long enough that my pizza is cold, so awhile. It seems strange to me that I didn't realize how long I was sitting here. Maybe I fell asleep? What's that sound? I hear Buddy again, that low growling that we heard for the first time earlier. The ferocity increasing now, and then nothing. He saunters into the dining room like nothing ever happened. I'm beginning to feel like Buddy is mad at me or something. Will a dog get mad at you for moving to a new house? After all, he was quite happy before.

ME

There is a tiny pebble in your shoe. You have taken your shoe off and thought you dumped it out thoroughly, but it's still there stabbing you with every step you take. You remove your shoe again and scrape at the sole with your fingers and you think you found the pebble. You bid it good riddance and flick it to the ground, only to realize that you are too late. You already have a blister forming from where the pebble rubbed against your foot. A pea sized bubble exists where before the skin was smooth.

And that is how it's going. I'm in a constant state of agitation at this point. The smallest thing sets me off and makes me seethe with rage. You're pissing me off, woman, and you will regret it.

RISSA

Peri and I are both starting our new routines today. We wave goodbye to Buddy, who looks at us longingly with sad eyes from the window. Again, I feel a little guilt about moving him from his former home. I know he will adjust in time. My commute to work is a little longer than it used to be, and Peri still has a bus ride, though hers is now shorter. You can't mess around with resilience, and keeping her in the same school with her friends is worth my extra time in the car. Again, I wonder how we got so lucky with this house and I'm feeling so much gratitude and relief. I was so worried that Peri would have to attend a different school. She would hate me forever, or at least for what seemed like forever.

We are again sitting down to dinner, salad and burgers tonight. I try to make conversation, but she eats her food in silence and then claims that homework is calling her. That's fine, I understand. She had to adjust to so much change, the biggest being the absence of her dad of course. After the divorce, he just needed a fresh start. Shared custody was always the plan, but when he announced he was moving across the country, well, that was the end of that discussion. She will visit him, and they talk, or rather text, but it's not the same. I suspect she feels abandoned by him when all he is trying to do is heal and regroup. I understand it, and also, it infuriates me to see my daughter hurting so much. So, I will continue to be here with her, providing a consistent and steady presence in her life, a safe place for when she's ready to move into this new chapter. Buddy has set the example for me here, showing patience and tolerance and unconditional love.

Sometimes I wonder if I have ruined her life and tainted her views on marriage and motherhood forever. She blames me too, even though all I did was grow out of the relationship. I dared to be honest despite the discomfort and the difficulty and the guilt. Everyone, or so it feels, has taken his side and tells me I have given up too easily, that I will be sorry, that I should stay till Peri is out of school. That's just it though. I want to show my daughter that she can stand up for herself, that she can be and do what makes her heart happy, and that she can be respected while she does it. After putting everyone else first for so long, it was time for a change. My happiness has been overlooked as frivolous and misunderstood as selfishness. Self-care is the opposite of selfishness, and until I put myself first, how could I possibly show my daughter what she deserves out of life? Now I try to live by example, a challenge for sure, but one I welcome.

Me

You had takeout from that shady food truck down the street and by the time you get home. You have to throw up and drop a load at the same time. Your stomach is convulsing and your throat burns, your eyes water and your nose drips. Your butt is raw from the cheap toilet paper you've got, and you'd give anything for some diaper rash cream or an ice pack. And then you have to heave again except there isn't much left in your gut, so you just lean forward over the pukey trash can that you grabbed and make a barking sound as you almost hope you can vomit.

I can't take much more of her. It's time for me to have a little fun and put her in her place.

Peri

I hate my mom; I can't believe how selfish she is. She wasn't happy with Dad, but so what? I'm not happy without him. See? Selfish! And Buddy hates it here too, I can tell. He's never growled like that before. And she is such a spazz lately, dropping her glass after passing out on the swing like that, so not cool. And the way she spaced out at dinner that first weekend here, I told her I was going up to my room and she just sat there looking like a freakin' zombie.

This morning, she was making all kinds of noise in the kitchen, and I found her emptying the pantry. Everything was on the floor, and she was muttering about the shelves.

I was like, "Mom, what the heck are you doing?" and she went on and on about how the shelves were trying to kill her.

Okay, lady, whatever you say...I guess she went in there to grab more oatmeal and a shelf fell. Then she said another came down right after she squatted down to clean up the goods that fell.

"The pantry isn't trying to kill you Mom, you just need to fix the shelve," I say above Buddy's barking.

It's becoming routine now whenever mom has one of her "episodes" for Buddy to do that growling and barking routine. It's almost like he's mad at her. You and me both, Buddy.

I hate my mom, but I like this new house. My room reminds me of my own private castle tower, with its tall windows and leafy view with just a little bit of sky visible. It feels so secluded, especially after I get home from school and Mom is at work still. Buddy is always happy to see me when I walk in. He eats his tail, his ears perk up, and he licks my face as I grab a snack from the kitchen and make my way upstairs. I like my big lavender room with the shiny wood floors. But I don't want my mom to know that. I'm still mad at her for changing everything on me so she can be happy. Where's your happy, anyway Mom? You don't look so happy lately.

I'm almost finished with my copious amount of homework when I hear a loud thud and a scream comes from downstairs. I run out of my room and down the stairs as fast as I can, and when I get to the downstairs bathroom, I laugh. I laugh hard and long and loud. My Mom is sitting on the floor with her pants and underwear down past her knees and the toilet is tilted to one side as if it were one of those goofy mechanical bulls you sometimes see at places.

"I don't know what happened. I had to pee and the next thing I know I'm on the floor and the toilet is like that," she says, pointing at the toilet.

She looks completely dumbfounded, and I rethink my laughter. I hand her a towel and give her a hand up off the floor. Luckily there is no water damage or leaks. She got lucky on that front somehow. The tilted toilet is quickly righted and then we make a call to a plumber because a tipping toilet can't be a good thing.

My mom just has this confused expression and is muttering to herself about pulling her pants down, starting to sit...trying to replay the moment she ended up on the floor. She is coming up empty. Okay, this is starting to get kinda scary. Is my mom, okay? Maybe she is sick, like, in the head? Or maybe she's having a mid-life crisis, or maybe it's menopause. All I know is that something isn't right, and even though I still hate my mom, I still kinda love her. After his growl and bark routine, Buddy is finally beginning to relax, or as I like to call it, come back to himself. He pads over to my mom and lays down at her feet. I think he feels bad for her. She rubs behind his ears and gives her a cuddle that melts me a little bit. Maybe if Buddy can adjust to our new life, I can too. Maybe.

RISSA

I can see it in her face. She's worried about me. Actually, I am beginning to worry about me too. I swear that shelf in the pantry was aiming for me, I swear it. And the toilet, it felt like it moved, like it bumped me up and off the seat. I just don't get it. I don't know what's happening to me. Maybe I should...no I don't need to do that, I'm fine. But maybe I should just be on the safe side. I'm going to do it.

I grab my smartphone and call my therapist. I started seeing her a few years ago when I was feeling depressed, stifled, unfulfilled, and looking for more out of life. She helped me see things more clearly, helped me reflect and reframe my thoughts into a vision for my future. After the divorce, she released me from therapy, and she let me know that I could return anytime I wanted, or in this case, needed. She picks up on the second ring and sounds surprised to get my call. Before she can even ask why I call, I launch into all of it. Like hot lava flowing down the sides of an active volcano, I tell her everything. When I get to the most recent event, the toilet, I think I hear her stifle a giggle, but I'm not sure because by now I'm crying.

She takes me through a brief guided meditation, as we have done so many times before. When I am finally calm and ready to hear her words, she asks me to remember my happy place, and to consider going there for a couple days. I am so glad I called her! That is just what Peri and I need, a weekend at the ocean. We both love it there and being on the sand, and by the water gives us a sense of rejuvenation and peace. "Thank you so much Louise! You know me so well."

With a smile in her voice and her typical gentle tone, she says, "Enjoy the sea, and Rissa, take care of yourself."

PERI

My mom has this brilliant idea to go to the beach for the weekend. Seriously? She has been a basket case lately, and she thinks this trip is a good idea. Maybe she is nuts after all. Whatever. Forced togetherness and all that, maybe I can at least get her to take me shopping. It seems like I just keep getting taller all the time and my jeans don't fit like they used to. It sucks being so much taller than everybody, as if being a teenager with divorced parents isn't enough.

Here's the thing: she is totally fine all weekend. And so is Buddy. He comes along with us and has none of his own episodes the whole time. We have lots of beach time walking and talking and playing in the water. We do a little shopping, see a movie, and we even have a dance party in our hotel room. It is almost like old times, and it has been so nice to feel that way again. That sense of connection, happiness, and being carefree. What if it's all in her head? What if she isn't sick? What could be causing all her problems?

I think back over the last couple of months and try to zero in on when all the weirdness started. The split from Dad wasn't it, because I remember that. She was calm and clear and apologetic, but sure of herself, even though I was so mad at her. Dad moving away sucked. We were both so mad and frustrated. That's all it was for her I think though, nothing weird like lately. When we had to move, she was sad, and I remember when she tried to pry the doorframe off with a crowbar and it wouldn't budge. It had my height marked on it since I was little. And all that time, we were able to talk to each other about it. I could say anything to my mom, even the hard stuff. But lately, she's like a different person.

The more I think about it, it all started when we moved into this house. That's when Buddy changed too. I just figured he didn't like the changes, but it's this house. The realization spreads through my brain like a drop of watercolor paint onto a wet page. And the timing couldn't be more ironic as the house comes into view upon our return from the sea. And as if on cue, Buddy takes his defensive stance, and I can hear the rumble radiating from his throat.

ME

Like a knife stabbing me in the gut, with a twist and a yank, I feel pain run through me like shock waves from an earthquake. The pain radiates from the center outward and throbs with heat and a hammering pulse.

She is back and I wish it just felt like that annoying song that I can't get out of my head, but her presence has become painful. She has invaded me fleas on a stray dog and made everything itch and burn. I will show her a burn like no other and be rid of her for good.

RISSA

Such a lovely weekend with my girl and Buddy at the beach, and I have Louise to thank for that. I'll have to send her a note of thanks. Sometimes it's just really tough to get out of my own way and see the obvious solution. We had a neighboring beach goer take some pictures of us together, and it was just lovely. I plan to frame one and keep it on the mantle in the dining room. I feel so light and free and relaxed that I almost don't notice the smell. I'm in the kitchen unpacking our remaining snacks, and the room smells like gas...I know I didn't leave the gas on; I am always careful about that since

I'm not used to having a gas stove. Our old house had an electric range, so it makes me nervous, especially having an easily distracted teenager in the house. Buddy is on the porch still, and he's doing that new thing of his.

The next thing I know, sparks are erupting from inside the microwave, and I scream for Peri to run as I get down low and roll away from the kitchen. I make it to the dining room and take shelter in the brick alcove that houses the old fireplace. I don't hear anything, but the volume is deafening at the same time. The initial explosion seems to have dispersed to the exterior walls, and I have a chance to escape. Unfortunately, my body chooses to be stuck in this moment. My joints are seemingly glued tight, and my hands and feet won't budge. It is then that I see my daughter, my Periwin, who says she hates me, crawling in from the front of the house toward me. She reaches under my exposed arm and hooks us together, and then she pulls. Linked together, we move along the floor to the front door and onto the porch to safety. All the while I can see poor Buddy barking. He looks so scared and also so protective. He is at our side as soon as we open the door, almost ushering us out of the house. We want to take a moment to catch our breath, but Buddy is forcefully herding us off the porch. All three of us make it to the street where neighbors have come to see what's going on.

PERI

I love my mom. When I saw the explosion, I thought I had lost her forever. I know she doesn't always act the way I want her to, or make the choices I think she should, but at least she's here. She is alive and in this hospital room with me and she is tearfully saying thank you for saving her, and I don't even mind when she reaches out to hold my hand. I can handle a little smoke inhalation if it means my mom will survive. After all, she has sacrificed so much for me already. Buddy is here too, coiled up at mom's feet. Looks like he feels the same way.

ME

I messed up. I wanted her out and gone, but I think I have ruined myself in my haste. I have been sitting here on this block for over a hundred years and I have become set in my ways. I was bothered by her, irritated to the point of distraction, and I let my discomfort and pain cloud my judgment. I should have just found a way to let her live here within my walls. I was such a handsome house with sturdy walls, a firm roof with a nice dry foundation. I should have just let her stay and found a way to get along with her. Because this is the end of me, and it's my own damn fault.

RISSA

The house is gone now. I plan to take the insurance money and build us our dream home, elsewhere though. We need a fresh start. It will be an opportunity to create the most lovely and cozy home that will be just for us, me and Peri, and of course, Buddy. He was trying to tell us something the whole time and I wish I had taken his behavior as the warning it was. And as we build our new home, choosing the finishes, materials, and colors that we love, we will rebuild our relationship. It will be slow and intentional, and we will be stronger than ever. I just have to be patient while she adjusts to our new home, our new life, maybe even a new puppy. I'm just so grateful that we have this opportunity. We almost lost each other, and I will never take for granted that we have this time together.

Jennifer Cyr is an early childhood educator with a background in Psychology and Human Services. Her work with young children has been ongoing since she was a teenager. Now in her 40's, she has been unraveling the pieces of her life that no longer fit, and she is finally becoming the person she was meant to be all along. Writing has been a vital part of the journey, and it has prompted her to share her thoughts in a way that allows her to connect with children and families in her community, culminating in the creation of her children's stories. The Honu and Kiyaya book series are stories that nurture the hearts and minds of young children, and that strengthen the spirit of the adults who love them. Most recently, Jennifer has made her debut as a poet reflecting on her midlife unraveling under the pen name Rylan James. This is her first psychological thriller, a long-awaited part of the journey.

Empty Nest

BY ROSE J MONAN

Can you ever really go home?

This is the question Thomas Geyer asks himself as he reluctantly returns to his hometown. After twenty years, Tom must reconcile his unease and alienation from his childhood with the responsibilities of providing end-of-life care for his estranged father. As Alzheimer's whittles away the man he knew his father to be, long forgotten memories of Tom's life at Lilypond Lane begin to resurface, piecing together a dark, terrible truth.

Tom looked back to where the bus vanished in the distance, foggy and confused as watercolor or a picture viewed behind grimed glass. He thought of London and the life he left behind in such uncertainty. Cara didn't want him to go. He didn't want to go—he *needed* to. Now, that life in London, his life with Cara, faded like words carved in sand when the tide draws in, disappearing with the bus in the Cumbrian fog.

The grinding wheels of Tom's suitcase against the sidewalk, *thud-thud-thud*ding over each furrow in the cement, sounded louder than they should against the quiet of the cozy suburb. Unease gripped him as he passed charming homes, their knee-high fences acting more to accentuate the manicured gardens than offer any sort of security for, surely, none was needed here. A flock of coots whimpered and clicked their beaks like ungreased wheels of a shopping trolley in the direction he was heading.

The bald-headed birds were one of the points of pride for the little village. Though generally rare in this country, they flock to the pond for which the town was named, their nighttime migration an annual spectacle for birdwatchers throughout the continent. Tom's father would call himself an old coot as he rubbed his bald head, imitating their call. He regaled the boys of Tom's Boy Scout troop with the Darwinian drama of the covert's lives—how they thrashed their fledglings to wheedle out the weak, ruffling the boys' hair with his knuckles.

"Survival of the fittest."

As Tom drew closer, he heard the soft buzz of flies, the chirr of beetles, the stirring of grass and rippling of water by the gentle wind telling him he had reached his destination. His eyes lingered on a patch of weeds sprouting from the sidewalk, withered by a spray of herbicide. He looked at them fondly, marveling at the resilience of unwanted things to persevere against adversity. He felt not unlike a weed bursting through stone as he approached the house.

His torso shuddered as he gripped his bags, still staring at the wizened plant before him, trying to chase the images from his mind conjured by the phone call two days prior.

The woman, *Elisa, was it*? She had explained that she called him three times before he eventually answered and, though her voice was soft and kind, the hint of frustration in her tone along with the news she imparted made his ears burn with shame against the phone.

The woman was a nurse – "Have you been informed of his condition by his doctors?"

No.

"Oh ... well, I'm sorry to be the one to tell you, and over the phone ... do you live far Mr. Geyer?"

A hesitant breath.

"Well, if you are able to come, the best time is now."

"Is he ... *dying*?" The question lingered in the air of his flat, in the space between him and the woman on the phone half a country away, thick like a storm cloud pressurizing the void between question and answer.

"Yes, Mr. Geyer. Your father is very ill." She sounded broken delivering the news. Tom smiled sadly at her sweetness as he thought this. The look in Cara's eyes as she tried to read his face and the sudden shift in the woman's tone flattened the slight smile from his lips into a grim line. "The Alzheimer's has reached an advanced stage. He has little motor control and needs constant care."

The heaviness creeping in around Tom pressed itself against his chest in the subsequent silence. When he spoke, it came out as a whisper.

"The hospital?" Desperation gripped his stomach, filling Tom with shame.

"Sir, your father expressed his wishes in his living will. He wishes to stay at home ... there's nothing more that could be done for him at hospital at this stage, anyway, I'm afraid ...."

Blood raged in his ears, thundering in the waiting silence. He turned away from Cara as her eyes needled his skin.

"Mr. Geyer?" Her voice pierced the bubble of anxiety inflating in his chest.

"Yes," he whispered.

"He has only a little time left. Your father needs you here."

So here he is— rooted to the walkway before his father's house, a weed in the concrete. It was a decision Cara told him he would regret, but, given how many of those he's made, why should that stop him now?

He faced the little house where he spent his childhood, smaller now than he remembered. In fact, all the houses on Lilypond Lane seemed smaller and closer together in their neat little curving rows.

The once bright red brick was dulled by a coat of morning rain sluggishly evaporating from where it had seeped into the stone. Vegetation sprouted in neglected gutters, tinging the grey roof green at the edges. Shuttered windows betrayed nothing of the house's contents or inhabitant. A sheen of grime encrusted the curves of the house number. 36. It struck Tom that he happened to be the same age as the number of his childhood home – a place to which he hadn't thought he would ever return when he left twenty years earlier. It was as if the house itself had predicted his return, had waited for the moment when he would darken its doorway again.

Tightening his grip on the handles of his luggage, Tom made his way up the path to the front door, navigating clumps of weeds reaching through the cracked cement. He paused, unsure how to proceed. Trembling, he rang the bell.

The woman greeted him, smiling with her whole face as she welcomed him into his childhood home. *Except her eyes*, Tom thought. *She has sad eyes.* He guessed that came with the job. It was the woman from the phone call. She wore a large name tag on her lapel spelling out "ELIZA" in unmissable black letters surrounded by small, glittering butterfly stickers.

Tom felt close to choking as the stale odors of his long-abandoned home invaded his lungs. As Eliza chatted, Tom held his breath, not wanting to let this place inside him. He'd left as soon as he could—only one day after exams. The need to get away from this house, from the memories within it, itched inside him. But now he was back and he couldn't say why. The sound of Eliza's sneakered feet on the carpet as she circled the front room, pointing out medications and equipment, made that same itch prickle up his arms, made him want to turn and leave without another word.

But before the thought could formulate fully, Eliza placed her hand on his shoulder. Like a bird perched on a rock, her touch was so light and soft against his rigid muscles that he felt himself soften toward her. He turned to meet her eyes and realized she was waiting for him to say something—an answer to a question he hadn't heard.

"I'm sorry, I ... what were you saying?"

"I understand this is a difficult time for you, Mr. Geyer."

"Please, Tom."

"Tom ...." She smiled. "I understand there is no other family to help you through this?"

"Oh, uh, no. My parents had me when they were older ... my mother died when I was born. Just always been the two of us."

"Losing a parent can be a traumatic experience, Tom. Especially alone."

She was a kind woman, but Tom wasn't interested in a therapy session. He hadn't worked so hard to cage those primal fears just to let someone start picking the locks.

"I'll be okay." He offered an awkward smile to evidence this claim, but it occurred to him it might be out of place in the home of a dying man and forced it from his face. "So, I guess just show me how I'm needed here."

"All right then .... Just know, he may not recognize you. Don't take it personally. It's the disease, not him."

Tom almost laughed thinking how he doubted his father would recognize him after all this time, regardless of his disease. The boy he'd been when he lived here was a stranger to him now, a mystery to him as much as his father had always been. He pictured his father: the dark eyed, steely man he remembered – his aquiline nose sharp and protruding as a beak; his foreboding, muscular figure and broad shoulders; his strong, heavy hands – and wondered if he would recognize him now either.

Eliza led Tom down the hallway. The surreal feeling of a stranger showing you around your own home struck him as he followed her past his old room on the left. He wondered if she knew how long it had been since he was last there. At the end of the hall, the bathroom door stood open revealing the yellow-tiled room he remembered, now fitted with white plastic attachments on the toilet and bath. To the right, the door to his father's room was slightly ajar—not enough to see inside, but enough to hear the mechanical respiration of a machine whose blinking green light reflected dully on the veneer of the door in the low light of the shuttered home.

"Knock, knock, Mr. Geyer," Eliza spoke with the sing-song lilting of one speaking to someone either very young or very old. She eased the door open. Its hinges whined as it yawned wide.

In the yellow lamplight, a shrunken figure barely emerged. A sullen lump laid unmoving under a bundle of pale blue hospital blankets on the narrow hospital bed along the farthest wall. Small, dark eyes fixed on Tom as Eliza flipped a switch on the machine at the foot of the bed, peering out over a plastic tangle of tubes attached to the mask clinging to waxy skin. The nebulizer whirred as it shut down, and a low rattling like the distant croak of a bullfrog bubbled from beneath the old man's mask.

"You've done very well with your nebulizer this morning, Mr. Geyer," she continued, gently slipping the mask from his father's face. His gaunt cheeks bore creases where the mask had been secured. "Your son has come to stay with you, Mr. Geyer. Isn't that nice? Your boy Tom wanted to see you."

Eliza moved to the other side of the bed, crouching beside the skeletal form, enunciating each word into his ear. She pressed a button, raising the reclined bed forward. The dark eyes glinted in the yellow electric light from the bedside table as the bed lifted the rasping figure upward. Tom thought the thin, age-weathered limbs might suddenly jerk upright and toward him like some horrible marionette. He reflexively moved backward, only to realize he had been standing with his back pressed firmly against the door jamb. His heel hit the wall behind him with a thud, breaking his concentration from his father's unyielding gaze. Eliza looked at Tom. He could read the question in her eyes and chuckled, stepping forward, hoping she wouldn't feel the fear emanating from his body.

"Hey ... dad." Tom offered weakly as he approached his father. The word felt foreign in his mouth. His nerves ricocheted through his body, threatening to rattle his limbs as he closed the distance between them. He smoothed back his hair with a clammy palm just to give his hands something to do besides tremble. His eyes rebounded off the various medical devices around the room: the plastic bag hanging behind Eliza's head; the clear liquid dripping through tubes tethered to the dark blue veins of his father's hand; his yellowed skin like a deboned, plucked chicken's hanging in curtains under the old man's chin which sagged with each shallow breath that escaped his slackened mouth; the foamed spittle collecting at the corners; Eliza's butterflies.

"Isn't it nice to see your son, Mr. Geyer?"

The old man only wheezed as Tom drew closer, Eliza gesturing him forward. Tom forced himself to lean in, half expecting his resistant body to creak like the old door which he was now keenly aware of being too far away for comfort. Tom's eyes moved over the tongue shivering in his father's wrinkled, gaping mouth, and traveled the furrowed contours of his face until they met his own sinister, shining gaze. His father's eyes had always been piercing—the intensity of their gaze almost violent. Now, a milky film enveloped the glassy globes set deep into his purpling sockets. The whites had an almost bluish tinge, traversed by a chaotic sprawling of blood vessels, some red, some brown, like waterways on a satellite map of some wild, untamed country. But even under the thick cataract, the old man's irises shone dark and dull like lumps of coal. They had always been nearly as dark as his pupils, giving the impression of not existing at all—his eyes resembling instead deep, dark holes.

"Hey, it's To —"

A gnarled, vein-mottled claw burst from beneath the blanket and grabbed hold of the lapel of Tom's jacket. Tom gasped, staring into the deep wells of his father's eyes, feeling as though he were about to fall into those dead, angry holes—into some unfathomable abyss.

His father wheezed out the words in a slow snarl punctuated by sharp, rattling breaths: "Wh—errrrre ... is ... my bo- oyyyy?"

He sputtered, stumbling over the machine at his feet as he pulled against his father's grasp, his eyes never leaving the gaze which sought to swallow him whole.

"Oh, Mr. Geyer!" Eliza closed her hand over the old man's bone-white knuckles. "Let go, Mr. Geyer, let go ...." Her voice faded in Tom's ears like the echo of a rock dropped down an endless well, beating against the walls of his fear-filled mind in fainter reverberations as his pulse beat in his ears, drowning out all else save his own dreadful heart.

"I'm so sorry, Tom." A purple butterfly glittered from the depths of the well. Tom blinked. The butterfly flitted its holographic wings under the lamination of the name tag. Eliza gave his arms a gentle squeeze—only then did he realize she had been holding him, guiding across the room. They were already halfway to the door.

The electric kettle percolated softly as he paced the linoleum, phone pressed to his ear. It rang and rang. Cara never answered. The kettle whistled as the 'call-end' notification bleated.

"Ah, look at my timing!" Meredith's full, pink face smiled as she waddled into the kitchen, nodding toward the kettle. She panted lightly as she smoothed the rainbow puzzle-piece patterned fabric of her scrubs which had ridden up above her protruding belly. She went by Merry, '*like Christmas*,' she'd chirped in her cheerful, lilting inflexion. It was a fitting name for a woman like her: rosy-cheeked and ever-smiling.

"Cuppa?" he asked as he removed two cups from the cupboard.

"Oh, please. Peppermint if you have it." The cushion of the seat wheezed under her weight as she lowered herself onto it. She leaned back into the chair, caressing her belly. "I just keep telling myself 'Only a little longer'!'" She giggled, her cheeks plump and shining.

It was her last day before maternity leave and it was evident in her carriage that she had pushed it off as long as possible. Tom was touched by her commitment to her work, to his father, when she had her own little family who she should be giving her time to, instead.

"You'll be a good mum." Tom poured the steaming water into the cups, embarrassed by the comment. He felt his face flush and was grateful to have his back turned as he bobbed the tea bags into the water. He didn't know why he said it.

"Why, thank you, Tom," she said softly, taken aback.

He offered her honey or sugar, which she declined. "Oh, thank you, dear, but I'm already sweet enough," she chuckled as she brought the cup to her lips, blowing the steam. Too hot to sip, she rested the cup on her belly, bobbing the tea bag as she allowed it to cool. "If I'm halfway lucky, this little one will be as good a son as you are, taking this time to be with your dear da'. What a lucky man he is to have you."

Tom cleared his throat. The flush returned to his cheeks as he took a sip of too-hot tea.

"I know, Tom ..." her brows knitted together as she spoke, "... it can be hard ... the way he is now." Tom occupied his mouth with another sip of hot, weak tea. "Remember him as he was, all the good memories you have together. That's what's important. Try to see him as he was in those good times ... not how he is now. He's still that man ... inside, I mean. It'll be easier that way. It really will."

A wet hacking like a dog coughing up bits of bone traveled into the kitchen from down the hall. Merry tabled her undrunk tea and lifted herself from her seat.

"Speak of the devil!" Tom moved to offer her assistance as she struggled against her weight, but she shooed him off. "All right, let us check on da' and see if we can talk him into a sponge bath."

"I'll leave you to it, then."

"Oh, actually, Tom, you'll want to come with me so I can show you the ropes."

"Me?" Tom felt the ghost of the old man's hand clutching his shirt. Since his first day back, he had busied himself with housework and tidying up the overgrown lawn with the rusted push mower on which he'd blistered his hands throughout his adolescence. He hoped his avoidance of his father's room had gone unnoticed by the nurses, otherwise occupied by the seemingly never-ending work of cleaning, feeding, caring for the soon-to-be deceased.

"Well, yes, dear. I'll be out of commission for a while, and it'll be just you and 'liza picking up the slack 'round 'ere."

"Right." Tom placed his cup by the sink. Unsure what to do with his unoccupied hands, he tucked them into his armpits, holding himself in an awkward hug that failed to offer comfort. "Right ...."

"Don't worry, dear, 'taint nothing to be embarrassed about. He changed your nappies when you was a wein, you're just returnin' the favor."

A growl escaped the old man's open mouth. Yellow mucus clung to his lower lip like a dollop of lemon jelly. The nurse cooed reassuringly at her patient, making small talk without expecting a response as she checked his vitals. The old man's gaze honed in on Tom, never leaving his target as the stout woman circled his bed.

"... and how would we feel about a bath today, Mr. Geyer?" She took his lack of response as acceptance and removed the blankets and sheets, tossing them into the waiting laundry basket on the floor. Beside it sat two plastic tubs, one nestled within the other. She pulled them apart, handing them to Tom.

"Now, I'll need you to fill both of these with some nice, warm water."

He was grateful for a moment of solitude as he filled the tubs, perhaps taking more time than necessary to return.

"First thing's first, Tom, I'm going to show you how to roll your father on his side." She gingerly rotated the old man's body, his pale, worn pajamas moving with him in a way that accentuated the sharpness of his protruding joints as the fabric draped over his bones. She had already spread a mat beneath him. The man simply stared, gasping like a fish on a newspaper waiting to be gutted.

She pulled down the loose bottom of his pajama pants, exposing a gauzy white diaper and thin, yellow-blue thighs. *Crrrtch.* She undid the Velcro fastening on his hip, revealing his withered backside. "We'll have you feelin' fresh as a daisy, won't we, Tom?"

Tom attempted a smile behind the hand he had unknowingly placed in front of his mouth.

Her chubby fingers worked the buttons of his shirt out of their holes swiftly, uncovering the sunken cage of his chest, each bone of his torso visible through the thin, sallow skin. She grunted as she lifted him forward into a sitting position, holding him with one arm as she slipped the arms of the shirt off one at a time, tossing the clothes into the laundry basket.

Merry waved a hand through the soapy water, testing its temperature, before soaking a washcloth until it was dripping.

"When you're cleanin' him between baths, you don't need it as wet as this, just get it damp enough to wet his skin and gently …" she touched the wet cloth to his forehead, "gently, work your way from top to bottom, front to back …."

She wiped the mucus from his mouth and agitated the cloth in the soapy water again to shake off the debris and swell its fibers with more soap. She moved from his neck to his shoulders and chest, miniscule bubbles settling in the deep grooves between the bones in his sternum, pooling in the hollow of his navel and between his distended hip bones as she worked her way down.

She navigated the wrinkled folds of his genitals with the cloth. Tom dropped his eyes to the swirling foam in the tub.

"Don't be embarrassed, dear," she whispered softly. "He don't know enough to feel that way himself, so there's no point in you getting' red in the face over it."

"No, I ..." Tom's voice was small, caught in his constricted esophagus. "I know ...."

"Now ... we can't leave you all soapy, can we, Mr. Geyer?" She hung the wet cloth on the side of the soap tub and drenched another in the clean water. She retraced her path over the old man's face. As she concluded her work on her patient's front, she handed the cloth to Tom.

"I want you to go over his hands again, just to get the hang of it."

Tom hesitated, water dripping onto the mattress.

"Go on, then."

He lifted his father's limp right hand. It was lighter than he expected and trembled as he held it, though Tom couldn't tell if the source of the shuddering was his father or himself. The skin was so much softer than he would have imagined his father's hands could ever feel, his once-strong grip now nonexistent.

Tom sopped the cloth gently against the skin, translucent like the greased wax paper of a butcher shop, which moved along with the cloth as if it might come right off the bones. Beneath the pellucid membrane, bulbous blue veins wove across tendons and bones. These were not the hands he remembered. These were the hands of a man already mostly gone, a man slowly disappearing before Tom's eyes. Even his bones felt unnaturally light – like the hollow bones of birds. Only the ossified, yellow nails extending beyond the tips of his fingers seemed to have any substance. Once trim and meticulously clean, they now grew thick and long, resembling the yellowed teeth of an old horse. As the water dripped from the tips of the nails, Tom imagined them digging into his skin and dropped his father's hand onto the bed.

"Careful, Tom, remember: gently, gently ...." Merry took up the other hand, washing away the soap that remained.

"Sorry ...." he mustered, wiping his hand on the thighs of his pants as he steadied himself.

"No worries, dear. We'll get there together. Won't we, Mr. Geyer?" She spoke to the dazed, glistening figure. "Now we'll do your back and we'll be nearly done."

She took the cloth from Tom, letting it float in the tub.

"Right. Tom, I'll have you lift him up just like I did when undressing him to get some practice in, then I'll soap him up and wash him off."

Tom didn't move from where he stood, immobilized by the thought of holding the bony body.

"All right, Tom?"

"Uh, yeah, right."

"Just as I showed you." She urged him on as he slipped his hands under his father's arms. His fingers shivered over the scapula protruding like featherless wings. He held his breath, turning his face away from the slack mouth wheezing into his ear as he lifted the man forward with less physical effort than it took to lift his soiled pajamas into the laundry.

He held his father upright, chest to soggy chest, as Merry scrubbed and rinsed his back. Tom wondered if his father could feel his heart beating.

"Well done, boys, well done!" Merry cheered as she returned the cloth to the tub.

Tom lowered his father onto the bed, imagining he could hear each excrescent vertebrae rattling, clicking into place. He exhaled slowly, his movements careful, until a hot breath licked his neck like the hungry, wet tongue of some wild animal against the neck of its prey before the fatal gnashing of teeth. At that, he expelled the breath held in his lungs, and with it a whimper, withdrawing to the foot of the bed.

The wet breath rattling within the sunken chest filled Tom's ears along with the rushing of his own blood as the nurse twittered merrily through the method of wiping the old man's ass with a wet wipe. He dropped his eyes from his father's magnetic, black gaze. The shadow of a smirk curled the folds of his father's mouth in a taunting, bemused grimace.

Tom volunteered to carry out the tubs and laundry as an excuse to escape the stifling room, scented now by fresh soap which failed to smother the smells of his father's slow decay.

In the laundry room, he poured more detergent into the basin than he needed, holding the open jug to his nose to inhale the clean scent, exorcizing the old man from his airways. He steadied himself on the washer after the lid clicked shut, pressing both palms flat against the metal as the machine rumbled to life. A torrent of water surged over the linens inside. Tom wished he could fold himself inside, submerge himself in the mechanical whirlpool, let it beat the memories and fear out of him and ring him dry, make him clean.

He reached for the phone in his back pocket. He dialed, and it rang and rang and rang.

Tom looked out at the curtain of fog lingering before the pond in the cloud-suffocated sunlight of the early afternoon. Though the mist clung all around him, he imagined he could see the glimmer of dappled light dancing on the water where birds agitated its stillness. The steam of his coffee mingled with the inland fret. Tom inhaled the thick, cool miasma, chasing it with hot, black coffee.

"What a day." Eliza's voice was as soft as the mist around them.

"Nothing like an English spring," he offered, turning toward the nurse in the doorway. She wrapped her cardigan around herself, folding her arms to ward off the chill.

"This really is a pretty place—even when you can't really see it through the fog," she chuckled softly, looking out to the distant spot where Tom had been staring. "You must have so many memories here." She spoke as if she were vocalizing an internal thought.

Tom hummed a terse acknowledgement over the rim of his mug. *Too true, that.* Memories as thick, as suffocating as the fog enveloping him. *No*, he wouldn't go there. It would be like trying to breathe in pond water—as soon as he dives in, he'll drown.

The feet of the matching lawn chair screeched as Eliza skidded it across the concrete patio to sit beside him. She shivered against the damp cushion, holding herself tightly as she leaned forward.

"Tom ...." He looked into her kind, sad eyes. "Times like this...they're never easy. But sometimes they're harder for some than others."

He leaned back in the chair, letting the condensation on the cushion soak through his shirt.

"Watching a person change so much—someone you love—from the way you knew them ...."

"I know." He cut her off. "Merry told me: 'Remember him as he was ... all the good memories...'." He expelled a sigh, pulled from his lungs by the heavy atmosphere, which disappeared into the fog.

"But some of us don't have good memories, do we?" Tom met her eyes, which held him gently in their gaze. "No ... I didn't think so."

Tom let his silence speak for him. They both turned their attention back to the wall of grey mist, the silence between them broken only by the distant chirps of unseen birds.

"English spring ..." Eliza murmured. "It's a transitive time ... summer coming but winter still holding on ...." She inhaled the dewy air, eyes closed. "But no matter how hard it tries to stay, summer's coming. Nearly here."

"Could've fooled me," Tom huffed into the mug as he sipped the dregs of his coffee. Eliza leaned forward, elbows on her knees.

Her voice was low, nearly a whisper, "In my experience, this is the time. When they go, I mean ... hospice cases." The atmosphere was still around them, close and intimate like a cocoon. "There's probably some scientific reason for it, I don't know ... they just don't tend to make it to summer. It's like something in them just isn't up for it. The winter wants to keep them, just holds on ... takes them with it."

"You think it'll be that soon?" His voice felt like that of a child as it left his lips.

"Every year, time and again ...." She watched Tom's features soften, his shoulders drop as the tension that seemed to hold him together began to release.

"Think it'll be a warm one this year?" He stared out toward the invisible pond. Eliza stood up, wiping the damp seat of her scrubs.

"Almanac says it'll be a scorcher." She pulled her cardigan around herself as she moved toward the door leading into the kitchen. As she passed beside him, she squeezed his shoulder. "Grab a jumper if you plan to stay out much longer. Winter's not gone yet ... don't go getting sick. Then I'd have *two* patients on my hands."

"I'll be in soon." He smiled at the nurse as he produced the phone from his pocket.

"I'll put a pot on for when you get in."

After the door slid closed, he tapped Cara's name in the digital rolodex. No answer.

Tom slipped the phone back into his pocket and stared out at the pond. A gentle wind tore through the fabric of the fog, creating an opening frayed at the edges like ripped, wet paper. Through the clearing, he could just make out the edge of the pond—a family of coots rippled the water with fluttering wings, flitting between the water's surface and bordering shrubs and trees bearing the first pale green buds of spring.

Two boxes arrived on the doorstep containing the remainder of Tom's clothes and belongings. There was no note, nothing needed to be said. Cara was gone. His life in London was gone. Now, all he had were a couple of boxes and the old man wheezing at the end of the hall. In two weeks, he had yet to unpack. He placed the boxes next to the open suitcase on the floor and sat on the bed. His thumb hovered above Cara's name on his phone's screen. He decided not to call.

Tom occupied himself with menial tasks, counting the minutes between visits from Eliza and Merry's replacement, Alice. She was a stern woman who spoke little, which suited Tom, but her efficiency made her visits shorter, the distance between them longer than he liked.

During one of those too-long intermissions between visits, a heavy thud from his father's room jolted Tom from his seat on the living room couch. He held his breath and listened, wondering if he could claim to not have heard it over the television when Alice arrived. He twisted the knob on the ancient television, hoping the volume would aid his alibi and drown out the thoughts in his head.

A violent clatter sounded over the voices shouting from the TV. She wouldn't believe he hadn't heard that.

He forced himself down the darkened hallway toward his father's door. As he reached for the doorknob, his hand shook. He closed his eyes as the door opened.

Convincing his eyelids to part, he saw the disarray on the floor beside the bed. Alice had set up a small television atop a wheeled table a few days before, setting it on a station constantly cycling through reruns of *Doc Martin*, *'Allo 'Allo!*, and *Waiting for God*, the last of which seemed darkly appropriate. Now, the television set laid on its side on the floor, playing an episode of *My Three Sons* for some American sitcom marathon.

"Get down, you'll frighten the quarry!" Meredith MacRae's girlish voice called out from the television.

The light emanating from the screen illuminated a cup, its water soaking the carpet, and a framed picture swept to the ground from the bedside table. The cup rolled to Tom's feet.

The old man glared at his son, still but for the shallow rise and fall of his chest with each strained breath. Tom retrieved the cup and bendy straw from the floor, retreating to the kitchen to rinse and refill it.

When he returned, the old man's eyes followed the straw as it bobbed side to side. Tom held his breath as he extended it toward his father. The old man's cracked, pale lips puckered and released around the straw as he sipped.

"We bird watchers all wear neutral colors. That way we blend in with the natural surroundings. It's called protective coloration." The television audience laughed. A wet growl reverberated within the cup.

His father freed the straw from his lips. He coughed, belching up a bubble of water which trickled through the deep wrinkle ravines around his mouth.

"I hope I didn't scare away any rare ones," the sitcom son replied.

Tom turned his attention to the floor, picking up the framed picture. It was his father and himself, aged eight or nine. A crack from the fall bisected the lower corner of the glass, carving through the wrist of his father's hand, which gripped the shoulder of Tom's blue polyester suit jacket. *"Blue for my blue-eyed boy,"* his father's voice echoed in Tom's memory. He beat his eyelids together, forcing it away.

He placed the picture on the table and kneeled to sop up the water.

"A pied wagtail?" the television voice projected across the floor. *"Found only in Great Britain?!"* A comical big band tune played the sitcom off, fading into an advertisement. Tom pressed the towel into the carpet, dabbing it dry as best he could.

A heart-halting coldness ran from Tom's crown like a cracked egg seeping under hair, over ears, down his neck. Fingers probed the thick, dark curls atop his head. For a moment he thought what he felt was only the memory of his father's touch, how he'd worked his fingers through his hair at bathtime, at bedtime, swimming at the pond.

"Myyyy ... boyyyyy ...." the wheezing croak above his head pulled him from the dark well of his reverie. The feeling was not a manifestation of Tom's memory. The touch was solid, present. The realization filled him with dread, shocking him as if the bony tips of his father's fingers were electrically charged. Tom gasped, falling back from his knees onto his ass in a desperate leap. Before he could distance himself, the old man's claw wrapped itself around the thick tendrils of his hair, holding him firmly in place.

"Myyyyy ... boyyyyyyy ...." Regurgitated water gurgled in his throat. His grip tightened, threatening to rip Tom's hair out by the roots as the old man convulsed in a fit of wet coughs.

"Get off!" Tom shouted, scrambling his jellied legs for purchase.

"MYYYY ... BOYYYYY ...." the old man growled, twisting Tom's hair in his hand. His clenched fist anchored him to Tom's scalp, pulling his gaunt frame forward, looming over his son's cowering body. Watery mucus spilled from his slack-lipped grimace.

"Let me go you sick, old fuck!" Tom desperately tried to pry the bony joints of his father's fist open.

"TO- OMMMYYYY ...." His face drew closer to Tom's, his tongue quivering in the horrible socket of his spittle-weeping maw with each ragged cough.

Tom was frantic, clawing at the talon holding him in place as tears burned in his eyes. That mouth, that ghastly, eager mouth advanced toward him. The battling voices of the television sets, his father's sickened snarl, the pounding of Tom's heart in his ears swirled into a deafening cacophony.

"LET GO!" Tom screamed, hot tears streaking his face.

"What's all this?" Alice's voice was shrill and arresting as she ran into the room, cutting through the chaotic scene.

The old man relinquished his grasp and Tom sprang to his feet, barreling through the bedroom door, nearly pummeling the nurse as he ran past her. He didn't stop running—through the front door, down the street, around the houses, past the pond. A raft of coots, rising into flight, cried and squawked in his wake. He ran until his chest hurt. The taste of blood filled his mouth.

As the light began to die, Tom made his way back. He saw the flashing lights of the emergency vehicle as he reapproached the house. From the pond, they backlit the little home, casting shadows across the field which reached out toward him. He didn't hear sirens.

His father's sheet-covered body exited through the front door as Tom entered through the back.

* * * *

In the chaos of responders swarming the little home, Tom sat still and silent at the kitchen table—an extinguished lighthouse in a roiling sea.

Alice answered questions and filled out forms. Eliza pushed a steaming cup of chamomile into Tom's limp hands. There was talking, Eliza was talking, but Tom couldn't hear the words through the fog that enveloped him, tingling against his lips and extremities.

She was the last to leave the house, refusing to abandon Tom until he had something in his stomach. He ate a buttered shrimp spread sandwich without tasting it, assuring her he would be fine. He just wanted to sleep. She left him reluctantly, promising to return first thing in the morning.

Tom stood in the doorway to his bedroom, seeing for the first time the thick layer of dust rimming the baseboards along the hallway. Someone had opened the shutters and curtains and, in the sunlight, he could see clearly the decay around him for the first time. He felt the grime sticking to his body -- the dried sweat, the smell of death in his mouth and nose, that feeling, *oh God* that awful, prodding feeling of those fingers in his hair. The sandwich in his stomach turned, shrimp and bile rising in his throat. He ran to the bathroom, expelling the contents of his stomach in the toilet.

Sweat trickled over his face, down his neck, with the ghost of his father's touch. He needed to be clean.

Tom entered the shower before the water warmed, numbed by his desperate need. He turned the temperature knob as far as it would go, filling a cupped palm with shampoo until it overflowed.

The water seared his skin as he lathered himself head-to-toe. Steam filled the room. He repeated the process, lathering and rinsing until he emptied the bottle and the water ran cold. Skin red and fingers pruned, he sank to the bottom of the tub, letting the cold water cascade over his body.

After an unmeasurable length of time, Tom stepped out of the shower and stared at his reflection in the mirror, naked and dripping. The curtains in the bathroom remained closed, the darkness that had fallen over the house in his father's final days remained here. Even in the muted light, he was struck by the image before him. He looked at the figure with horror and pity. Who was this broken man wearing his face? The image of his father's wet, naked body imposed itself over his own and Tom reached for a towel, rubbing the terry cloth into his eyes.

When he looked again at his red-eyed reflection, a glint of light at the bottom of the mirror drew his attention. It burned in the dimness of the bathroom like the spotlight cast by a magnifying glass on an immolated ant by a cruel child.

Tom stepped aside and followed the shaft of light, given form by the surrounding darkness and life by motes of dust caught in its trajectory, to the opposite wall where he found its source. He wiped a pruned finger over the shower's ceramic tile until the tip found a small, circular recess. About waist-high, a key-sized hole was carved into the center of the tile, camouflaged by the details of the pattern.

Tom's breath caught in his chest. Unaccustomed to the light and stinging from shampoo, he blinked his eyes wildly to adjust as he ran down the hall, readying himself to enter his father's room.

The opened curtains bathed the room in light, transforming the space before him. Tom searched the wall shared with the bathroom. The lower shelves of the bookshelf were cluttered with books and magazines. On top, bird calls were arranged in a row, his father's birdwatching binoculars placed centrally among them. Three framed pictures hovered behind them, fixed to the wall by large pendant hooks. First among them was a yellowed clipping from the local paper reading "Birders Flock to Lilypond" above a grainy picture of black and grey figures, the details of whom were identifiable only by Tom's memory. His father stood to the right of the Boy Scout troop, peering through the camera with binoculars, his face obscured save his crooked smile.

The rightmost picture was a reproduction of the painting Tom recognized from his father's favorite book, *The Art of Audubon*. The American coot glared at him, feet and beak poised for attack. A chill ran through him. Looking to the center picture, that creeping chill solidified like a block of ice in the pit of his stomach. Faraway blue eyes stared through him from the face of his younger self. The glass reflected his own wet torso over the bare upper body of the boy in a bathing suit. Beside the child's stony face dangled a limp fish, held aloft by his pale sapling arm.

Tom was lost in the eyes of his former self, forgetting why he was there. The fleeting shadow of a bird passing by the window shook him from his fixation. He moved his eyes to the hook from which the picture hung. The tarnished brass made the clear glass bead at its center glow in comparison. Tom leaned forward and touched a finger to the bead. It swung to the side, revealing an empty space bored into the wall. Through it, Tom peered through the shower and saw the tiles reflected in the bathroom mirror.

The phantom touch of his father's fingers dug into his brain, prying open the locks of his caged horror, clawing through the gaps in his memory. He had to fill it. His mind raced as he tore into the bathroom. He pulled the mirror toward him, swinging the medicine cabinet open. Hands shaking, he located the toothpaste, squeezing it onto his fingers. Trembling, he stepped into the shower and smeared it across the tile, filling the hole.

He was patching a wound decades past healing. He reminded himself his father was dead, those clawed hands are crossed over his corpse, his dark eyes cataracted by lifelessness, now forever unseeing.

He returned the items to the cabinet, slamming it shut with all his strength. Part of him hoped the mirror would shatter. Instead, when he opened his eyes, he faced a blank wall, another small hole drilled through it. The force of closing the cabinet had rebounded through the plastic, releasing it from the wall on a second row of hidden hinges.

Through the hole, Tom saw a fishbowl perspective of his own bedroom warped in the view of a convex looking glass.

Leaning on the wall for support, Tom turned the corner into the room, searching the wall with his hands until his eyes caught the glint of a glass bead. At the center of the brass hook, it stared back at him like a clear, penetrating eye. From the hook hung a heavily lacquered cockeyed crucifix, whittled in years past for a Scouting badge.

"*You sick fuck ....*" Tom whispered, staring into the glass eye. He suddenly felt his nakedness and pulled clothes over his wet body.

The next days were a blur of bureaucracy punctuated by silent, sleepless nights. Eliza handled the brunt of the logistics, removing the hospital bed and equipment, contacting the funeral home, and composing the obituary, only bothering Tom for his signature when it was needed.

He stuck around like a weed in winter, having no other place to go. The house was Tom's now, but even as he finally unpacked his belongings, he felt like an unwanted visitor.

The black suit he found in one of the boxes was wrinkled and paled on the shoulders from dust. He hadn't worn it in years. Why hadn't he thought to pack it himself? He put it down to carelessness, though perhaps when he packed his suitcases, he hadn't really come to terms with the journey he was taking—with the old man's impending death. In a way, he still hadn't—listening for the rattling breaths at the end of the hall, feeling eyes watching him through the walls, anticipating that horrible skeletal form to emerge from the shadows.

A gentle rapping on the door preceded Eliza's soft voice, "Ready, Tom?"

"Yeah ... just about."

"I'll fix us tea before we go."

He couldn't do anything about the suit but his shoes, scuffed and creased from Cara's haphazard packaging, desperately needed a shine. He'll be looking at them all afternoon at the service and decided to do something about it.

His father's room seemed bigger without the bed, but still Tom felt claustrophobic, easing the collar of his shirt with his finger as he approached the closet. His father's scent lingered in the clothes folded on the shelves. The smell threatened to choke him and he loosened his tie. He spotted the shoeshine box in the far back corner.

"All right, Tom?" Eliza peered in.

"Ah, yeah, sorry. Just need to shine my shoes ...." He smiled gratefully at the nurse, holding his scuffed dress shoes aloft.

"Oh, right. Let me get you some paper." She was gone from the hall before Tom had time to look up from the worn, wooden box. She returned with the local paper, freeing leaves of advertisements. As she flipped through the pages, she stopped, sighing sadly. She carefully folded the page over, presenting it to Tom. "You might want to keep this."

Tom's father stared at him from the page. Even through the blurry pointillist newspaper image, those dark eyes bore into him. Below the portrait read:

Thomas William Geyer

Born in the city of Birmingham on December 18th, 1938, Thomas William Geyer departed March 19th, 2024 in his home in the town of Lilypond Lane. Having spent his youth in the service of Her Majesty's Royal Air Force, Mr. Geyer retired to the countryside to engage in his favorite hobby of birdwatching and to raise his only son, Thomas Geyer, II.

He is preceded in death by his loving wife, Lara, and succeeded by his son, Thomas.

A service will be held at St. Mary's Church at 11am on Monday, March 25th, 2024. In lieu of flowers, Mr. Geyer has asked for any donations to be sent to the Lilypond Birders' Society.

Tom turned his attention to his shoes as he placed them on the crinkling leaves of paper.

"I'll save it for you ...." Eliza removed the obituary.

"Thanks." Tom looked up at Eliza as she placed the remainder of the newspaper on the side table. "For everything, I mean."

Eliza simply smiled her sweet, sad-eyed smile and left the room, obituary in hand.

He worked away at the scuffs, smoothing out the wrinkles, until the toes shined mirror-like. Tom stared into his own reflection in the leather, the heavy scent of polish making him dizzy, less from the fumes than from the memories they invoked. Firm fingers gripped the nape of his neck and suddenly were gone. Tom gasped, dropping the shoe onto the paper and knocking the tin of polish onto the carpet.

"Shit!" He whispered, reaching for the stack of newspaper on the table. As he pulled it down, a loose advertisement glided through the air, touching the ground on the floor of the closet. Tom reached for the paper, only realizing when his fingers touched the edge that the corner of the paper had disappeared behind the wall.

Hesitantly, he slid the paper out to reveal the hidden corner, then pushed it back through the crease between the closet floor and wall, watching it vanish again.

Sweat slicked his palms as he placed one on the back wall of the closet, feeling the faintest movement as he did so. Cold sweat crept up his body as he tossed the clothes onto the floor, wrestling the shelves from their ledges. As the last shelf thudded on the carpet, he pressed his stained hands against the back wall, shifting it aside with all his strength.

"What was th-?" Eliza burst in, breathless. Over Tom's shoulder, a dark chamber extended beyond the closet wall.

The tea kettle screamed in the kitchen. Neither of them heard it above the shared shock of Tom's discovery.

Tom reached for a spiderweb-draped chain swinging from the ceiling of the hidden room. He pulled it, illuminating the space with the weak, buzzing glow of a bare lightbulb.

Before him, Tom faced rows upon rows of shelves, reaching up to the ceiling of the alcove. On them, a vast collection of orbs was displayed, each cradled in its own porcelain cup. He steadied the swinging light and stepped into the hidden room to inspect its contents. They were eggs—of every imaginable color and size.

"Must have been a collector as well then?" Eliza offered. Tom could only respond with a sharp exhale. "Why do you think he hid them back there?"

"I don't know ...." Tom muttered as his eyes scanned the shelves. On the bottom shelf, just above the dust-caked floorboards, was a row of metal boxes. He removed one with trembling grease and sweat-slicked hands.

Easing open the box on rusted hinges, he discovered a stack of folded papers. As he removed the first bundle from the box, a photograph slipped from its folds, followed by a small paper square. Tom lowered himself to the floor, retrieving the fallen papers. The first was a photograph, old and weathered at the edges, of a man in a uniform. The face had been cleanly excised, leaving an empty square.

The smaller piece was a square bearing his father's face. Tom pieced the smaller photo into the hole of the other. In size, it fit perfectly, but the lighting and background didn't match.

He unfolded the papers: identical copies of his father's discharge papers. Or, *nearly* identical. The first two contained the name he knew — the last ... was different. "William Allen Adams." The name was foreign to Tom, but the "W" in the signature at the bottom, its sharp points like the fangs of a snake, was unmistakable. It was his father's.

He looked again at the contents of the box, trying to make sense of it all. There were more papers, more signatures, more photos missing faces. At the bottom, he found a stack of photographs bound together with a rubber band which disintegrated as Tom pulled it away. Each pair of photos bore a striking resemblance to the next: a lone, faceless man, each body a different shape and size; then a faceless man with his father's shoulders, a pregnant woman beside him. The woman, however, was different in each picture. He searched their faces. Most were young, desperate looking girls with swollen bellies and sad eyes.

Tom carried the other two boxes to the bookshelf at the end of the room. He opened the second box. A picture he recognized stared up at him. His own bright blue eyes looked up at the camera, two tiny teeth just barely bursting from his gums as the baby smiled, a rubber duck floating around his baby-fat thighs in the yellow bathtub.

As Tom picked up the picture, his fingers brushed against something soft, making him drop the box with a clang onto the bookshelf. The bird calls rolled around in the aftershock.

Reaching again for the photograph, Tom turned it over, revealing a lock of dark, curly hair adhered to the back with yellowed tape. A shiver prickled from his fingertips to the top of his head. There were more pictures of Tom: as a baby, a boy, a teenager. Some he remembered. Most he didn't—candid shots, taken from strange angles. Here he was sleeping, there he was catching frogs. At the bottom of the pile, the familiar pattern of the yellow bathroom tiles surrounded the photographs' unknowing subject as he brushed his teeth, washed his hair ....

Tom's heart fluttered inside his chest like the wings of a trapped bird against a windowpane, wild and frantic. He threw the photographs aside, opening the final box.

More photographs. Several bundles held together with rubber bands were stacked on top of each other like decks of playing cards. He broke the band on the first deck, staring at an unknown infant's face. On the back of the first photograph, a lock of blond hair brushed his finger. He watched the baby grow into a child as he flipped through the pictures.

There were so many of them. So many little boys locked away in this rusted metal box. He feverishly removed each stack, digging, unsure what he was looking for or if he even wanted to find it. His fingers found the cold metal of several rings and a yellowed envelope. Tom unfolded the envelope, emptying the contents onto the shelf. A collection of licenses spilled out. Again and again, he saw the old man's face smirking under the lamination. O'Brien, Walker, Brown, Davies, Clarke, Hughes, Adams ... Geyer.

There were more licenses. Women's licenses. The women in the pictures from the first box. Tom searched the faces and names: Elsie, 17 years old; Maryanne, 18 years old; Olivia, 17 years old ... his fingers shook as he picked up the next card.

Lara.

Tears welled in Tom's eyes as he looked into those of his mother. She was young and pretty though rough around the edges, with bright blue eyes and curly hair teased high atop her head. She wasn't an old woman ... *in 1988, she was 16.*

"Oh, Tom ...."

He had forgotten Eliza altogether. When he turned to face her, red eyes brimming with fear, she held the stack of Tom's bathroom pictures. Pain creased her brow as she lifted her glassy eyes to meet his. He felt the tear rolling down her cheek in his gut like a fist reaching up through his stomach and into his soul.

He turned away, shoving the photographs and papers back into the boxes before she saw any more.

"We ..." his voice quaked. He cleared the salted iron taste of grief from his throat before he continued, "We better get going ... if we want to get there in time."

"Tom ... you don't ...."

"I do, though." It came out harder than he meant it to. "I mean ... I have to get it over with."

Eliza nodded, pressing her hand on Tom's chest as he fought to control his breath.

"I'll start the car. Come out when you're ready." She wiped the tear from her cheek as she turned to leave the room. Reaching the doorway, she remembered the photographs in her hand and placed them facedown on the table.

The service was sparsely attended. Eliza and Merry flanked Tom in the front pew, Merry's son babbling and cooing against her breast. Theirs were the only faces Tom recognized. The older couple a few pews back were undoubtedly church folk—the type who attend every service.

As Eliza and Merry led Tom down the aisle, he noticed a man watching him from the furthermost pew. He was stout with sharp eyes, a soft face, and a bushy, bristling mustache like the broom of a chimney sweep. Their eyes met as Tom exited the church.

The weedy congregation stood around the front lawn of the church as the casket was wheeled out through the double doors and into the hearse that would convey it to the crematorium.

Ashes to ashes.

The hearse rolled away, disappearing over the crest of a hill. The nurses spoke softly around him, offering their condolences. Tom pulled away from the clutch of women, walking across the lawn.

"No, let him go," Eliza's hushed voice trailed in his wake.

He looked out at the serene field dotted with lichen-covered stones bearing the unintelligible names of the bones beneath them. A faint, pained twitter called out from the overgrowth beneath an ancient, knotted oak. Tom followed the sound, dew dampening his ankles as he moved through the grass.

At the roots of the tree, he spotted a feathery nest. Shards of egg littered the shell of woven twigs which had once kept them safe. At its center screeched a pale, pink fledgling. Its useless wings trembled as it cried out through its shivering beak. The bird's cries wrenched a sob from Tom's lips. He heaved and shuddered; tears streamed his cheeks.

A black figure swooped between him and the fledgling, circling the nest and cawing menacingly as it drove toward the chick.

"Shoo! Get away, ya bastard! Shoo!" The mustached man sprinted through the grass, whipping a handkerchief through the air, driving the black bird off its prey. "Damned things," he muttered through his mustache. He delicately scooped the bird, nest and all, into his calloused hand with his handkerchief. "Nasty little bastards, they are. Go after the nests of other birds, eating the eggs. Damned things."

Tom was silent as he watched the man cradle the newborn bird.

"Junior, is it?"

Tom blinked, wordless.

"I mean, son of, er ..." he gestured with his free hand in the direction of the church.

Tom cleared his throat. "Y-yes. Yes, I'm Tom."

"Well, I'm sorry, son, for your, er ... loss." The man seemed at a loss for words but rooted where he stood, bird in hand, as if wanting to say more.

"Thank you .... I'm sorry, have we ...?"

"Met? Oh, no, I doubt it, son. No ... you see, I saw the picture in the post. Of your old man, that is. Never thought I'd see that face again, I'll tell ya."

"*Only for your funeral*," Tom murmured to himself.

"What's that, son?"

"Uh, sorry, 'Only for your funeral' ... something my father used to say about when a man should get his picture in the papers."

"Ah, right," the man chuckled, adding, "he would, wouldn't he?"

He stared at Tom with smiling but inquisitive eyes. The bird chirped in his palm.

"I didn't know your dad, son. I'm an investigator, you see. I recognized his face is all and, well, I'm sorry for the timing but ... I need to ask about his collection."

Tom felt a weight fall from his shoulders, the tension releasing from his chest. Throughout the service, he saw the faces of those women, those boys, the rows and rows of eggs, the rings, the hair. Eliza hadn't seen the worst of it, only *he* knew what the old man had buried in those boxes. The weight of that knowledge was suffocating. Tom looked at the quivering bird in the mustached man's hands, how gently he held it. His eyes found the man's searching gaze and he took a deep breath.

"Which one?"

Rose J Monan holds a BA in Comparative Literature and Italian Language and Literature from Smith College along with a background in journalism and publishing. She hails from Lusby, Maryland, the setting for her upcoming debut novel Runes in the Kudzu. Rose loves to explore local history and folklore, weaving these stories into anything from historical essays to fictional tales of horror. She currently resides in Carrboro, North Carolina with her husband, Ray, and two cats, Mcleod and Nox. When she is not writing, Rose can be found making art, baking for family and friends, enjoying nature, or conducting research for her next writing project.

To find out more about Rose's upcoming releases, follow her @Rosejmonan on Facebook and Instagram.

Long Weekend

BY AMBER LACIE

An escape, some place where no one knew me, a place to lie low until everything blew over...I had been looking for such a place for months.

When my great-aunt passed away, she left me everything, including her picturesque estate. Funny how fate just happens that way. I found myself surrounded by perfection—perfect houses, perfect nei ghbors...or at least that's what I thought.

Turns out sometimes perfection is only on the outside. The inside is darker...frightening.

The only question I have is who is more sinister? The neighbors...or me?

THURSDAY

Lynn was on her third lap around the pond, seemingly carefree, lost in thought as she ran. If the sweat marks on her shirt were an indication of the heat outside, today was another sweltering summer day. I sipped on my late morning coffee, watching her from my window while I enjoyed the cool air conditioning. As she passed in front of the house, the next-door neighbor stepped off his porch with his gardening tools in hand. It was the same thing every day. Lynn ran. Mark gardened. Rissa walked her dogs. It never differed.

How my aunt survived as long as she did in this perfectly posh subdivision was beyond me. Lilypond Lane had perfect houses with perfect landscaping and perfect people. The way they all stuck to their routines and greeted each other with forced smiles and vacant eyes creeped me out. My heebies had been jeebied. If I did not need somewhere to crash for the time being to escape my life, there was no way I would have taken up residence in my deceased aunt's house. I need anonymity and peace, even if it was to be short lived.

It was strange walking through her house without her here. Sure, it had been a year or so since my last visit, but nothing had changed. Every bit of the decor was ostentatious, expensive, and as peculiar as she was. It screamed Eliza Pruitt. You would never know looking at the house from outside there was a four-foot-high by eight-foot-wide, golden, bejeweled peacock waiting to greet you just inside the entryway. Nor would you be expecting a thick, black leather canvas with red velvet roses and deer antlers dipped in 14-karat gold to be the main focal point of her sitting room. And yet, there it was hanging above the mantelpiece. Just one more thing I would have to figure out how to sell before putting the house on the market. The realtor was insistent about removing as much of the decor as possible before listing it. I had never sold a house before and, according to my knowledge, which I gained from watching television, it was not an abnormal request. What he said to me the day we met to put everything into action still echoed in my mind.

"People need to picture themselves in the house, Elowyn. They won't be able to do that with," he paused waving his arms towards random items. "Whatever this is. It's got to go. Either store it or sell it."

Was I procrastinating by being a nosy neighbor watching everything out of the large window in the kitchen? Absolutely. I would deal with it eventually just like I did with everything else in my life, begrudgingly and late. Taking another sip of my coffee, I eyed my deceased aunt across the room from me. The white marble elephant that held her ashes was placed on the table so it could "*enjoy the intriguing view*" per her request. When, or if, I sell the house, I was to take her ashes with me and dispose of them "*in a great manner when you should feel the timing is right.*" Whatever the hell that meant.

Another odd remark in her will was for me to take in the ambiance of her newly finished office downstairs. It was something I had ignored previously, but my sleep had become more fleeting the longer I stayed in this house. When I brought it up to my therapist, she suggested tackling some things I was putting off might help. Perhaps my mind was restless because I had too many open-ended projects. A list of three things laid at the tips of my fingers as I tapped them idly. The first thing was to enjoy a late morning coffee.

Second, was to start packing up the office. I would not be enjoying the ambiance so much as packing it up. The third item was to start cataloging items to sell. I had no use for most of her collection, nor did I have an attachment to the items.

I had just put my mug into the sink when I heard keys in the front door. To my knowledge, besides the realtor, I was the only one with a set since I had the locks updated when I moved in. My heart skipped a beat in my chest as my nerves climbed into my throat. Quickly reaching for something to protect myself, I pulled a knife from the wooden block beside the sink. My breath stilled in my chest as I stepped through the doorway of the kitchen and into the hall leading towards the front door, where once again I heard keys attempt to turn the locks. A dark shadow in the shape of a person loomed outside the stained glass.

"Who's there?" my voice wobbled. The turning of the handle stopped, the shadow stilling. "Hello?"

"Hello?" a soft feminine voice parroted back to me. "Is there someone there?"

My grip tightened on the knife I was holding as I leaned closer towards the glass, trying to peer out through the menagerie of shapes and colors.

"I could ask you the same. This is my house. State your business or leave. I will call the police." As the words fell from my lips, I grimaced with embarrassment. Calling the police should have been the first thing I did, but curiosity lured me here over logic.

"I'm sorry. My name is Vanesa Jackson. I'm with National Care Associates. Could you open the door so we could speak face to face?"

National Care was the name of the company hired to care for my aunt in the end. At the realization of my mistake, I quickly stepped back into the kitchen, placed the knife on the counter, and rushed back to open the door. A short, round woman with mousey brown hair looked up at me holding up a badge hooked to the lanyard around her neck.

"As I was saying, my name is Vanesa. I was the supervisor who handled your aunt's case. I just wanted to check in and offer our condolences as well as gather up anything we may have left behind."

I paused waiting for a second to see if she would recognize me, but when it was clear she didn't, I invited her in. "Right, um, come on in. I'm Elowyn, Eliza was my great aunt."

"Oh, we didn't have any family on record for her."

"I don't know anything about that, but she was my great aunt and I'm here now. If you'll just follow me." I led her down the main hallway into another that led to a small sitting room. Since I had already begun to clear the room out, it was the most normal looking one in the house. I motioned for her to sit on the small sofa while I sat opposite her in a leopard print chair. "Before we get into anything, can I have the key you were trying to use please?"

A look of shock passed over her face before she quickly regained her composure.

"The key? Right. Of course. I don't think that will be necessary as it didn't work." She smiled sweetly.

"Still. Imagine my shock when a random stranger tried to gain entry to my home. Surely, you understand. If you could also explain why you were attempting to enter the home of a patient you know no longer occupies it, that would be great." I smiled back, trying to replicate her own sticky sweetness.

"I'm here to collect the items left behind by the caregivers, of course. Bedding, some minor personal items, and a medical binder. They should be in the room the caregiver stayed in. As Ms. Eliza is no longer with us, I thought I'd just hop on over to pick them up. Just making sure I cross all my t's and dot all my i's. I'm sure you know how it is."

"Yes, well, I don't. The guest bedroom has already been emptied and all items were given to my aunt's lawyer to deal with. Perhaps you should be meeting with him, and while you're there ask him what the courts justify as breaking and entering for future references."

"I do apologize. I realize we have gotten off horribly on the wrong foot. I was unaware of the lawyer's involvement. Do you have a name or number for them? Also, would you mind if I just took a quick look in the room? My employee keeps insisting she left her diary here. She won't stop pestering me about it."

Standing, I brushed my hands on my jeans and nodded back towards the hall we just entered through.

"I have a card for him in the kitchen. I'll show you the room, but you'll have to make it quick. I have things to do and to be honest this is all rather unnerving especially since I'm still dealing with the loss of my aunt." She nodded and followed me to the small guest room with light gray walls. The bed had been stripped bare. Only the mattress was left on the platform frame. The drawers in the nightstand and dresser had been completely emptied out, along with the closet. She inspected every corner but found nothing. The room was bare, with no décor or sense of belonging to it.

"As you can see, it's empty. Everything is with the lawyer. Come on. I'll get his number for you." I waited for her to leave the room before pulling the door closed. "Just down the hall and to the right. You'll see the kitchen. It's the room with the fridge."

I followed her down the hall making sure she followed my directions, but then I veered off, turning into a doorway that appeared to be a closet, which led to the kitchen through a different door beside the pantry. I had just placed the knife back in the block holder when she walked in the room. She eyed my movements, arching her brow as if to question how I arrived before her and why I was touching the knives.

"You should always be prepared to defend yourself. You never know who might try to use an old key to get into your house." I chuckled to myself enjoying her look of shock as I pulled his card off the fridge. "Here you go. Now, let's get you on your way."

As soon as her car faded from the drive, I called the lawyer, letting him know what happened and to ask if we had in fact changed the locks. He assured me the locks were updated and he would be dealing with Vanesa personally. The next thing I did was order video doorbells and some security cameras to place around the house. I was not going to take any chances. Deciding to forgo packing up more stuff for the day, I crawled under the blankets in my bed and spent the rest of my day binging movies and stuffing my face. Did I waste a perfectly good day? Probably. But procrastination was what I did best.

FRIDAY

Boxes, tape, and a permanent marker were laying on the floor beside me as I dug through the closet in her office. The antique desk was going to be the next item for me to tackle. Aunt Eliza had a thing for calligraphy and swans. At minimum it was the going theme for this room. The number of pens, tips, inkwells, feathers, and swan statues in the closet alone was insane. There was even a swan made to hold a pen in its mouth. It was morbid looking with the pen going in through the top of the head and coming out of its beak. The swan looked less like it was holding it and more like it had been impaled by the pen. I had spent the better half of my day removing the art hanging on the walls, all but one picture that was above the desk, and emptying the closet shelves. Her obsessive swan collection had spilled over into the need for an obscene amount of paper, evidenced by the three full boxes I had found of origami swans of varied colors and sizes.

Reaching above me, I pulled down a heavy box. I spun to set it gently on the desk but tripped over one of the boxes of swans and ended up dropping the box haphazardly. It fell onto the top of the desk with a loud thud breaking off one of the corners.

"Shit!" I gasped and reached for the piece, trying to fit it back on. It was then I noticed it wasn't broken, it was *meant* to come off. A small brass circle the size of a pencil eraser inlaid in the wood trim was revealed by the false covering. After messing with it for an obscene amount of time, I came to two conclusions.

One being the brass part must have been some sort of trigger mechanism. What it did was still a mystery.

Two being Eliza had secrets.

After yesterday, my nerves were already heightened. Adding in some odd furniture and paper swans sent my brain into overdrive as I peered around the room trying to figure out what it all meant. I had already removed most of the contents of the closet, so I began pulling open the drawers of the desks looking for more clues but came up empty handed.

Deciding that I needed a break, I headed upstairs to make myself a late lunch. Perhaps if I came back with fresh eyes, something would stand out to me. It was just after two o'clock when I sat down to enjoy the salad I had made myself. My eyes focused on the movement outside the window on the sidewalk. Rissa was walking her dogs. Soon the mail would arrive and the neighbors would all make their way to their mailboxes with vacant gazes, false greetings, and perfectly whitened teeth. I hated this part of the day, but I did my best to partake in it. I needed to sell this house and I didn't want difficulty with the neighbors. I could at least appear to be social even if it was for only a few minutes a day.

After finishing my lunch, I washed my plate and stepped outside onto the grand front porch. I had barely made it down two steps before the mail truck had already moved on from my house and onto my neighbor's. Rissa was chatting with Mark about his garden as I grabbed the few pieces of junk mail inside the box. As I walked up towards the front door, I heard someone call my name.

"It's Elowyn, right?" I turned nervously, finding a happy and bouncy Rissa walking towards me. *Why are her steps always so springy?*

"Yep. That's me." I gave her my best half smile. I had been using my legal name since I moved and, so far, no one had questioned it. To them I was just Elowyn and that was exactly how I wanted it.

"I just wanted to say I was sorry about Eliza. She was always so quiet. We were all shocked when we heard she passed. I noticed her nurse came over the other day. Everything okay?"

Wait a minute. "Nurse? Who do you mean?"

"Uh, I think her name was Vicky or Vanesa. Yes, that's it, Vanesa. Short, plump, and plain looking thing. She lived with your aunt for a while. She used to bake us all cookies, but then she just stopped. I guess your aunt must have taken a turn then. We just stopped seeing her. I didn't even think about her being gone until I saw her stop by. I got worried you might be sick too. You're not, are you? There's not some weird diseases or something in that house is there?"

Vanesa wasn't the employer then. She was the employee. She would have had time to prepare and gather all her things if she were taking care of my aunt. Why would she come back? What was she after? Yesterday had already felt odd to me. I wondered for a second if Rissa knew how helpful the information she just gave me was. Then again, I was certain her dogs were more intelligent than her so perhaps not.

"No weird diseases. She just came by to offer her condolences and check on me. Sweet, I guess, even if I wasn't expecting it."

"Oh, okay. Good. That's good. I mean, not your aunt dying, but being disease free. We wouldn't want a plague spreading among us. That would be awful." Rissa crinkled up her nose causing her freckles to disappear in her botoxed face before turning around bounding back down the drive. Her dogs jogged closely behind her to keep up. As I opened the front door, I looked over my shoulder to spot Mark spraying his grass green with paint. *What artificial hellscape am I living in*?

Aunt Eliza had a beautiful, mirrored bar set up in the dining room with gorgeous crystal ware. Grabbing a bottle of white wine, I grasped a crystal wine glass and poured myself some. It had a crisp, delicious flavor. I was enjoying it too much to leave it upstairs, so I grabbed the bottle along with my glass and headed back down to the office.

The bottle was empty. By the looks of my empty glass, the wine was a little too good.Balancing on the leather desk chair, I attempted to grasp the corner of the last painting still hanging in the room. I slipped and caught myself by grabbing onto the frame.

My fingers slid down the side, stopping when they hit something metal. *Are those hinges?* The frame was firmly anchored to the wall with metal clasps that closely resembled a door hinge.

Take in the ambiance. That's what Eliza wanted me to do, right? What better viewpoint than from her desk. I plopped down into the chair I was using just moments ago for a ladder as my gaze raked along the walls and details of an empty room. The wooden trim alone was exquisite. That's when I saw it: my next clue.

Right above the picture, carved beautifully into the ceiling trim, was the word 'Ambiance.' I was on the right track, but I was missing a piece. My fingers danced softly along the edges of the desk stopping only when they found the brass mechanism. Previously, I had tried to push it in, but maybe I need to pull it out. Feeling along the inside of the metal circle, I found a ring that I could pull down, so I did just that. A loud click echoed in the empty room and the picture I was trying desperately to take down before was now pushed away from the wall on one side by a few inches.

"Aunt Eliza, you sneaky bitch." I grinned slyly to myself as I made my way to the picture, pushing it completely open and revealing a perfectly varnished nook containing a leather journal. Chills spread up my spine and down my arms as I held the journal in my hands, knowing this was probably the last thing my aunt held dear to her before her passing.

Written in ink on the pages inside were dates with the names and activities of my great aunt's neighbors. I made myself comfortable at her desk as I began to read page after page of happenings around Lilypond Lane. I quickly learned everyone had a routine. They also had secrets, terrible secrets. My great aunt was nosey and crazy enough to write them all down...including some *interesting* facts about Vanesa. After snapping some pictures of the inside, I put the journal back where I found it. In the wrong hands, it could be devastating. I needed to talk to someone about this, and soon.

It was after eight by the time I got back from the lawyer's office. His suggestion was to hand the journal over to the authorities, let them investigate, and let the law take it from there. Since when has the authorities or law ever worked efficiently or in a timely manner? My worries were Vanesa taking off before the investigation could begin, before she could be charged.

I wasn't like my neighbors. I wasn't perfectly poised. No, I was angry, vengeful, and had no problem calling people out on their bullshit. The only thing I had left to do was figuring out how to get Vanesa to make a visit to the house tomorrow. Once that was done, everything else would just fall into place.

SATURDAY

A neighbor had sunk more than one long, body-shaped bag in the pond at the center of the houses. At least five by Aunt Eliza's count. Lynn ran every day to stay in shape for her husband who was having an affair. Little did she know it wasn't Rissa he was interested in. He had been sleeping with their neighbor Mark for the past six years. One time, things went a little too far when Lynn's husband invited his nanny to join in. She had come running out of the side door late one night with Mark hot on her heels with some kind of long-handled mallet in his hand. Eliza never saw the nanny again. Coincidentally, that happened at the same time Mark had decided to give up croquet and was spotted selling his set to someone in his driveway. Even stranger was the garden that appeared overnight in Mark's yard. Perfectly pristine. Almost too perfect. Almost plastic. According to my aunt, some of the plants were.

I continued to read the journal, gasping here and there as I lost myself in the sudden twists and turns. The journal was better than any mystery-thriller book I had read in years. The parts on Vanesa, however, were bone chilling. Turns out she had a thing for the dramatics. She had accused my aunt on several occasions of not paying her enough. When my aunt argued back, Vanesa had decided to punish her.. My aunt who had no issues moving around was suddenly in and out of the hospital from random falls and experiencing unknown bruising. The doctors wrote my aunt a slew of prescriptions to help with headaches, dizziness, pain, etc. Vanesa kept them all locked away. Any time Eliza made even a hint at recovering fully, a new accident would befall her. Soon the bruises turned to broken limbs and fractured ribs.

My aunt's writing on the last page had sealed Vanesa's fate.

"They were checking my leg today. Vanesa left me alone with the nurse to answer a phone call. I quickly grasped the nurse's shirt and begged her to help. I don't know what will come of me asking. I need

someone to see what's happening. This isn't like me. I know who I am and what I'm capable of, this falling business isn't me. I just know when we get home, Vanesa will make my afternoon tea, and everything will be lost to me. She's killing me. I just know it. Lord, please, let someone listen to me."

It was a month after the last entry when my great-aunt Eliza left this world. She knew everything about everyone so, surely, she had to be right about Vanesa. There was one way to find out. I closed the journal and put it back in its place behind the frame in the office once again. Vanesa would be there any minute. I had called her early this morning informing her I had found some interesting and expensive items that I had no use for, offering them to her as a thank you for the wonderful care she had given Eliza. The stupid nurse took the bait hook, line, and sinker.

No sooner had I come back upstairs and made myself a glass of ice water than the doorbell rang. My guest had arrived. I shook off the last of my nerves, brushing the wrinkles out of my shirt and slacks before opening the door.

"Vanesa, I'm so glad you could come."

Her round face smiled up at me sweetly returning my greeting. "Of course, it's no problem. The company would do anything for Eliza. She was so loved by us."

By us? Keep the lies coming, sweetheart. I know what you did.

"Great, do come in. I'm going to grab myself something to drink before we get started. Would you like something?"

"I'm fine. No, thanks."

"Right. Well, it's just a few things in the kitchen I boxed up for you."

She follows me into the kitchen while I pretend to fill my glass of water. I moved slowly, listening to her 'ooh' and 'awe' over a few random items I grabbed as a distraction. I needed to drag out our visit before moving onto the next step of my plan.

"Vanesa, did you work closely with Eliza?"

Placing my glass in the sink, I spun to look at her. Her round hands with stubby fingers gripped what looked to be an expensive hand mirror she had found in the box as she looked up at me.

"Uh, occasionally. Why do you ask?"

"No reason, really. Did you know she loved to write?" She shook her head at me, and I continued, "No, I guess, you wouldn't. It was more of a hobby of hers, I think. She has these letters downstairs in her office. I think…" I paused for a moment scrunching my face up as I pretended to search for the right words, "I don't know exactly who they are for, but I think they're letters missing from her will. Something about payments rendered or being corrected. I don't know. I was hoping, if you were close to her, you might be able to help me decipher some of it."

Vanesa's eyes widened, crowning almost cartoonishly at my carefully crafted lie. *Come on little fly, follow the honey.* It was hard to maintain a look of indifference when all I wanted to do was relish in my enjoyment of her being so easily conned.

"I could try. Where are they?"

Nodding towards the doorway, I started walking into the hall. "Downstairs in her office. Come on, I'll show you what I've put together so far."

The shuffling of her footsteps on the wood floor let me know she was following me. At the top of the stairs, I hesitated, looking at Vanesa standing eagerly beside me with the box from the kitchen in her hands.

"For such a nice house, she didn't really keep up with everything did she?"

"What do you mean?"

"I mean, just look at that railing. Gorgeous hardwood floors, and a shotty iron railing. She should've fixed that. It makes me nervous. You know?"

Vanesa shifted the box on to her hip and then took one step down followed by another, tugging on the iron railing with her free hand.

"I guess. It still seems secure to me."

"Hmm. Are you sure?" I took one step down, and leaned towards the railing where she was holding on. "It would suck to fall down them, wouldn't it?"

She swallowed as looked over her shoulder at me, "Yes. It would."

I nodded in agreement and leaned back to make it seem as though I was going to give her room to continue down the stairs. She took a step down, furthering herself from me, while I pretended to take another step up to give her space. Relaxing her shoulders, I could see the tension ease from her body as she went to take another step. The corner of my lips curled into a sinister smile as I turned around and shoved her hard from behind. Her body bounced several times on the hard wooden stairs before hitting the marble landing. Her head bounced just once with an awful, loud *crack*. The box she was holding, along with its contents, scattered around her.

"Oh, no. You fell. Here,moment, let me help you." My monotone voice held no alarm as I stared down at her unmoving, clearly dead body. "Oh, Vanesa, you're making a mess. Just look at all that blood. Someone is going to need to clean this all up."

Unnervingly calm, I walked back into the kitchen, picking up my phone and dialing 911. My voice shook and cracked where needed, real tears streamed down my face, and I recounted the horror I found when I heard Vanesa scream. The lovely operator stayed on the phone with me until the police and emergency services arrived. Everyone was so consoling. By the time everything was said and done, I had been hugged by several officers, had been given a blanket by the EMS since I was obviously shaken, and had signed a few autographs. I had done my best to keep my identity hidden when I moved in. All I wanted was a break from the press hounding me daily about my recent breakup. I sniffled as the last of the officers said goodbye for the evening.

"Now, Miss Kathryn Kelly, I know this must be hard for you. Taking your time from the big screen to help sort out some family matters, and then this happens. You poor thing. I promise we will keep this under wraps."

"No, press?" I sniffed again, batting my eyelashes.

"No, press. Everything is situated and cleaned up. You have a good evening, Miss Kelly."

I wrapped my arms tightly around him, hugging him as though my life depended on it. "My name is Elowyn Kathryn Kelly. You can call me Elowyn. Thank you, officer."

"No worries, ma'am. Get some rest if you can."

Wiping a stray tear from my cheek, I nodded as he walked away. One benefit of being a famous Hollywood actress was fame; another was being able to cry over nothing at the drop of a hat. I was a silver screen sweetheart. They never once questioned my motives. When they were long gone, and it was just me in the house again, I shrugged off the blanket, tossing it on the couch. I poured myself a glass of wine and went to bed.

It had been a long time since I had felt a thrill like I did that night. Maybe I wouldn't sell Aunt Eliza's house. Maybe, just maybe, I would keep it after all.

Sunday

My Great Aunt was right: the neighbors were dangerous company to keep, but damn, they were exciting to watch. I flipped the journal open to a new page marking the date at the top right corner.

Lynn was on her third lap around the pond, seemingly carefree, lost in thought as she ran. If the sweat marks on her shirt were an indication of the heat outside, today was another sweltering summer day. I sipped on my late morning coffee, watching her out my window while I enjoyed the cool air conditioning. As she passed in front of the house, the next-door neighbor was stepping off his porch with his gardening tools in hand. It was the same thing every day. Lynn ran. Mark gardened. Rissa walked her dogs. It never differed.

Indie-Award Winning Author Amber Lacie is about all things books, glitter, and shenanigans. Never without a book or caffeinated goodness, she's managed a husband that worships at her alter and two awesome kiddos, all while pumping out tales of love and suspense. Growing up in Chicagoland, she's seen the nitty, and knows the gritty. As for love and home, that landed her in Beverly Shores, Indiana where she dreams up adventures for her characters so that you the reader can explore new bends in the road. Buckle up.

To find out more about Amber's books, you can reach her on Amazon: https://www.amazon.com/author/amberlacieand Instagram: https://www.instagram.com/amberlacieauthor

Epilogue

BY ROSE J MONAN

Now that you have read these stories, have seen beneath the suburban façade and peered into the dark soul of Lilypond Lane, you may be thinking: "Well, that couldn't happen in my neighborhood." Perhaps you think our little village uniquely evil. Perhaps you comfort yourself by calling these stories fiction.

But how well do you really know your neighbors? Do you really know what happens behind closed doors?

Perhaps the only difference between this neighborhood and your own... is that the secrets of Lilypond Lane have come to light.

Like many small towns, on Lilypond Lane one woman pulls the strings. This is the story of the witness to all the crimes and horrors you have just read – the blackest heart of Lilypond Lane, its most corrupted soul. This is the story of how those horrors came to be.

This is the story of the witch of Lilypond Lane.

The evil here didn't start with me. It existed before I was even a tadpole in my mother's womb—long before the first brick of

Lilypond Lane was laid. You see, this town grew from another's demise, centuries after the horrors of that which destroyed it faded from the minds of men. But the land... the land never forgets.

The first village man built on these fields was called Gast-ham, a homage to the Spirit that pulled the pilgrims here. You can feel Him, still—though now He lingers just below the surface. He calls some of us in and pushes others away, communicating subconsciously with the darkness within us all like a terrible psychic soul magnet. He was stronger then, in that godforsaken age. Those first settlers, their souls open and raw from their fearful journey across the continent, heard His call and followed.

They practiced the Old Ways, letting the blood from their lambs feed the soil in thanks for His fruitfulness. They honored the Spirit and reaped His beneficence, though they knew not His true name. As the generations prospered, they soon replaced the Old Ways with the new religion, denying Him His rites and sacrifices. But He would hold them to their contract.

Death came to the village. It crawled across the continents, bursting from blackened pustules and weeping sores. The people felt safe in their hamlet, far removed from the diseased populations. But He called Death to them to affect his retribution. As Death stood at the boundary stone, He offered the people His mercy. Donning the visage of a beggar, He wandered the paths carved into his land. From door to door, He extended His hand. Each of His children forsook him, turning the beggar away. His rage grew along with His hunger, insatiable and burning. It was then He met Death at the boundary stone, welcoming him to His land.

The villagers' skin erupted in boils, blood foamed from the mouths that had once so greedily suckled from his teat. Panicked, the burning began. They lit the thatched roofs of the first infected. But He would not allow them to contain His revenge. He felled trees across the roads and gusted the embers from the burning homes across the rooftops of the village. He reveled in their fear and pain as the inferno consumed them.

By morning light, all that remained was ash and smoke. He opened the skies and rained down on the land, hissing as water met fire and earth. The ungrateful souls of the villagers seeped into the soil. He absorbed them all, letting them feel His hunger.

He waited as centuries passed, feeding on the lone wanderer, occasionally feasting on the blood of men in wartime when they marched across His domain, imbued with the stench of fear, gunpowder, and their glorious deadly gasses. But it wasn't until I found Him that He could feed as His hunger desired.

War came again to the continent—one for the entire world to remember. I was young then, a traveling nurse. But I was raised in the Old Ways and saw the power of our country's adversary, his vision and its possibilities. As I traveled from camp to camp, removing bullets and appendages, I sought out more knowledge about Him—what part I could play in His great design.

The chaos of war provided my education. So many men came into my hands for care. Most were not expected to survive and, therefore, would not be missed when I used their blood and bodies in my alchemical experimentation. I was only just mastering my craft when the war came to an end, cutting off my resources.

Before the final camp disbanded, I was at least able to perform the ritual which would start my life's work—making *you*.

I didn't think it worked, at first. The flames of my cadaver-fat candles barely flickered as the soldier's blood pooled around their wicks, there was no sound in the night as I finished reciting my evocation. I thought I had failed and, that night, I fell asleep feeling emptier than I had ever known.

That was when He spoke to me. Newly strengthened by the bloody battles, His voice echoed through my body. He needed more blood, more souls. He needed me to feed Him.

When I awoke, I left the camp and started walking. I traveled smoldering moors and battle scarred plains until I found Him.

I knew Him at once. A great, gaping maw in the land screamed for me. It was the scorched earth where the village once stood—barren, still, but surrounded by verdant fields and woodland.

I took to the city, plying my surgical skills in seedy back rooms on pathetic young women to remove the unwanted products of their one-night unions with soldiers now dead or otherwise unlikely to return. The little money secured me the land, and the leavings I collected fed my Master while His plan unfolded.

Eventually, I found some nameless, faceless corporation to build our little town, eager to drain soldier stipends into mortgages. It was one of the construction workers who gave me the idea to fill in the pit. We pumped the basin full of fresh water, creating the idyllic pond that would draw the people in. When it was filled, I invited the young construction worker to christen it with me. He was more than keen when I stripped off my clothes in the light of the full moon. I waded in and felt my Master's power. He was electric against my skin. I'll never know if the man felt Him too when we entwined ourselves in His waters. I was so overcome by His ecstasy as He worked His way into me with the water, as I pierced the man's flesh with my fingernails, as I held him under the water, giving him to my Master.

I thought that would be the final step, but it didn't take. Families flooded into the homes around His lilypond and the occasional missing child satiated Him. I tried again and again and again, but my womb was barren. My Master told me *I* would be the Mother of His New Flesh. It would be through *me* that He would walk once more among men. He knows all... but how can a barren woman bear His child?

As my body aged, His power weakened. He still called the darkest souls to Lilypond Lane—and, oh, did they come and oblige—but His voice faded until I could hear Him no more, left only with the aching feeling of His magnetic pull, left to my own devices.

I almost gave up, almost opened my veins in despair for my failure. But as I pressed the scalpel against my wrist, the glint of the metal summoned to my mind the answer to my question. I realized then: I have all the tools, the supply, I have evoked my Master with less experience than I now possess... I could mother His New Flesh without a womb of my own. There are ways. *Old Ways....*

I scoured the dusty shelves of bookstores and libraries until I found a grimoire with a promising recipe. I attended every service at the nearby church, every potluck, barbeque, and fete at Lilypond Lane. I donned flowery dresses, baked pies, volunteered with the Ladies' League. I created an image of a sweet old woman and passed unnoticed, as women my age often do, and all the while, I readied myself for the ritual. I whispered allusions to my post-war practice over tea with the stuck-up Christian bitches who soon sought my skills to alleviate their daughters of the embarrassment of unwed motherhood.

I scraped away their shame—my hopeful vessels for His New Flesh. Five times, I attempted the ritual. Five times, I failed. My hands trembled, my eyesight blurred as nature began to reclaim me through age, but I had to try again. I knew this would be my last chance... I could feel the cold breath of Death aching my marrow. I knew he would not wait much longer.

It was then I made pilgrimage to Chetham. In the library's audit room, I saw my Master's face, hewn in wood, smiling down on me from the crux of the ceiling panels. His glorious jaws joyfully devoured a nonbeliever. The librarian spoke of superstition and architecture but I knew this was no ordinary chimera—this was the true face of my Master, proudly overseeing my work. I found the book among the ancient tomes, chained with iron to the stacks where pretty little things with black lipstick and cobweb fishnets posed for Instagram. I had it pulled for me and delivered to the old oak table where He once revealed Himself to the famed alchemist, John Dee, burning His hoofprint into the wood. I traced the grooves of His hoof print with my fingers. The feeling was electric—like that first time I bathed in his waters. My fingers burned again as they found the page. He was showing me the way.

Had my fingers not felt like the tips of a Hand of Glory, burning as if ready to combust, I would have passed it by. It was not the recipe I sought... but another evocation, not unlike the one I first performed by the light of those soldiers' burning fat on that fateful night when I first heard His voice.

I transcribed the page word for word and sent out a silent prayer, gazing up at the carved wooden image of my Master before I returned to Lilypond Lane.

It took some time to find the right tools, to press my own paper from the pulp of the tree that overlooked the pond, its roots drinking from His waters. I cleared my kitchen table of the primrose-patterned place settings. I laid out the paper from the sacred tree and lit the candles I still kept from our first meeting. Reciting the words He spoke to John Dee, I carved His sigil into my left palm. The flames guttered, then swelled into great pillars of burning light as I read the final words of the incantation. I pressed my bleeding palm to the virgin parchment and, for an ecstatic moment, I felt His hand upon my own, sweeping it across the page. The unnatural light seared my retinas. A suffocating, inky blackness drowned my vision. His hands closed my eyes, anointing me. When I opened them again, the lights had died to their natural glow. I gazed at the page bathed in my own blood. As I traced where I had carved his sigil on my palm, I discovered it was no longer there. He had healed me. I marveled at my restored flesh in awe of His power until the bloody page stole my attention. The smears receded before my eyes… the parchment was absorbing my offering. I watched, rapt, as the paper was made pure once more. Then… it happened. The words began to appear—words written in my blood, written by my Master's own unseen hand.

When the flames burned out, I had my recipe.

Through the New Flesh shall I be born again of myself, of my land, of my waters, of man's blood and pain.
Mother of the New Flesh, grow my spirit a cage so that I may be freed of my earthly prison – freed to walk among men and turn their souls toward my Darkness.
Walk, my Pilgrim, the breadth of my domain. Let my waters guide you to the artifacts of my touch upon this place. Work the craft I have taught you with these remnants of my Power – through them, I shall be Born again.
Ashes of a Soul Incorporeal and Discontented
The Wyrm-Maddened Mind
Tooth of the Beast who devoured his master
The ever-breaking Heart
The Ear haunted by the sound of Violence
The Tongue that has tasted human Flesh
The Eyes of the Beholder, one White, one Yellow
The deposed Crown of an Innocent
The Right Hand of the False Prophet
The Womb of the Matriarch
Devil's Berries, Six by Six by Six
The Ledger of My Works upon this Land
The Foot of My Faithful Pilgrim
Mother of the New Flesh, this Trial is yours alone to bear. Serve me.

I traced my fingers over the words until they were numb, hoping to feel the shadow of my Master's hand, turning the words over in my mind. Where would I find all my snips and snails and puppy dog tails? If only His needs had been that simple....

I wracked my brain and suddenly it came to me: *"the Beast who devours his master."* It was an unforgettable event, even here. That doctor, with his shiny cars and fancy gadgets, who built the first of the McMansions in the newest development on Lilypond Lane, encroaching ever closer to my Master's waters—he was surely the "master" of whom He spoke. And the beast... I knew where it was but it wasn't alone. How would I know which one was the *right* one? My Master provided my answer: *"Let my Waters guide you...."*

I jumped to my feet and pulled my cookbooks from the shelf beside the range. *The Ladies' League of Lilypond Lane Recipe Book, Country Cooking, Pies and Pasties*—I tossed them across the kitchen, their pages fluttering like giant moths in the candlelight as they flew. My heart pounded as I uncovered the laminated booklet. *Recipes*, it read in my own handwriting. Unassuming and painfully ordinary from the outside, the contents contained within enumerated the many tricks I'd picked up while honing my craft. Remember, dear, *never judge a book by its cover.*

In its pages, I found the spell I needed. I collected water from my Master's lilypond in my thermos—not exactly the most fitting receptacle, but I would need to blend in. The city zoo stank of sweating tourists and excrement. These places fill me with unease—how the caged beasts stare, wide-eyed, as if I'm the one behind the bars. Luckily, I found the creature's enclosure devoid of spectators. You could only just make out their bodies below the murky waters of their artificial swamp. Ensuring I was alone, I removed the cap of my thermos and pierced my finger with the back of my earring, squeezing until a fat drop of blood fell into the water.

It rippled as I whispered the sacred words. My blood did not dissolve, but formed into a solid ball, swimming in frenzied circles until it stopped at the 10 o'clock position. I followed the trajectory of the blood drop and watched as the shadow in the swamp rose to the surface. The creature's eyes emerged, wet and withering in their gaze as they turned toward me.

The beast glided toward where I stood at the edge of his enclosure, the blood drop tracking his movements like the arrow of a compass. Water trickled from his scales as the crocodile crawled from the water's edge. His great jaws yawned wide, almost smiling. A muddy, reptilian stench emanated from the cavernous mouth stretching open just beyond the bars. With trembling hands, I reached into the cavity. A deep rumbling came from the pit of his body. The creature laughed as my fingers pried a yellowed tooth from his gums.

I pocketed my totem, wiping his slime on my floral skirt. A shudder reverberated through my body when the crocodile's jaws snapped shut. The beast turned back to the water, smiling as he looked back at me before disappearing into the muck.

One down.

Invigorated by my first success, my next target came to mind almost immediately. I was replacing the scattered cookbooks on their designated shelf when the identity of my next totem became clear. *The Ladies' League of Lilypond Lane Recipe Book*. Of course! Sandra never would share her secret recipe, the favorite of many a potluck. How crafty she thought she had been, thinking she had everyone fooled. And she did... everyone but me, of course. Then again, how many people know human meat when they taste it?

I visited my old friend at her new home. Sandra slumped in a wheelchair, withered by age and weight loss. She wouldn't have even noticed me—dazed and delirious, stuck in her own self-pity—had she not smelled my offering. How her eyes glistened when the warm meat and pastry awakened her senses. They had her on a vegetarian diet, poor thing. What she wouldn't give for just one more taste, she told me. So, I made my case and, unsurprisingly, she agreed.

I gave her more than a taste—I sat beside her as she devoured the entire pie, dark sauce dripping from her wrinkled, quivering lips.

"I can die happy now," she told me as she dropped the fork into the empty pie dish, bloated and euphoric in gluttonous ecstasy.

She reclined in her chair, tipping back her head in blissful resignation. I made my cut deep and fast—a final gift to an old kindred spirit. She gurgled as the blood flowed and I wondered if she enjoyed the taste of it as it filled her throat and lungs.

When her convulsions ceased, I pulled my prize out through the bleeding gash, sawing it free. The bloody muscle oozed, mingling her blood with the saucy remnants of the pie when I dropped it into the dish, covering it with foil.

❧ ❧ ❧ ❧

It was some time before the next success in my scavenger hunt. The totem announced itself in the early hours of a hot night. A thundering blast reverberated down the lane, waking me from a fitful sleep. Sirens and the smell of fire found their way through my opened window. I watched from my porch as the blaze lit the night sky like an early, orange dawn. It wasn't until I saw the ashes carried on the wind, falling like black snow, that I realized what I needed to do.

I consulted the water and, sure enough, the blood pointed toward the smoldering carcass of the house down the lane.

I waited until the fire engines left and onlookers dispersed. When I was alone with the still-smoking remains of my neighbors' home, I slid off my slippers and walked through the ashes. Among the ruins, I found a single picture, barely singed by the inferno. Two women—a mother and daughter—smiled at me from the glossy image.

I had heard about Rissa and Peri, though I had yet to meet our new neighbors. I heard the whispered stories about their troubles—the mother's odd behavior, the endless stream of plumbers. The woman had confided in a member of the HOA about how the house seemed to have a mind of its own. It seems she was right. Our very own Amityville. I smiled as the embers warmed my feet. I used the photograph to scoop the ashes into a Ziploc baggie and returned home to consult my Master's list.

❧ ❧ ❧ ❧

Looking between my list and the picture I stole from the fire's ruins, something about the mother and daughter echoed in my mind. I closed my eyes and moved my finger in circles, bringing it down on a random spot on the page.

"*The Wyrm Maddened Mind*." Of course, yes! Poor little Paige, orphaned in a moment of madness. I just read about her sentencing in the paper—she would have so many years ahead of her locked in that penitentiary.

I knew how I would get what I needed. Bible in hand, they let me walk right in. The pretense of praying with the lost souls and my unassuming appearance persuaded the guards to overlook my bag as they checked me in, and thankfully so, for if they had found my instruments, I might have ended up as an inmate rather than a visitor.

They took me to her solitary cell. She had been there since her imprisonment began to protect the other inmates from her violent outbursts. I assured the guard I would be fine on my own with the girl, being she was confined in a straightjacket. After rambling on and on about the "glory" and the "power" as he stewarded me through the prison's halls, he was more than ready to take his leave of me.

Paige regarded me, wild-eyed, as I stepped into the cell. Dark circles ringed her eyes and her hair was matted in damp clots around her head. When she saw the bible in my hand, she turned away, rubbing her head furiously against the wall of her cell. It was then I realized the damp in her hair and on the walls was not sweat, but blood.

I opened the bible and read aloud: “I am a wyrm, and not a man: a shame of men, and the contempt of the people....” The girl turned, watching me with her maddened gaze.

Her lips began to move and sound slowly followed as her chant crescendoed: “Worm, worm, worm, worm....”

“Yes, the great Wyrm, the Serpent, devouring all, the unbreakable circle...”

“Worm, worm, in my brain, worm in my head, in my brain, in my head, worm, worm...” the girl rubbed her head violently against the wall, widening the dark, wet stain.

“You let Him in, Paige. You let the Wyrm inside.”

“Worm, worm, get it out, out, get it out!” She pounded her head against the wall. I ran to buffer the blow, placing my hand on the bloody side of her head. She nuzzled my hand, seeking to use my fingers to scratch that insatiable itch.

“Listen to me!” I whispered coarsely. I could hear the distant jingle of keys as the guard grew closer, attracted by the sound. “I can remove Him, but you must play along!”

The girl’s eyes widened with hope and she shook her head, consenting just as the guard came to the doorway.

“All right in here, ma’am?”

“Of course! This lost soul has consented to a baptism so she can be found again. Glory be to him!” I responded, moving my hand from the side of her head to the top. “Will you join us for the ceremony?”

“Er- no thank you, ma’am, on duty...” and with that, the man was gone again.

I unpacked my tools and got to work. The trauma resulting from the girl's incessant rubbing effectively numbed her scalp, and she offered no resistance as I peeled the skin from the front of her skull. She continued to mutter under her breath as I bored into her cranium with the trephine, only stopping when the circular piece of bone detached.

Her eyelashes fluttered lazily. Calm overtook her tortured face. Using my sugar spoon, I reached into the opening, swirling through the soft matter. I removed a spoonful of her pale, pink frontal lobe and deposited it into the awaiting jam jar I had washed out that morning.

Floating in the pond water in the jar, I marveled as the pink organ faded to foggy grey.

The source of her affliction now extracted, pain flinched the girl's eyebrows as I rejoined her scalp with my needle and thread. Luckily, she could do little now but grimace as I completed my operation. When I finished, I smoothed her matted hair over the incision.

As I smiled down at the girl, a single, grateful tear rolled down her cheek, landing in her slack, silent mouth.

Siren chasing might as well be the official pastime here on Lilypond Lane. The morbid curiosity gets to us all, given how often they scream through our quiet streets. Now, however, I have a purpose beyond my own amusement when I join the throng of rubber-necker.

As they pulled the young man from the pond, his cracked skull weeping brain matter and pond water, I watched the faces of my neighbors rather than the wonderfully gruesome scene on my Master's banks. She stood out at once—she was the only other person whose eyes were not fixed on the boy's body. Not only was she not looking, her eyes were pinched closed as if in pain... her hands covered her ears, protecting them from what I do not know as the crowd was hushed, silent in their terror and awe.

I knew her face. I had seen it in the framed pictures hanging in Camilla's home. Camilla was an odd bird. Such a sweet tooth that woman had, but there was something sour, something dark just below the surface. Perhaps that's why I liked her so much—that, and her generous pours in her boozy hot chocolate. What was the girl's name...? Katarina...? Yes, that was it.

It was only a matter of days before the invitation for dear Camilla's funeral arrived. I attended, of course, watching the girl from my pew. She was paler now than I remembered, shaken and perturbed. Haunted.

At the reception luncheon, I was able to corner her to test my theory. I found her tucked into the corner of Camilla's oversized couch, occasionally twitching as if alerting to an alarm only she could hear. When I dropped myself onto the cushion beside her, her body trembled. She calmed as I made small talk. "Oh, what a lovely service... don't you just look the spit of her... have you tried the cucumber sandwiches?"

I reached for the bowl of walnuts on the table and squeezed the shell between the tongs of the metal cracker. *Crack*. The girl's eyes went wide as her hands shot up from her lap to cover her ears.

"No, no, no…" she soothed herself as she trembled. That useless mother of hers pulled her away to some private room, but I knew I had found my next totem. Before I could retrieve it, however, I will need to find another: Devil's Berries.

In a town like this, I did not doubt I'd find my Master's fruit in one of the many white picket gardens along the lane. I took my thermos as I walked the curving road, following where the blood waters led me.

It was not the type of house I had expected. Yes, generally the homes here are well kept, even picturesque, but to see that savage, deadly fruit growing on such a perfectly trimmed bush came as a surprise.

The woman toiled amongst the flowers, snipping branches in millimeter increments with her pruning shears. Her white gloves bore not a single mark of the immense work it must have taken to achieve such perfection from dirt and leaves. A woman like this certainly knew what grew in her garden, yet among the lilies and roses, there they were… how very interesting.

I waited for her to finish her work and reenter her home, following some silent ritual involving turning her doorknob seven times before she could open it. When I heard the water running inside, I let myself in through her garden gate, careful to step lightly so as not to make a sound as I walked the gravel path winding between her plants.

I held my breath, listening for any movement inside the house as I approached the perfectly square bush by the door. She was running a bath, I could do as I pleased without interruption.

I plucked my 18 berries, beautifully black, their skins shiny and taut, close to bursting from their contents. Surely, she will notice the loss of so many berries, but what would she do about it? I laughed to myself as I pulled a red rose from the bush by the gate, inhaling its sweet scent as I closed the gate behind me.

A few days later, I sought out Katarina. She was hesitant at first but softened when I presented my thermos of hot chocolate and slipped the bottle of rum out of my bag. I poured the chocolate into mugs as we sat in her kitchen. When I twisted the cap of the rum, the seal made a soft *crack.* Katarina jolted in her chair, hands flying to her ears. As they did so, she shook the table, causing the hot chocolate to slosh out of her mug.

I cleaned the girl's mess, comforting her as I did so. I told her I could clean up other messes too... *bigger* messes. I know she knew what I meant. I told her bits and pieces—about the craft, my nursing days, about how I have healed broken people using the Old Ways.

So trusting, she was. Though, maybe that was more the effect of the belladonna steeped in her chocolate than anything else. Either way, she went with me willingly to the bedroom where I laid her down and watched her drift to sleep. When peace overcame her haunted expression, I removed my scalpel from my bag. At least now the poor thing will never have to hear whatever haunts her again. Though, she'll want to grow out her hair to cover up the empty space where her ear once was.

❧ ❧ ❧ ❧

I watched the waters in the bowl every night and in my thermos throughout every day, waiting for the blood to lead me. It was a lazy Sunday when it moved again.

I knew the house where it led me, but the occupant I had known was long gone. I didn't recognize the woman rushing to the sleek car in the driveway, at first. Later, I would find she was the chubby, sullen little girl who once lived there years before. I waited as she peeled out of the driveway and disappeared down the lane before I made my way into the house. It reeked of mold and fresh paint.

The blood dove to the bottom corner of the thermos. Navigating piles of rotting newspapers and unpacked boxes, I found the stairwell to the basement. Faint, pathetic whimpers called me deeper into the basement. The blood swung frantically to the side, indicating a rusted metal door, caked in dust and cobwebs.

I found the latch and pulled. The rusted hinges screamed open, flooding the black recess behind it with the buzzing fluorescent overhead light.

She cowered, cradling herself, as she rocked on the floor beside a bare mattress. The young woman blinked doe-like eyes, bloodshot and fearful as they adjusted to the light. Shock overtook her tear-stained face.

"Who are you?" she managed through sniffles.

Curious. One would think a woman in a place like this would run into the arms of any stranger willing to open the door to her prison. I asked if she was well, if she needed help. Her answer was stranger still.

She assured me she was fine, begged me not to call the police, not to get involved. When I mentioned the other woman, heat rose in her cheeks.

"She didn't hurt me. She didn't mean it... we- I had an accident. She'll take care of me when she comes home. She loves me... she's my wife."

Ah, my broken, bleeding heart.

I could have used the hammer resting on the shelf, or offered her some water dosed with belladonna. But, looking into the woman's eyes, I knew none of that would be necessary. Instead, I pulled up a folding chair to the mouth of the door. We spoke of love, of need. I asked her what the other woman could do to lose her love. She took no time to answer.

"Nothing."

"And does she love you back?" The question registered like a gunshot in her heart.

"I know she does..." she trailed off, her voice warbling with uncertainty.

"But does she love *you*... the way you love her? Does her heart break for you?" The woman looked back at me dumb, numb, vacant. "Do you want her to?" My words illuminated a light behind her eyes, a hope kindled in the darkness of her unrequited grief.

"How?" Her voice tremored.

"You must give her your heart." Oh, am I not clever?

"She has it! She's always had it!" Tears sprung anew. "I can't prove it anymore than I can rip it out myself and hand it to her."

I merely had to smile and wait as she absorbed her own words.

"I'll do it- I'll do it and she'll know... she'll never doubt me again." She stood in her prison, shaking with excitement. She whispered to herself. "Then she'll miss me...."

She only managed two deep cuts before the blood loss weakened her too much to continue. When she fell to the ground, her bloody hands falling limply from the handle of the blade, I did the rest.

I closed the door behind me, wondering when the curvy woman would discover her wife, what she would do about it having put her down there herself. In the weeks that followed, police never came. The house never hit the market, so she must have decided to stay. I guess it's true what they say: *home is where the heart is*.

The blood stirred again on the hottest day of the summer. I feigned reading a trashy paperback by the lilypond as I watched the women at the nearby house drink themselves into a stupor. Every single one of them ate too little of the charred barbeque and drank too much of the cheap wine—all except the stoic older woman watching them all. She carried herself with an air of significance, graceful and light regardless of her age and the heavy, clunky jewelry weighting each arm.

The women deferred to her and she imbibed their attention with the same fervor with which they drowned themselves in wine. I had watched them all arrive one-by-one for their weekend retreat. They wanted to be healed of their individual, private wounds and thought this woman, this *impersonator*, could heal them.

I lingered after the ambulances left with the last woman. The false prophet switched on a dime, playing dumb to the EMT's as if she were just an ordinary housewife with a crystal collection, not the cunning thing she really was. When she saw me, I watched her change back into that cunning woman she was at heart—cunning sees cunning.

She welcomed me into the now-vacant home and offered me a glass of herbal iced tea. Surely, she didn't think I would be that easy to get rid of. I took the glass and smelled its contents.

"Verbena, mint, apple..." she raised her thinly painted eyebrows as I described the concoction, impressed. "... and the faint but unmistakable odor of fly agaric." I placed the glass between us, holding her gaze.

"I see you know your herbs." She made an attempt to seem unperturbed.

"I know much more than herbs." I smiled. "As do you, it seems."

The woman smiled coyly, arching an indignant eyebrow.

"I have a gift-" the woman was poised to begin some oft-recited diatribe. I didn't let her.

"No, dear. *I* have the gift." With all her pomposity, she recognized the truth in my words and knew not to argue. "Why are you here? I mean *here*—on Lilypond Lane."

"I am leading a retreat-"

"No, dear. Not anymore, at least." I chuckled. "I mean, what *brought* you here? If you had any trace of the gift, you would know, wouldn't you?" A violent blush rose in her cheeks but the woman fought the muscles of her face not to betray her rage. "Oh, don't feel bad, dear. Not everyone is born with the gift. Some people have to earn it."

"Oh?"

"You didn't just come to Lilypond Lane... you were *brought* here. By Him." There was a pregnant stillness between us. "I can't see why..." I sighed, "based on your work here... but it's not my place to question His plan. And, yes, it seems you *are* part of His plan."

"And what 'plan' is that?" she intonated the quotations, as if I couldn't see through her sarcasm, couldn't see her hunger for power, that hunger which already had her eating out of my hand.

"The ritual to ordain the great prophet of His word, of course. Clearly, He has chosen you. Have you really not felt Him calling you to the helm of His ministry?" Her eyes glinted as a smile crawled along the wide edges of her mouth.

"Of course I've felt Him. Why else would I come out to the suburbs!" Lying comes easily to this woman. I had to restrain myself from laughing—she had no idea what lurked in this little suburb.

"Clearly... well, shall we get started?" I placed a bottle on the counter beside the sweating glass of untouched iced tea. She eyed it nervously. "Your communion—sage for wisdom, rosemary for clarity, mint to facilitate communication with His Spirit... I'm sorry there isn't much ceremony to this—you know how few we are in numbers these days. That's why we need you ordained now, the sooner the better, to be our priestess, prophet—our leader."

What reservations her better judgment held onto were wiped away with those last words. She drank the potion down fast—and thank Him she did or she might have tasted the distinctive almond flavor of the heaping helping of arsenic.

I instructed her to hold the prophet's pose: to raise her right hand, extending three fingers, before lowering it onto the table between us, pointing her fingers down in our blasphemy of the trinity. That was when the arsenic began to take hold. Her eyelids shot open, eyes bulging in terror as her throat constricted. She shook as bloody foam frothed from her lips. Before she could move, I retrieved the heavy butcher knife from my purse and swung it down on her wrist, severing her hand with a single, bone-crushing blow.

The arsenic closed her throat against her screams. Spittle sprayed from her grimacing mouth and blood jetted from her severed stump with each pump of her heart, receding as her pulse faded into nothingness. I left her face-dow in her own pooling blood.

I turned over the phrase in my mind: *"The Eyes of the Beholder, one White, one Yellow."*

Lilypond Lane had no shortage of Peeping Toms, any one of them could be my *"Beholder."* But *"one White, one Yellow"*... what could that mean? I had a hunch about the identity of my voyeur. He had lived on Lilypond Lane for some decades and was rarely, if ever, seen without his binoculars.

But as I surveyed Thomas Geyer's house, the blood was still in the waters of my thermos. That was until one balmy early spring morning. It had been frigid and wet for days on end, but the first buds were starting to force their way through the chilled bones of the barren trees.

I watched as they wheeled Thomas Geyer's sheet-covered corpse out of the home. The blood followed the ambulance as it disappeared down the lane.

I followed my Master's compass to the funeral home, where the corpse was being prepared. I was lucky the old man was set for cremation following a closed casket—the eyes I needed would still be there when the mortician finished his work and no one would be the wiser once I finished mine.

Once the final attendant left, I let myself in. Though he locked the main doors, the loading bay must have slipped his mind. It was all too easy to follow the blood to the simple pine casket. Inside, Geyer's arthritic claws were crossed across his chest, his sallow, grey face, sunken by age and lifelessness, was set in a grim frown.

I pried the lid of his right eye open, revealing the bumpy eye cap the mortician had inserted to keep the corpse's eyes closed. Leveling my scalpel under its edge, I popped it out, revealing the milky white orb beneath it. *"One White."* I needed the eyeball intact, so I pocketed the blade and retrieved the melon baller from my purse. The enucleation was swift. Once I applied enough pressure to slip the melon baller into place, the cataracted eye popped right into the cup of my instrument. Twisting away the connective sinew, I freed the eyeball from its socket with a satisfying *pop.*

However, when I removed the eye cap from the second eye, the orb staring back at me was white, not yellow... this wasn't right.

I opened my thermos and consulted the blood. It swirled again before pointing back in the direction of Lilypond Lane. I packed the gaping, raw socket with cotton before replacing the eye cap and closing the cadaver's eyes, leaving everything to appear as I had found it. I had one eye but, now, I needed the other.

As I approached the home, the blood stilled. It wasn't time. Yet.

Only a few days passed before I was led to there again. The pretty nurse I had seen before and the old man's son, Tom, Jr., left in mourning clothes for the funeral.

The blood instructed me through the house and into the old man's room. It stank of antiseptic and shoe polish—polish-stained newspaper by the closet marked the smell's origin. The blood prompted me to open the closet where I discovered the back wall had been opened, revealing a hidden room. What secrets this town holds.... I marveled at the collection before me. Eggs. *"Yellow eye,"* of course! But there were so many of them, which one could it be?

I let out a frustrated sigh. Gathering myself, I looked at the floor where I saw a metal box, the lid partially open. The blood's trajectory indicated to it. Inside, I found pictures of children—babies—little curls of hair taped to the reverse side of their photographs. The aged tape released the shiny, black lock from the first photograph. It was so soft between my fingers. When I closed my eyes, I could smell that sweet baby scent between the strands.

I looked to the blood again and, to my shock, it swam in circles as if searching. I pocketed the lock of hair and held my thermos with both hands. The blood suddenly stilled, pressed against the side of the receptacle, pointing to the window.

There was nothing there. I patted the wall, hoping for some hidden latch to another secret room but found none. The blood vibrated violently in the water, nearly jumping out of the open mouth of the thermos.

I ran out of the room, down the hall, through the kitchen, following the blood across the yard and to the water's edge. I looked around but saw nothing in the morning fog nestling the pond. Then, I heard it. Something rustled inside the dew-soaked tall grass on the bank. As I parted the grass with my hand, a blood-red eye burst from the overgrowth followed by a sharp squawk screamed through a bone-white beak.

The terrible bird lunged toward me, fluttering its wings and holding out its chest. Swinging my bag, I shooed it away. That whining squawk echoed across the pond as it reluctantly withdrew from the brush.

I parted the grasses again, finding the treasure the bird had attempted to protect. Nestled in the grass was a single, speckled egg. "*Yellow eye.*"

Three ingredients remained and time was waning. I couldn't rely on my own cunning anymore. I took to keeping a bowl of His water on my kitchen table. My blood sank like a lead weight to the bottom and rested there for days while I waited for a sign.

One calm evening, I sipped a nightcap in the low light of my kitchen. It was late, and I intended to tuck in shortly when I saw the waters ripple. The blood swirled in a manic spiral, winding my nerves up as I followed its frantic movements. It vibrated urgently in the 2 o'clock position.

Donning my dark overcoat, I pulled on the wellies beside my door and carried the bowl out into the night. The blood led me forward, winding down the lane and through backyards and gardens until I found myself at the backdoor of Cecil Wallace's house. Knowing the old man's reputation, I had to stifle a snort when I heard the pounding steps of approaching feet progress toward the door. I crouched down in the hedge as a gaunt, filthy woman threw the back door open, a little girl barely keeping up behind her as she pulled the child through the darkened threshold. Another woman, reeking of urine, followed.

I assumed I would only have a matter of seconds before police arrived. My heart pounded.

The three huddled together, struggling for breath between sobs. Their own personal drama was the perfect distraction as I stopped the door with the toe of my wellie before it closed and slipped through the door unnoticed.

It was too dark inside the house to see the blood, but I only had to follow Cecil's voice to find my prize. I made my way through the basement as quickly as my wellied feet could carry me until I met the locked vault door, my heart sinking as I appraised its impenetrability. I whispered a prayer to my Master and, lo-and-behold, He answered—not in words, but with a mechanical *click*, unlocking the vault. The heavy door creaked open and old man Wallace's groans grew louder.

He ceased his wails when he saw me. Oh, how he begged me to pass him the keys at my feet. Pleading, playing the victim, spinning a tale of imprisonment by a deranged gang of home invaders. I only laughed at the old man. "I know you, Cecil," I chuckled, "and you are right where you belong."

His eyes darkened, and he raged against his cage. The blood pointed to the door at the end of the room and I followed it, ignoring the curses shouted after me.

"Oh, Mr. Wallace, you have been busy," I taunted as I took in the macabre collection. But what among these things would I need? I consulted the blood, moving the bowl around the room until it jumped in the water. This was it. Beside Cecil's throne of bones, a little cup of tea rested atop a stack of books. This was not an ordinary teacup. The cranial sutures gave it away immediately. I held the little sawed-off calvaria in one hand and my bowl in the other.

"Deposed Crown of an Innocent."

I had no time to celebrate my victory, expecting the police to swarm the home at any moment. I dumped its contents onto the floor and tucked the tiny skull into my jacket, preparing to outrun the coming sirens. But, as I stepped back into Cecil's garden, all was silent in the darkness. No one was coming for him. Chuckling to myself, I took my time returning home, enjoying the stillness of the night. If only my sleeping neighbors knew what was coming.

I only had two more totems to go. It was no surprise when the blood led me to Eliza's house. That nosey old bitch was always watching—a certified busy body. She must have kept a ledger. What *did* surprise me was the spectacle I witnessed when I rounded the bend to her home.

What a performance that girl gave. I nearly believed her myself. But, while crocodile tears may move a policeman, I'm a bit more cunning than that. I did my research on Miss Elwyn—or, as the officer referred to her, Miss Katherine Kelley.

Actresses always are the easiest targets. All that glitz, all that glamour, that all-possessing need for fame. *That* was my way in. No need for any big messes here, by the time we've finished our tea, she'll hand the book right over.

It was harder than expected, though, to receive an invitation. The damned girl made me talk to her through a video camera by her doorbell before she'd even open the door. In the end, I feigned interest in the old woman's hideous décor. Apparently, the girl was eager to sell—I hadn't expected a Hollywood type to have taste, but this girl was full of surprises.

When I came clean about my interests not lying in her great-aunt's kitschy furnishings, but, rather, her ledger, she asked me to leave, glancing at the knife block on the counter more than once. She must know what the ledger contains.

"What use is an old woman's diary to you now?" I smiled calmly.

"What use is it to *you*?" Oh, this one has spunk.

"Do you know what it contains?" I saw the question she wanted to ask in her eyes: whether or not *I* knew its contents and, if so, how? "Do you think having it—having the knowledge in it—will do you any good? Give you any *power*, perhaps?"

"Leverage is leverage." The girl crossed her arms, as if she wasn't itching to grab the nearest knife.

"Ah... 'leverage'... yes, leverage can be a useful tool. But only if the people you wield it against can benefit you. And who, dear, on Lilypond Lane, could be of any benefit to a big Hollywood actress?"

"How did-" clearly she thought her oversized sunglasses were enough to keep her incognito. "Who do you-?"

"Who do I think I am? Oh, darling, I'm the woman who can help you go from starlet to star. J-Lo to Joan Crawford." She laughed, snorting as the laughter erupted from her.

"That's a new one. What were you, the third-string seamstress for Judy Garland or something?"

"No, dear. I'm no one." My candor stilled her laughter. "But I can make you a deal. It's a deal all the greats have taken. Crawford, Garland, Taylor, Kelly... *Monroe*. Do you really think a man with a face like Humphry Bogart's could be a leading man on talent alone?" I had her attention now.

"What? Are you gonna offer me stardom in exchange for my soul?"

"He doesn't need your soul, dear. You have what you so eloquently term as 'leverage.' He'll give you eternal fame, a star never-fading, and you can keep your soul. All he wants is your book."

"How do you even know about-?"

"I know nothing but what *He* tells me... and *He* knows All. About. You. He knows why you're still hiding out here. He knows that your star is fading–nearing burnt out from what I hear." I tut consolingly. "And what a shame. With that little something special, you could have been somebody."

I turned to leave. I barely made it to that grotesque golden peacock before she stopped me.

"What are you going to do with it? With the book...?" She chewed her lip, deepening the lines starting to form around her mouth.

"Why, I'm going to boil it, dear."

Like I said, the easiest targets.

This was it. The final totem before my own.

I waited for this one until the very end. I needed to ensure everything else was in order. Things like ears and tongues keep quite well in the freezer with enough foil, but the womb–that had to be *fresh*. Now, nearly nine months since the night my Master wrote to me, it was time to make the new Matriarch's acquaintance.

Usually, I would have had to contend with a whole vicious brood before I could get to her, but the new girl made things so much more streamlined, cleaning house just before the time came to meet her.

The beautiful thing about this particular psychopath is that she knows she's a psychopath. She saw the sickness in her family and she wiped them all out. But that narcissism, that defining characteristic of a League blue blood, wouldn't let her turn the gun on herself. She would see their line end with her but that sickness just wouldn't let her pull that trigger.

"Don't worry, dear. I understand."

"How could you understand? I've never even seen you in the League—how do you even know about us, about me?" She wasn't shaken by my knowledge of what she was and what she had done, but hostile at my presumption to question it.

"I was a member once upon a time." I thought of the first Matriarch, my dear departed cousin. We both learned from our grandmother, though she had clearly been the family favorite. I learned the Old Ways while she decided to make something new. But now we see how well that worked out....

"They don't just let people out. You would know that if-"

"Of course, you're correct, generally speaking. But, alas, they found no use for me."

"And they just let you, what? Retire?" She held her head high but the tightness of her muscles as she crossed her legs and arms evidenced her unease.

"Oh no. In fact, I'm still quite busy with the work the League makes for me."

"How's that?"

"I have a particular skill they find themselves in need of calling upon whenever one of their young men... loses his senses."

"What skill is that?"

"I clean up other peoples' messes. I've cleaned up quite a bit for your family over the years, in fact. Do you know how many of your nieces and nephews I've scraped out of girls in the last decade alone? Honestly, I've lost count."

"You're an abortionist...."

"Among other things. But yes, that is my only remaining use to the League after I failed my initiation. I couldn't carry a child to term, either, so holding onto me for the breeding was pointless." I saw a twinge of discomfort pierce through Aimee's body at the mention of motherhood. No doubt, that was to be her fate until this dark horse turned the whole game on its head. Good for her. "For as proud as we Leaguers are, it's such a barbaric practice, isn't it? We all defer to a woman, our Matriarch, our unquestioned leader, but the rest of us women are treated as nothing more than chattel to be sold off and bred out to that season's winning stallion. Shameful.... Well, anyway, I was put out to pasture when I couldn't conceive. Lucky me."

"Lucky you...." I watched the gears begin to turn in her mind.

"You know... I don't have to tell *you*, though. You're a bright young woman."

"Tell me what?"

"Well... the Matriarch isn't expected to just lead. She must build the family line."

"I answer to no one. If you haven't noticed, I'm the only one left of the line."

"Of *your* line, dear. But what about the others? Do you think they'd allow your house to end with you? When they have sons and brothers ready to stud?" A shadow of fear passed over the girl's face as my words sank in. She knew I was right. "You *could* fight them off, of course, I know. Look what you've done already! But they won't stop trying. How long do you think you can keep fighting?"

"What do you propose I do? I assume you have a proposal."

"What if you couldn't give them what they're after?"

"If I couldn't conceive...?" She paused, considering the options before her. "And you could do that?" I nodded solemnly over my teacup as I drained its contents. "When?"

"No time like the present."

I made quick work of it in her kill room, stitching her up nicely after I was done. I left her with a bottle of oxycodone and my best wishes, taking her unwanted womb in my medical bag.

I had little time to prepare the final item before my appointment arrived.

Sinking into the bathtub, I tied the tourniquet tightly around my ankle. Anesthetized only by the adrenaline of being nearer to seeing my Master reborn, I got to hacking.

I filled my largest pot with my Master's waters. As the temperature rose, I added the totems. I held Katarina's ear to my own like a seashell, hoping to hear the ghost of whatever horror haunted her for myself. It was cold against my skin and silent. I dangled it by the sterling silver hoop piercing the lobe above my nearly completed potion.

A knock came to the door. Dropping the ear into the pot, I hobbled away from my bubbling brew to answer it. The pinched-faced church lady clutched her daughter's shoulder, her eyes darting around in search of onlookers.

"Come in, come in."

I recognized the girl as one of the noisy teenagers in Katarina's old flock. She was subdued now, nervously stepping into my kitchen as I shuffled toward the stove.

"Your foot-" her mother began.

I looked down to my bandaged stub. Blood had begun to seep through the gauze.

"Nothing to worry about. Diabetes, you know...." I mashed the black berries in my mortar as I spoke, emptying them into the pot. I ladled a spoonful of the steaming brew into Cecil's teacup, offering it to the girl. Her nose wrinkled at the smell. "You'll need to drink that up before we get started. You'll regret it if you don't."

"There's no narcotic in there, is there? No painkillers?" This woman truly detested her daughter.

"Just some herbs to relax the womb and purge the blood." I turned to the girl, still staring at the cup. "And there *will* be blood. Blood is cleansing—don't let it startle you." Her eyes were wide with fear. I leaned in to whisper in her ear, "And there's a bit o' something to take the edge off."

The girl forced herself to consume the concoction. I watched it burn down to her belly as she swallowed. The mother took the cup from her daughter, turning it in her hand.

"What an unusual piece..."

"Rare bone China," I smiled, taking the skull back before she had a chance to inspect it further.

The ritual had now begun.

I carved His sigil into the tender flesh, her mother holding the girl down on my table as I worked.

"Pain purifies," the woman repeated as I continued my work, removing the growth from her womb.

I couldn't get the pair out of my kitchen fast enough. My wound was weeping through the wrappings, making me dizzy. I had to complete the ritual now, as the full moon climbed to its zenith.

Inside the still-warm womb, I placed the fleshy blob I had just secured. Over it, I laid the rich, yellow yolk before filling the womb with my broth. I threaded a needle with that unknown child's soft, black hair and sewed the organ shut. The neat, little bundle just fit in the teacup. I ladled more brew over the homunculus and recited my infernal prayer.

In the full moonlight, I made my way across the field to my Master's waters. They were dark and still as if waiting for me, reflecting the cold, white moon: a beacon drawing me in.

Navigating weeds and rocks, I stumbled toward His grassy bank. His waters were cool against my bleeding wound.

Lifting the living seed to the sky, I recited the words again and again. On the sixth repetition, I lowered the teacup to the surface of the waters. It floated--its contents glistening in the moonlight.

When I spoke the final words, the still surface rippled. The ground beneath me rumbled. The tremor grew, reverberating through my entire body, creating a whirlpool in the previously calm waters. The homunculus spun in the teacup at the vortex of the waves, picking up speed until it became a blur, then was sucked down into the water.

The water was now inky black—impossibly black—thicker than velvet, deeper than space. In the center of the pond, a small light glowed. It was a flower, a lily, perched atop a broad lilypad. It glowed from within its closed petals, radiating an ever-intensifying light. It pulsed and throbbed and, with it, so did the petals of the flower which melded together, reconstituting their organic matter into a beautiful, pulsing organ.

The chirr of beetles rose in a cacophony of sound, echoed by lightless thunder which boomed overhead. The horrible concert swelled until my ears rang. With a final *BOOM* of thunder, the flowering seed disappeared into the black water and everything was still once more—silent....

The blackness withdrew from the water surrounding me, pulled toward the center of the pond.

I felt faint.

Had it worked? Did I fail? Where was my Master?

A crown of black curls emerged from the water. Then, I saw Your face for the very first time.

Your big, dark eyes found me and You knew me at first sight. How Your young arms splashed in the water as you made Your way toward me, how Your legs trembled beneath You as I raised You to the bank.

And there I saw You in all Your Glory: a bonny young boy with bone-white skin, ash-black hair, and eyes so dark, so bottomless.

I took off my cardigan and swaddled You in it.

"My Master, my son... I loved you at once."

"Oh, dear God!" A woman's scream rebounded off the houses.

"What is-?" A burly, bearded man started, coming to his horrified wife's side. He followed her gaze to the figure by the pond. The caution tape cordoning it off had been broken. The two loose ends fluttered in the breeze around the moon-silhouetted figure.

"She drowning it! She's drowning that baby!"

The woman's voice cut through the fog, drawing the old woman's attention. She attempted to run, clutching the infant to her chest. The bearded man soon caught her, holding the woman firmly by the shoulders as he took in what he saw.

She was drenched in water, seemingly having emerged from the pond, and clutched the infant to her breast. It was still and silent as she growled, "Get away! He's mine!"

"Lillian?" He recognized the old woman in the moonlight. It was the woman whose post he had taken up on the HOA board, Lillian Ayers. But the woman before him was not the woman he remembered. Lillian's hair was unkempt, her eyes feral as pond water dripped down the furious lines of her face, contorted by a maddened rage.

"He's mine! Don't touch my baby!" Spit flew from her lips as she clung tighter to the infant.

"Lillian, it's me, Caleb!"

"Don't touch him! He's mine!"

"Lillian... that baby isn't yours. You have to let go... let me take him. It'll be okay...." Caleb gently closed his hands around the wet bundle.

"No! He's mine! My Master made him for me! I'm his mother!" She tried to wrench the baby away from his grasp, but Caleb held on, his grip firmer than he realized by the adrenaline coursing through him.

Caleb's wife screamed as he pulled the child away from Lillian. The old woman held onto the infant's tiny hand protruding from the cardigan, forcing the arm to detach from the silent, unmoving bundle.

He fell backward onto the grass, cradling the baby in horror. Lillian's scream curdled his blood. His stomach sank as she discarded the infant's stiff limb in the grass, lunging toward him.

Cradled the child in his arms, he turned away from the assault, protecting its body with his own as the old woman beat and clawed his back.

The commotion alerted the policeman who had dozed off in his cruiser at the entrance to Lilypond Lane, stationed there since the contamination had been discovered earlier that day. The officer tackled the old woman, wrestling her to the ground. She kicked her bloody stump feebly as he secured the handcuffs around her wrists, blood weeping onto the wet grass.

Caleb rolled to his side. Hands shaking, he unwrapped the cardigan, petrified of what he was about to witness within the swaddling.

"Is the child alive?" The cop shouted.

"I-" Caleb's eyes widened as they scanned the contents of the cardigan.

"Sir! Is the infant breathing?"

"No..." breathless, he struggled to get the words out.

The officer recited several codes into the radio clipped to his chest as Lillian wept.

"It- it's *a doll*.... It's just a doll...."

Caleb fell back onto the grass, catching his breath.

A mud-stained, one-armed babydoll laid before him. Twigs, leaves, and shredded bits of paper filled the holes of its eyeless sockets and protruded from the opened seam running down the length of its abdomen. He picked it up, if only to prove to himself it was real. Pond water seeped from the sodden cloth of its body and hollow plastic limbs. As Caleb's grip tightened on the doll, a mechanical child-like voice called out:

"Mama... mama."

Rose J Monan holds a BA in Comparative Literature and Italian Language and Literature from Smith College along with a background in journalism and publishing. She hails from Lusby, Maryland, the setting for her upcoming debut novel Runes in the Kudzu. Rose loves to explore local history and folklore, weaving these stories into anything from historical essays to fictional tales of horror. She currently resides in Carrboro, North Carolina with her husband, Ray, and two cats, Mcleod and Nox. When she is not writing, Rose can be found making art, baking for family and friends, enjoying nature, or conducting research for her next writing project.

To find out more about Rose's upcoming releases, follow her @Rosejmonan on Facebook and Instagram.

A note from the authors

Thank you so much for reading The Secrets of Lilypond Lane. The QR code above will take you to Amazon to leave a review. Reviews are so important for authors and they help other readers find books they'll love.

We hope you'll check out the authors' other works, and we look forward to delighting you with new stories in the years to come.

www.ingramcontent.com/pod-product-compliance
Lightning Source LLC
Chambersburg PA
CBHW030340310726
48979CB00001B/116

* 9 7 8 1 0 6 8 7 6 0 0 1 3 *